PRAISE FOR
THE SOFI SNOW NOVELS

"An action-packed kick in the pulse. Mary Weber kills it with this conclusion to Sofi Snow's story. You will hit a point where you just. can't. stop. reading. And when you finally turn that last page, you'll be ready to jump into round two."

—NADINE BRANDES, AWARD-WINNING AUTHOR OF *A TIME TO DIE* AND *FAWKES*, FOR *RECLAIMING SHILO SNOW*

"Weber creates a fascinating future with a captivating gaming aspect, complicated political and personal relationships, and a constant watchful alien presence. Readers will wonder what will happen with each turn of the page. Suspenseful and romantic, this intense story should intrigue teen and adult fans of Caragh O'Brien's Vault of Dreamers series."

—*RT BOOK REVIEWS*, 4½ STARS, TOP PICK!
FOR *THE EVAPORATION OF SOFI SNOW*

"A cool vision of future Earth that realistically reflects an increasingly multicultural world."

—*KIRKUS REVIEWS*, FOR *THE EVAPORATION OF SOFI SNOW*

"The fan-fight world itself is intriguing, and as Sofi deals with Miguel and tries to recover Shilo, this offers the best of both science fiction and romance."

—*BOOKLIST*, FOR *THE EVAPORATION OF SOFI SNOW*

"A smart, intriguing adventure of high-tech futuristic gaming. Mary Weber takes readers on an intergalactic journey intertwined with complicated family issues, politics, loyalty, secrets, and betrayal."

—WENDY HIGGINS, *NEW YORK TIMES* BESTSELLING
AUTHOR, FOR *THE EVAPORATION OF SOFI SNOW*

"Mary Weber spins a compelling tale with lyrical beauty and devious twists. *The Evaporation of Sofi Snow* is the kind of book teens and adults will devour and talk about—endlessly."

—JONATHAN MABERRY, *NEW YORK TIMES* BESTSELLING
AUTHOR OF *MARS ONE* AND *ROT & RUIN*

PRAISE FOR
THE STORM SIREN TRILOGY

"There are few things more exciting to discover than a debut novel packed with powerful storytelling and beautiful language. *Storm Siren* is one of those rarities. I'll read anything Mary Weber writes. More, please!"

—JAY ASHER, *NEW YORK TIMES* BESTSELLING
AUTHOR OF *THIRTEEN REASONS WHY*

"*Storm Siren* is a riveting tale from start to finish. Between the simmering romance, the rich and inventive fantasy world, and one seriously jaw-dropping finale, readers will clamor for the next book—and I'll be at the front of the line!"

—MARISSA MEYER, *NEW YORK TIMES* BESTSELLING
AUTHOR OF THE LUNAR CHRONICLES

"Intense and intriguing. Fans of high stakes fantasy won't be able to put it down."

—C. J. REDWINE, AUTHOR OF *DEFIANCE*, FOR *STORM SIREN*

"A riveting read! Mary Weber's rich world and heartbreaking heroine had me from page one. You're going to fall in love with this love story."

—JOSEPHINE ANGELINI, INTERNATIONALLY BESTSELLING
AUTHOR OF THE STARCROSSED TRILOGY, FOR *STORM SIREN*

"Elegant prose and intricate world-building twist into a breathless cyclone of a story that will constantly keep you guessing. More, please!"

—SHANNON MESSENGER, AUTHOR OF THE
SKY FALL SERIES, FOR *STORM SIREN*

"Weber's debut novel is a tour de force! A story of guts, angst, bolcranes, sword fights, and storms beyond imagining. Her heroine, a lightning-wielding young woman of immense power and a soft, questioning heart, captures you from word one and holds tight until the final line. Unwilling to let the journey go, I eagerly await Weber's (and Nym's) next adventure."

—KATHERINE REAY, AUTHOR OF *DEAR MR. KNIGHTLEY*, FOR *STORM SIREN*

"Mary Weber has created a fascinating, twisted world. *Storm Siren* sucked me in from page one—I couldn't stop reading! This is a definite must-read, the kind of book that kept me up late into the night turning the pages!"

—LINDSAY CUMMINGS, AUTHOR OF *THE MURDER COMPLEX*

"Don't miss this one!"

—SERENA CHASE, USATODAY.COM, FOR *STORM SIREN*

"Readers who enjoyed Marissa Meyer's Cinder series will enjoy this fast-paced fantasy which combines an intriguing storyline with as many twists and turns as a chapter of *Game of Thrones*!"

—DODIE OWENS, EDITOR, *SCHOOL LIBRARY JOURNAL TEEN*, FOR *STORM SIREN*

"Readers will easily find themselves captivated. The breathtaking surprise ending is nothing short of horrific, promising even more dark and bizarre adventures to come in the Storm Siren trilogy."

—*RT BOOK REVIEWS*, 4 STARS, FOR *STORM SIREN*

"Fantasy readers will feel at home in Weber's first novel . . . Detailed backdrop and large cast bring vividness to the story."

—*PUBLISHERS WEEKLY*, FOR *STORM SIREN*

"Weber builds a fascinating and believable fantasy world."

—*KIRKUS REVIEWS*, FOR *STORM SIREN*

"This adventure, in the vein of 1980s fantasy films, has readers rooting for the heroes to smite the wicked baddies. Buy where fantasy flies."

—DANIELLE SERRA, *SCHOOL LIBRARY JOURNAL*, FOR *STORM SIREN*

"Mary Weber's debut novel reflects an author sensitive to her audience, a stellar imagination, and a killer ability with smart and savvy prose."

—RELZ REVIEWZ, FOR *STORM SIREN*

"A touching and empowering testament to the power of true love and of knowing who you are, *Siren's Fury* is a solid, slightly steampunky follow-up to the fantasy-driven first book that will leave you with a sigh—and a craving for the next volume in the series."

—USATODAY.com

"A perfect conclusion to this delightfully brave trilogy, *Siren's Song* will leave you eager to read whatever falls from the pen of talented author Mary Weber next."

—*USA TODAY*

"This series comes to a close with an intense pursuit of good by evil, with the fate of all in the hands of teenaged Nym. She is consistently inconsistent in her feelings and fears, truly human in her characterization, and a champion accessible to readers who can identify with her insecurities."

—*RT Book Reviews*, 4 stars, for *Siren's Song*

"If you're looking for your next fantasy series, definitely pick up The Storm Siren Trilogy. The story, the characters, and the writing style impressed me so much, and I can't wait to see what the author has in store for her readers next!"

—*Love at First Page*, for *Siren's Song*

RECLAIMING
SHILO SNOW

OTHER BOOKS BY MARY WEBER

The Evaporation of Sofi Snow

THE STORM SIREN TRILOGY

Storm Siren

Siren's Fury

Siren's Song

RECLAIMING SHILO SNOW

MARY WEBER

THOMAS NELSON
Since 1798

Published in Nashville, Tennessee, by Thomas Nelson. Thomas Nelson is a
registered trademark of HarperCollins Christian Publishing, Inc.

Thomas Nelson titles may be purchased in bulk for educational, business,
fund-raising, or sales promotional use. For information, please e-mail
SpecialMarkets@ThomasNelson.com.

Publisher's Note: This novel is a work of fiction. Names, characters, places,
and incidents are either products of the author's imagination or used
fictitiously. All characters are fictional, and any similarity to people living or
dead is purely coincidental.

Library of Congress Cataloging-in-Publication Data

Names: Weber, Mary (Mary Christine), author
Title: Reclaiming Shilo Snow / Mary Weber.
Description: Nashville, Tennessee : Thomas Nelson, [2018] | Series:
Evaporation of Sofi Snow ; 2 | Summary: Sofi Snow, the most wanted
teenager alive, travels to the icy, technologically brilliant planet of Delon,
but as she tries to find her brother Shilo and warn those on Earth of Delon's
dark designs on humanity, Sofi feels herself unraveling and questions the
very existence of reality.
Identifiers: LCCN 2017045022 | ISBN 9780718080945 (hardback)
Subjects: | CYAC: Science fiction. | Virtual reality--Fiction. | Brothers and
sisters--Fiction.
Classification: LCC PZ7.1.W425 Re 2018 | DDC [Fic]--dc23 LC record
available at https://lccn.loc.gov/2017045022

Printed in the United States of America

18 19 20 21 22 LSC 5 4 3 2 1

*For the almost 30 million precious humans
currently being trafficked and enslaved . . .
We hear you.
We value you.
We are coming for you.*

THE TAKING

FOUR YEARS TO THE DAY AFTER THE ALIEN PLANET ARRIVED above Earth, Sofi's papa had collapsed on the rickety front porch of their buttermilk-yellow farmhouse. The suffocating heat from the late-August eve had dragged the two of them outside while Shilo slept on the Best Couch—christened as such due to the sagging divot created from years of use that cradled one's body like a velvet glove.

The child's light snore had been drifting through the window, while the humid warmth kept Sofi and her dad sipping iced tea on the creaky swing just to create a bit of hot breeze. The radio played old Twenty One Pilots songs and the fields played cicadas. Sofi thought how funny it was that those bugs could barely last a winter but the species as a whole had survived the Third and Fourth World Wars.

Which was about all one could say for the human species as well.

They'd survived.

Two minutes later Sofi heard a soft gasp and looked over as Papa's heart sputtered, then squeezed.

His writhing limbs went limp as his body slipped off the

1

aged, weathered seat, and Sofi screamed and dropped her cup, which shattered across the white wood porch planks.

She tugged Papa's sallow head into her lap and focused on drawing deep breaths. As if she could breathe for him and inflate his sagging chest. Her brown hand wrapped around his big farmer one as her tears drip-dropped on his cheek and trickled into his bristly beard.

"Call your mother," he mouthed. "She'll take care of you."

"No, she won't." Sofi shook her head. "Papa, please don't leave. Don't go."

Papa's gaze twitched and widened on her small face as she hovered before he moved it away toward the moon and her dead half sister, Ella's, star—until his focus settled glassy-eyed on the shiny planet, where it stayed. As if in indication of something more, of something ten-year-old Sofi already knew:

Somehow the aliens were responsible. And, eventually, they'd be the death of them all.

Then in the next breath he was gone, and she and Shilo were suddenly alone.

Sofi pulled out her inhaler and sat there sucking in its mist—scared to yell for help because the only help around was the kind that helped themselves to anything that wasn't theirs.

The cicadas stopped chirping. The breeze stopped whispering. And Sofi stopped believing in anything beyond her own two hands and the brother currently still burrowed and snoring on the Best Couch.

The following morning her CEO mom sent down a coroner from the Corp 30 office in Manhattan's metropolis.

"Heart gave out," the man said, voice squeaking like the porch board he stood on.

Sofi glowered. As if she hadn't just told him the exact same thing five minutes ago. As if his professional assessment changed anything or made it any more real.

He bit his wet cigar and stared down at her. "So why didn't you call your mom last night when it happened?"

Her small fingers stroked her brother's hair as Shilo let out a sob and pressed his head against her side, his body wrapped like a fist around her scrawny chicken legs. "Would she have come?" Sofi growled.

The man took the corpse. Took a last look at Sofi and the five-year-old boy, both who glared at him like he was the hand of Satan. Then strode to his fancy hovercar, mumbling that a nanny would be sent out this evening, on order of CEO Inola.

Except thirteen hours later it wasn't the nanny who appeared.

It was something else entirely.

And it took them before anyone noticed.

INOLA

Update: Sofi Heather Snow, age 17

- FanFight Gamer, Daughter of Corp 30's CEO
- Reclassified Status: Imminent Terrorist Threat #1
- Required Action: Alert for immediate worldwide dispersal

THE MOMENT EARTH'S UNITED WORLD COUNCIL OFFICIALLY placed seventeen-year-old Sofi Snow at the top of their Imminent Terrorist Threat list, a siren went off in the circular downtown building, and she became the most wanted teenager alive.

Corp 30's CEO, Inola, stood next to the podium in the center of the room located in the heart of Old America's shiny Manhattan metropolis and eyed the sea of raised hands. All of which had just finished voting her daughter onto that list.

The fact her daughter was currently on another *planet*—let alone the one that'd mysteriously appeared near Earth in 2031, eleven years ago—didn't matter. Nor that its humanlike society was capable of annihilating humanity in a heartbeat.

If anything, that was the point.

Sofi had found a way up to their icy, technologically brilliant environment from an Earth that was, in many ways, still broken and rebuilding. Meaning she was far more capable than Earth's leaders had accounted for. And the clock was ticking on what she'd do next.

She'd already been there over thirty-six hours.

When the resulting siren went off, ringing through the United World building and making half the council members in the room jump, Inola didn't flinch. Didn't move. Didn't do anything other than observe them all with her cool, calculating gaze. Even as the sound meant that texts were being sent to every tech-head, soldier, and peacekeeper, warning them of Sofi's new status.

A terrorist of the most dangerous sort, the messages would read.

"A brilliant mind that could hack our darkest secrets," the messages would mean.

"The girl who might just start a war with the Delonese," the Council was really saying. "And we need them far more than we need her."

A moment later those raised hands dropped, the three hundred faces suddenly looking Inola's direction—some in humility, others in victory—as the alarm shut off and her own Corp 30 vice president, the perfidious Ms. Gaines, stepped from the podium after demanding the vote.

Inola let a smile flicker around her lips. She swept her gaze over the lot of them before lifting it to the room's single ceiling window through which the shiny ice-planet glittered just beyond the day-lit moon. *Sofi, a threat?*

They can't even begin to fathom.

Tick, tick, tick, tick . . .

SOFI

SOFI ACCIDENTALLY BIT HER TONGUE AS MIGUEL'S ARM SNAPPED across her chest, pressing her short frame back into the thin shadows of the medical room, three stories beneath the ice-planet's wintry surface. The storm of alien boots and voices surged and frothed, then crashed with clipped heels in a wave down the narrow hall toward the spot where she and the nineteen-year-old ambassador stood. "Have they been located?" "They're not to reach the surface!" "Find them before they engage with the populace!"

Stay still. Stay silent. Sofi's breath stuck to the sides of her lungs, like frost on a window, waiting to crack against her rib cage at the grief keening through her bones. Her stomach threatened to retch all over again.

This alien planet had looked so crisp and peaceful in its orbit beside Earth's moon—like a snowflake glittering against the black backdrop of space. Who would've known the metallic world beneath its crust was so barbaric?

So calculated.

The siren continued blaring.

Sofi thrust her emotions down and slid her hand to Miguel's arm as a robotic voice rose above the rest. "The sensors in the vent-wing just triggered; it might be them! Return Ambassador Alis to Lord Ethos while we apprehend Girl-Sofi."

The instructions were followed by an abrupt silence.

"C'mon, keep going," Miguel murmured. "Search another sector."

An elongated second went by. Then, as if in response to him, the cadence of shuffling boots resumed and the officers stamped away in their matching strides, scraping against Sofi's spine. She wanted to toss a giant bowling ball in their direction, just to watch them all topple like the monstrously efficient pinheads they were. *Good gad, they're heinous.*

Miguel exhaled beside her and shifted his tall, broad physique to tap his earcom. "Vic, you there?" he whispered to his Artificial Intelligence assistant. "We're going to need a hand."

What? No. Sofi dipped a thick brow up at him with a single shake of her head. They needed a hand, yes, but they needed a search of this room more. "Miguel, we can't. This room—the beds . . ." her voice faltered.

His black eyes stared down at her as if to say that was precisely why he was anxious for them to leave. As if he knew too well what this space was doing to her—what it'd already *done*—and he wasn't about to let the Delonese or this place do it further.

She blinked and glanced away, and waited for his arm to drop before pulling the handscreen from her pocket and focusing on the dim display. His concern triggered that chaos of emotion she was trying to ignore. She cared about others. She didn't need them to care about her. Particularly not him. He'd been despicable eighteen months ago and now—truly decent. She didn't have time to process that paradox. Especially in light of the chilling reality in front of her.

She steadied her shoulders and lifted her attention to the large, lengthy medical space with its rows of shower stalls sectioned off by clear plastic curtains that had once held her and her younger brother, Shilo, strapped like animals on the med equipment.

Experiments, her mind whispered.

Child abductees. Her lungs gulped.

Shilo.

Her throat clamped down over his name as if to protect it from the very air in here.

"Hold on, guys." Vic's voice erupted in their earcoms. "I'm trying to pull up more specs, but the Delonese are tracing me."

Sofi ignored the AI and moved her scrutinizing gaze to the spigots attached to the white walls beneath white halogen lights, each overlooking med beds with straps that spread out eerily, like arms waiting to embrace her and anyone else the Delonese decided on.

How long had those straps been waiting—days? Hours? And how many kids had been trapped on those med beds during the past seven years since she'd been strapped to one as well?

Avoiding the uneasy tilt of Miguel's lavender-haired head, Sofi brushed past him farther into the room while the heat of his gaze followed her. As if he was calculating how to secure her from the trauma of what this place meant about her and everything she knew.

Or rather, the realization that they apparently knew nothing at all. Thirty-six hours spent mingling with the human-looking aliens on the surface of Delon, and her entire world and history had just been shattered by this one underground room.

"Sof?" Miguel's tone was taut.

"It's fine. I'm fine."

He made a sound but didn't argue. He didn't have to. They both knew she wasn't fine—wasn't anywhere close to it. But she couldn't just stand there in her hot mess of newly discovered not-fineness. *Do it and get out, Sof.*

She gritted her teeth and searched each stall—as if her brain needed proof that she and Shilo weren't still among the ghostly whimpers the place echoed with and that there were answers to all of this. The Delonese had brought and kept her here. According to her memories, they'd destroyed a portion of her life here.

What exactly had they done to her? What other memories was she missing? How much time had she spent inside this planet through the years?

And where were the other kids who'd been taken with her and Shilo back then?

Her chest quaked as her mind drifted toward suggestions—repressed images bubbling to the surface—while her feet carried her to the metal hoverbed she'd once occupied. Then to Shilo's stall—where the sanitized smell and the memory of him, along with the others, were enough to make her gag.

She couldn't recall the rest of their faces, just their screams as a seven-year-gone memory erupted of her brother looking up and meeting her gaze.

"*Sofi?*" his small five-year-old voice had said. "*I want to go home now.*"

She ground her jaw as the image faded, and glanced back at

Miguel, whose expression was an apologetic mix of worry and the need to hurry. He shifted from one foot to the other before tipping his soft gaze toward the door. The siren's *whir* was growing louder. The boot steps and long, unblinking faces would be returning.

She nodded. Looking around wasn't giving her anything concrete. Just hazy memories. What she needed was better access to the Delonese's data stream.

After a last glimpse, she strode back, reaching Miguel as the alarm abruptly shut off and the wall to the right flickered and hissed.

The room gave a soft *zap*, and its halogen lights blacked out. Leaving her and Miguel encompassed in pitch dark.

Alone.

"Sof, we need to get out of here." Miguel's low voice breezed against her hair through the sudden silence. But her mind was already fading backward and a memory was exploding— unwanted, uninhibited—buried so deep she hadn't even known it existed inside her seventeen-year-old soul until too late . . .

THEY HAD COME TO EARTH AT DUSK, CRAWLING ACROSS her farm like predators in search of prey.

Sofi had been out securing the barn, as best as a ten-year-old could, to keep up the appearance she and Shilo weren't there alone and that Papa hadn't been dead for twenty-two hours.

Creeping sounds that began this morning among the trees at the edge of the fence were growing louder—people watching, waiting to see if it was true. And to see what they could steal. Because everyone knew kids fetched as high a price as old meds and food seeds these days, especially on the black market. And everyone around those parts knew Corp 30 CEO Inola's kids would pull a good price indeed.

Sofi swallowed and tried not to look at the tree line from between the barn slats. Mama should've known not to leave them—should've had the coroner take them with him. Or more accurately, should've cared enough to come fetch them herself rather than leave them to their fate.

But what was new? The woman sat in her shiny Manhattan office building hundreds of miles away, and even more emotionally distant, as the space between their Old North Carolina farmhouse and the border to the rest of the messed-up world dissolved into nothing.

A rank smell filled Sofi's nose.

She frowned. The scent was different from that of the scavengers or starving neighbors.

Peeking between the barn window shutters, she blinked, then froze as the smell morphed into something unmistakable. It reeked of metal and medicinal labs.

The Delonese were in the yard.

Giant, perfectly fashioned men whom Earth's upper class found intriguingly fetching, dressed in thin gray boots and slick coats, bare of any facial hair or expression, were spread across the field and driveway. And they were coming closer.

She hadn't even heard their craft.

Her lungs rippled. She slipped back, gripping her shaking fist around the hammer she'd been using. *Keep going*, she said in her head. *There's nobody here.* Except the determination of their steps said they knew better.

Suddenly, a shadow passed by the shutter, throwing darkness

across the slatted evening light. Sofi slid the tiny tool into her boot and scrambled for the farthest corner of the barn.

At least Shilo's in the basement where I told him to stay 'til I finished.

A hand scraped the wall, making her jump.

Voices.

She curled into a ball—trying to clamber inside her ten-year-old skin—as if she could shrink her bones and muscles and lungs small enough to roll inside herself. Even as fear spiked a blasted signal and caused her asthma to kick in, ill-timed as all get-out. *No, not now,* she told her lungs. *You've got to work for me.* She squished herself against the wood siding and fumbled in her pocket for an inhaler.

Not there.

Her throat tightened. She breathed in slowly. One breath, two breaths, she inhaled an infinity of breaths and focused her attention on a couple of fireflies illuminating the ceiling as fingers scratched at the barn's sturdy door and her breathing became shallow. She could almost imagine their ears listening for movement, matching it to the smell of human flesh. If they could smell at all.

You'd think they'd be dead from their own medicinal odor by now if so.

Tears filled her eyes as Sofi tried to inhale again, while her body strove not to move.

It didn't matter. The moment they broke in, her gasping exploded and gave her away. Her chest imploded as her world shrank into that feeling that there wasn't enough oxygen on Earth to keep her alive.

At least Shilo isn't here. Her eyesight blurred as her lungs caught fire.

C'mon, Sofi, focus.

She couldn't. She was going to pass out. She needed air.

At least Shilo is safe.

And then they were on her, reeking like sterile, huge plastic people that looked half doll and half human in her gasping-for-oxygen state. She shrieked but there was no sound, and then her throat collapsed somewhere between seeing their unblinking faces and having a bag stuffed over her head.

Which was when she heard him.

His tiny voice carried hesitant across the yard. "Sofi?"

Shilo?

No! Oh please no! Shilo, run!

The instantaneous boot shuffling said they were already going for him.

"Leave him alone!" she choked into the bag's cloth. She lashed at them with the violence of one who'd recently known the taste of death. She kicked, wheezed, and mentally swore every curse word she'd been taught never to say, while her chest felt near the point of ignition.

She lunged out in her sightless state, hands trying to break free from the clammy fingers pinning her wrists. Tearing off the bracelet Shilo'd made her as she yanked at what felt like an icy void around her. Sobbing. "Fine, take me, just leave him alone, please."

But her hands and voice moved nothing, and those two fireflies full of light and life and everything warm were the last things in her mind before the tears and suffocation took her out.

3

MIGUEL

AMBASSADOR MIGUEL EDWARDO PEREZ II WAS ABOUT TO BURN this ice planet down.

When the lights in the Delonese room slowly fluttered back on—low and eerie—the first thing he looked for was Sofi's face. The first thing he saw was the crushing horror spread across it, as whatever memory was accosting her coated her skin in sweat. His anger cracked and flared and he muttered to Vic, "On second thought, let's just blow this place to toast."

"Yeah, still trying to reaccess the blasted maps, dude."

He kept his voice low. "Any idea how long that'll take?"

"Probably faster if you'd hold on to your panties and—"

Right. *Mantener la calma.* He looked back at Sofi and touched her shoulder to stir her. She didn't blink or move. His frown deepened.

"Okay, seven-point-five minutes."

Miguel didn't respond. Just straightened and, keeping his body between Sofi and the door, turned to mentally assess the maze of underground hallways they'd come through to reach this room. Which ones would make the best path out?

The crossway led to the other medical quarters where they'd found the group of young kids an hour ago. All drenched in terror and urine, scared out of their wits, waiting for the Delonese experiments to start. They'd snuck the poor children onto a shuttle for Earth, only to turn around as soon as it'd left and find this room—and the seven-year-old recorded video of Sofi that Vic uncovered, and her memories that went with it.

That vid . . . Sofi'd been so young. He winced. *Get her out of here, Miguel.*

Firming his jaw, he squeezed her shoulder again as boot steps struck metal grates somewhere down the outer hall. "Sof?"

Her face moved toward his voice.

"We're still on Delon in the med room," he said quietly. "I'm just not sure where you are at the moment."

Her pupils flickered. She shifted, and a second later her eyes cleared. She connected her expression with his and nodded, her owl necklace fluttering against her damp neck. "I'm here."

He smoothed his hair to hide his relief. "Good. You alright?"

Another nod. "Just a memory from when Shi and I were taken from the barn." She shifted her pointy chin as if to squelch the ache in her tone, then dropped her eyes to the handscreen she held. "I need to find Shilo."

"*Sí*, but I think first we need to get us out of here." He offered Sofi her tech-bag just as the room's white wall beside them clicked, as if it were a comp monitor turning on, and flashed static across the length of it again. It buzzed and flared through the dim room, then lit up like a telescreen.

What the—?

A Delonese voice rippled from the wallscreen into the room surrounding them. Their earcoms translated in unison:

"Citizens of Delon, please give your attention to this short update."

The buzzing wall plastered a close-up of Sofi's face across it, followed by the camera angle panning out to show a pic of her in a tech-room three days ago at the Fantasy Fighting Games back on Earth.

Miguel recognized it. The scene was from an hour before the bombing that had taken out a good portion of the arena and contestants, including Shilo. Or so they'd believed. Miguel had been up in the stands in his *cabaña*—level three to be precise— with his plethora of celebrity admirers while Sofi was working down in her team's virtual reality room. The pic changed to one overlooking the live gaming arena, where Shilo and the other players had combated.

He sniffed—*This distraction is not helpful*—and turned back to Sof, who must've caught the look on his face because she slid a hand along her bag's strap in agreement and spun to leave just as the voice continued in its precise, unemotional tone. "One of our guests, known to all as the hugely popular gamer Sofi Snow on Earth's FanFight field, is currently lost here on Delon. We're asking for your assistance in locating her, both for her safety as well as your own. Her mental stability is currently questionable."

Sofi slowed. Her eyes narrowed and her expression sharpened to anger right along with his.

Ah.

There it is.

It was the same look she'd offered at their first meeting a year and a half ago—when she politely told him off, and rightly so because he'd been a disgusting cad back then. Her initial dismissal had left such a clear impact, he'd been unable to function right for the rest of the night. And despite their now impending weird-death-by-aliens, he wouldn't want to be with anyone else to experience such a thing. He knew what she was capable of.

What they were both capable of.

"Nice of them to get the whole hive on board," Sofi muttered. "You ready?"

He offered her a furtive smile, which she returned before she nodded and pushed through the door to the hall. The sterile smell stung the nose and the dim glow of the lengthy white ceiling caught her dark hair as she tossed her long ponytail over her shoulder. "Alright, best-case scenario we find a tech-space to cement ourselves into their system. From there I can tag team with Vic before we search out Shilo."

She tapped her handscreen. "Ranger, you there?"

No response.

Miguel shook his head. The hacker guy's vid feed from Earth had shut off ten minutes ago and hadn't reappeared since. "I couldn't pull him up eith—"

The narrow, tall walls on each side buzzed loudly and turned on like a strobe effect, all the way down the corridor, with shadows cast at odd intervals. Floor-to-ceiling telescreens lit up, mirroring the one in the room they'd just exited. They looked like advertisements from a metropolis. Except now they were showing a vid—one from yesterday morning in which Sofi was stepping off the shuttle on Delon. It followed her entering their vetting area where she'd been quickly scanned and questioned along with Heller—Sofi's FanFight tech friend who'd betrayed them.

The Delonese voice came back on as they turned down a second hallway. "While Girl-Sofi went through our vetting system yesterday upon entry to our planet, we were unable to finish the process. We need to do so immediately."

Miguel's neck prickled. He picked up his pace to stride nearer her. At the time, he'd found yesterday's entry process oddly swift, especially considering only he and Earth's other ambassadors were allowed anywhere near this planet. Now, in light of everything they'd just seen . . .

He doubted very much they'd made a mistake in how they vetted her.

Miguel glanced at the medical rooms they were moving past. The Delonese hadn't minded him bringing her here. They'd wanted her. Probably saved them a trip to retrieve her like they'd supposedly done with her brother.

The question was—why? And why *now*?

He tapped his earcom as they reached the hall's end. "Vic, you ready?"

Sofi slowed and turned her wide cheekbones and delicate nose his way, triggering a muted emotion of longing in his chest. He kept his face sterile, ignoring her beauty as her dark eyes hardened. "You know what kind of further tests they're speaking of?"

"They didn't clarify at this morning's meeting." He held her gaze. *They didn't have to*, was what he didn't say.

Sofi slung her bag higher on her shoulder. "Right. In that case . . ." She moved her small hand and tapped her own earcom. "Vic, I'm on. My head's clear and I'm gonna need—"

A sensor on the metallic door in front of them clicked. Sofi uttered a soft "You've got to be kidding me" as it gave a *swish* and slid up to open onto a balcony that overlooked the giant interior of the planet—which wasn't a planet at all, as they'd discovered a few hours ago, but a massive spherical space station.

Sofi retreated, pushing Miguel back. "Did I mention I hate this place?" she hissed. "I say the minute we grab Shilo we leave, then light it up."

He couldn't agree more, but he lifted a teasing brow and looked down at his handscreen, accessing the door coding she'd created. "I seem to recall you saying that at a party once. It didn't end well either." He waved his comp in front of the door to shut it, but without luck.

She snorted and swiped a thumb across her own handscreen. "That's because I didn't intend it to end well." Sofi suddenly eyed him. "And neither did you, if the police reports were to be believed."

With a smirk she pointed her comp at the door.

The thing stayed up, staring like a gaping eyeball onto the inner workings of Delon.

"Crud. Let me recalibrate."

Miguel nodded and shoved aside the brief amusement along with the internal nudge that every moment put them in great danger. *I know. We're trying.* Instead, he stood silent as Sofi worked her tech genius, and assessed what he could see of the enormous station from their spot hidden in the shadow within a hall that was probably one of a thousand identical-looking hallways in this small catacomb section alone. *Where do we need to get to?*

Where indeed.

The thing might as well have been a freaking beehive. Each level lined with a complex system of rooms and openings shaped like honeycombs that led to who knew where, all filled with whiteness. White rooms, white doorways, and a metallic framework of stairs and walkways in perfect unified layouts assembled into the five levels he could see—two above and two below where he stood, all set facing inward in a perfect square like a hotel complex. All beneath a vast black ceiling, mirrored by a black void below that one could fall into forever. The chasm likely led to one of the planet's cores or fusion engines.

Admittedly, the place was beautiful. With its detailed, lacy use of silver and glass and black metals that gave way to those white interiors reflecting from each room. Probably would've made the place feel rich and sterile if not for the dead bodies kept in glass vats in the med quarters they'd snuck through earlier.

Sofi tried again to get the door to shut. Nothing. "Okay, forget it." She attacked her comp again as the screens outside, along the station walls, started to flicker with pics of her face. Hordes of tall, unblinking, human-looking Delonese were already assembling to study them, like drones.

"Girl-Sofi is believed to currently be with beloved Earth ambassador Miguel."

"Yeah, yeah, we know," she mumbled, poking her device.

Delonese Lead Ambassador Lord Ethos's voice echoed through the station so loudly it rumbled the grates beneath their feet. "We ask all citizens who locate them to alert us immediately, in order to return them to their shuttle before it leaves."

Miguel looked at Sofi. They weren't going to let them anywhere near that shuttle. "Sof, are you still able to track where each Delonese is in this place?"

"Already on it."

He nodded and tapped his own handheld. And kept his voice down. "In that case—Vic, I'm pulling you on-screen."

His handcomp dinged, and a tiny holographic head popped up a few inches off of it with short red hair and glassy blue eyes couched in thick lashes that, even in this situation, expressed herself as being the fanciest artificial intelligence he knew. The flame lipstick she wore around puckered lips only solidified it.

The AI popped a virtual wad of pink bubble gum. "Okay, I've managed to work back in, but—"

"The best thing would be to reaccess the station's system from somewhere in here," Sofi whispered, still working on her own screen. "Can you find us the safest place with a portal?"

The AI paused and cocked her head as if assimilating the requested data as fast as she could. After a moment—"Not without your tech friends, Ranger and Heller. Ranger's been shut out, and Heller's, well—a traitor. And the Delonese are rewriting the codes you created, Sof."

"Explains why our tech keeps going out." Sofi's voice was calm even as her shoulders stiffened at Heller's name.

Miguel peered past the hall entrance at the Delonese citizens all standing in lines, still frozen in front of those telescreens. They needed to move. "Vic, just get Ranger online and find us a place to hole up. We'll have to hack their codes without Heller."

The AI blew her fake pink bubble gum to the size of her sassy face and let it pop. "You got it."

Sofi nudged his arm. "Miguel." She held up her handscreen that now showed her program pulled up, displaying a mass of lights representing every single Delonese's location in this giant section. He squinted. A single group of them were converging on his and Sofi's location. Their voices were growing louder along the balcony, clogging his earcom's translator. "We don't have time to wait for the maps," Sofi murmured. "We need to get to a tech-room *now*."

The Delonese soldiers were suddenly bearing down right

beyond the hallway. Their words growing clearer than the others.

Miguel stepped back and swiped his screen so Vic's face disappeared, and he started pulling Sofi down the hall where the lights were dimmer—toward one of the side rooms.

Too late. The boots stopped with a sharp snap in front of that main hall door.

Diablos. He stalled and pressed them both against the video wall beneath one of the thin shadows. Only to hear a chuckle as soon as their bodies touched the smooth surface.

The thing vibrated, then morphed into a shot of their faces.

"Hello, Ambassador Miguel and Girl-Sofi. Nice of you to appear."

4
—

INOLA

"ALL IN FAVOR SAY *AYE.*"

From the front row, Inola added her voice to the day's final decision before acknowledging CEO Hart's gaze across the circular room. The broad, sixtysomething-year-old man with a mole on his left cheek gave a slight brow raise, which she met with the slip of a nod while keeping her wiry posture relaxed.

His tiny eyes hadn't stopped darting to her and her Corp 30 vice president, Macy Gaines, since Gaines had pushed the vote to name Sofi a terrorist. Inola sniffed. Nor had he stopped slugging back those drinks in front of him, as confirmed by the glassy eyes and reddening snout.

If she didn't know better, she'd say his darting gaze was part of the flirtatious coaxing he was known for, rather than an insistent need for reassurance. Reassurance of what? That both their Corporations' endeavors would remain intact? That Gaines's exploding a bomb on Inola's children was forgiven in light of the "greater good"? Or that Inola's private Delonese genetics program was desperate enough to keep paying Hart for his continued investment?

She fought the urge to laugh. *What a mess.* The man had no idea what was quite likely about to befall them all.

If he did, he'd be more concerned with their lives at the moment than with their business arrangements. *Good gad.*

Inola caught view of Gaines, half hidden behind two Eurasian senators. She was shifting in her seat, like a coyote trying to hide a dead squirrel. Inola forced herself to ignore it and tuned back to the podium. *Focus. Pull the facts before you act.*

"The ayes have it," announced the UW chairperson. "Let the record show Corporations 24 and 30 are banned from participating in the Fantasy Fighting Games until all investigations of their players, the bombing, and integrity have been concluded."

Inola nodded agreement as murmurs of approval hummed through the air.

"Chairperson, if I may." A senator from the back stood. "Of course Corp 30 would agree—and thank you for that, CEO Inola. But considering it was Corp 24 whose player set *off* the bomb—as now seen by every person here—why aren't we placing a full embargo on Corp 24 instead of just freezing their sport's privileges?"

A number of members among the crowd, as well as those sitting in via telescreens attached to the ceiling, added their agreement. So did Hart.

The chairperson lifted his hand for silence. "A full embargo didn't earn the required votes, thus sanctions will not be handed out yet."

"Then perhaps we should revote. Because I'd argue their Altered device hitting the market this week will wreak havoc in the hands of the public. The panic it'll cause will only make our peacekeepers' jobs harder and possibly start a war."

Altered. The "wonder wand."

Somebody had been bound to create it. A Delonese genetic detector that could instantly read a person's DNA for alien additions or influence. Despite the fact there was no evidence of humans ever having their DNA "altered," the ongoing fears after the aliens' arrival eleven years ago were still alive and well. As were the protestors taking up every corner of her streets in reaction to the Delonese attendance at the games.

The chairperson's hand went up again. "The UWC has launched an investigation into the ramifications of the Altered device on Earth and Delonese relations. *That* is the current decision. Although . . ." He peered in the direction of Corp 24's vice president now standing in for their newly fired CEO. "Let me be clear that we as a united body strongly discourage its distribution."

He glanced down at his notes. "Annnnd it appears, with that, we have concluded our morning meeting. So I bid you all a good day."

The delegates waited for the gavel to fall before breaking into a mass of voices—some, like Gaines, arguing more strongly for the embargo on Altered, and others suggesting they shut down Corp 24's and 30's entire United World privileges until it was proven they'd no involvement with the FanFight attack.

"Or at least until Sofi is retrieved and taken into custody from Delon," Corp 5's CEO murmured.

Inola disregarded him and slid her seamless amaranth coat on.

"Madam Inola!" Gaines's voice clipped out higher than necessary as she strode over, her silver hair matching her tone in height—in what Inola's dead husband would've called "Politician's wife hair," due to the fact that at one time, every politician's wife in the old south had sported a permed bouffant hairdo and worn a blue blazer. The irony was not lost on Inola. *Political hair, and a heart consigned to hell.*

Gaines stopped in front of her. "Even though our Corp 30 players have been excluded from the Games, I assume we'll still see you at today's FanFights? Or shall I attend on behalf of us to show our support for the other Corporations?"

She'd said it loud enough to gain half the room's attention.

Inola sniffed. *Nice play.*

She'd always known the thirty-year-old woman was a shark. It's why she'd hired her. But using the circumstances to hedge her way into Inola's CEO seat? Not going to happen. Inola had built this company, and she'd be shanked if the same woman who'd privately confessed to the bombing last night, before publicly pushing today's vote to blame Sofi, was going to steal it away.

She put on a smile. "Thank you, Gaines. You may attend if you'd like. Regretfully, a number of *urgent* items have arisen in need of my attention—not the least of which is our ongoing United World communications with the Delonese, the bombing, and the internal care of my Corporation in order that we may continue to support the other Corps in areas that are vital. Please be sure to enjoy yourself, though."

Gaines's already narrow expression shriveled beneath that silver hair. A second later she eased back and nodded. "Of course. As you said, I too am looking out for our Corporation's best interests."

Before the woman said more, Inola moved on to the senators, ambassadors, and vice presidents who'd already flocked around, in their usual hopes of staying in her good graces.

"Madam Inola." A senator from the Eurasian region reached out a hand. "We're *so* sorry about Sofi. I can't even imagine how difficult this must be."

"To be betrayed by your own daughter," another crowed. "Let us know if we can do anything."

"I'm shocked I'd not heard about Sofi hitching a ride to Delon," Senator Finn murmured, close to her ear. "Had I known, be assured I would've contacted you."

Inola's brown skin bristled. The young Icelandic senator, with a preference for keeping his head bald and encouraging his fans to run their hands over it, had practically thrown Sofi to the wolves during Thursday's United World meeting by being the first to suggest her responsibility for the bombing and murders. The theory had taken root in those who loved nothing better than seeing Inola taken down a notch. And in those who lived for drama as long as it didn't personally affect them or their kids.

However . . .

Considering Finn and Ambassador Alis were near inseparable—and Alis had been on the second shuttle to Planet Delon yesterday—

Did Finn know about her kids, then? Did he know who'd really planned the explosion, and why?

She watched his expression carefully and said evenly, "Thank you, Senator. Have you heard from Ambassador Alis? I know she was a last-minute addition due to another's illness."

He shook his shiny head. "No. But since she and the other ambassadors are due back tomorrow, I'm sure we'll know more then. I'll contact you the moment I receive news, of course."

Straight. Clear. With no hint of apology.

She nodded. Considering her position granted her immediate

updates, his offer was superfluous. But his physical clues had answered her question. While he obviously hadn't heard from Alis, he knew more about the situation than he was telling.

"For what it's worth, I hope she's okay." His voice dipped low in feigned virtue. "Your daughter, I mean. And that all this chatter"—he glanced around—"isn't true."

She offered him a sharp smile framed in blood-colored lipstick that said she'd remember this. Especially when it came time to further, or ruin, his career. "Enjoy the fights today."

She returned to the group in front of her and pretended to check her handscreen before looking up. "My apologies, but if you'll all excuse me, my car's waiting."

She stepped through the crowd, trying to ignore the pressing aura of hunger that was near insatiable. Always. For her attention, her appraisal, her investment in their never-ending projects—when the truth was, there wasn't enough of her to go around. And for whatever reason, that reality was something they couldn't understand.

That at some point, she just had to say no.

She'd learned it two years after taking over Corp 30. Otherwise her work would suffer and those depending on her would end up like—

A shallow lump moved into her throat. *Like* what? *Sofi? Shilo?*

The familiar discomfort flared. For the mother she'd been versus the mother she could've been.

Shoving it down, she firmed her jaw and slipped out of the round room's private exit where her hovercar was waiting in the sunlight, with a door that opened at her approach.

"Afternoon, madam," Jerrad, her head security officer, said.

Inola slid into the back, where the late-morning rays momentarily played across the seat, then let the door close behind her, engulfing her into the car's cool, dark cocoon. "Afternoon, Jerrad. We'll head home, please."

"As you wish."

The black-haired officer was of her generation—meaning old enough to have lost two fingers on his right hand before science could make new ones and to have refused to trust any vehicle to command itself—pulled away from the United Corporations Building and onto the steamy streets. He swerved around the Manhattan traffic and businesses and extra crowds in town for the Games.

The city rose above them—*her* city, thanks to her Corp's nearly single-handed restoration of it following the Fourth War—glittering in all its tall, majestic skyscraper glory. The buildings made of glass and flex metal were covered with giant telescreens advertising everything from prepaid flights to Delon, to cancer creams, to the new homes she'd built to help deal with the persistent homeless issue. And, of course, advertisements for the final round in the FanFights that were set to resume in a few hours.

Jerrad slowed the car at a stoplight, and Inola lowered the window a few inches to catch the homey scent of steamed whale-fish and soy sauce from one of her preferred street markets. And caught site of a FanFight advertisement scrolling across the tall silver building ahead.

"Tune in to the Fantasy Fighting Games tonight!" A robotic voice floated off of it.

"For eighteen months now, they've brought our world together like never before! And this season is no exception."

The robot was right—they *had* brought the world together. Inola herself had been at the helm of the FanFight creation, seeing it as the natural progression of a world raised on video games, sporting events, and i-reality superstars. Half virtual reality, half live action—the Fantasy Fights consisted of real players duking it out in a glorified Roman coliseum while gamers controlled arena nanobots from behind the scenes to create live, interactive scenarios. And for the kids who won? They earned relief from poverty and empty lives.

But for Inola's kids?

It'd kept them safe from the Delonese noticing them too much.

Until last week apparently.

She kept her chin leveled with the road as her car began to move again and the ad switched to display the massive outdoor stadium with the background music pulsing. "Tune in to see why it's the biggest turnout in its eighteen-month, three-time history! With over ten thousand in the stands and a million more watching as players fight for their future in the arena! And the winner goes on to the Fantasy Five to fight challengers from around the world—challengers of your choosing—in the ultimate match!"

Inola frowned. The lump that'd been tickling her throat swelled and she shut the window.

"Am I to assume you won't be attending the fights, madam?"

"Correct. I'll be working."

Jerrad eyed her through the mirror. "Working on *work*-work or *them*-work?"

She didn't need to see his full face to know what he meant.

In the quiet dim of the car, that throat lump grew—carving toward her stomach with an ache she'd not experienced since losing her daughter Ella. Before she'd left her husband, Ben, and her little family to come save the world.

Before she'd made a deal with the Delonese that she could not take back.

She blinked and tried not to bank on the sliver of hope Sofi had given a few days ago. That Shilo was somehow truly still alive and a measure of her family still existed. She shut her eyes. *Sofi, you know how to work this. You've trained eighteen months for this. Figure it out.*

Lifting her chin, Inola poured a glass of 9's latest chardonnay, took a large sip, and settled into her wide black seat, then slid her thumb over her handscreen. "Has there been any news, Jerrad?"

His brown eyes didn't move from the road. "None as yet."

She nodded and pulled up her private security firm, of which Jerrad was in charge.

And typed:

Double the priority cybertag on Gaines and Hart. I want to know everything they say, do, and who they speak to.

The reply came within seconds. Done.

She peered at the faces that'd popped up with Hart's and Gaines's names. The deception in their eyes. In their smiles.

In what they'd done.

And double the guard on Inola for the next two weeks. Jerrad's voice verbally texted his instructions, which showed up on her screen the second they left his mouth.

She blinked her approval. It's why she preferred him. He knew how to care for her when she was busy caring about everything else. She set the handheld down and flipped on the car's news screen.

"In a last-minute decision, two Corporations were barred from this afternoon's Fantasy Fighting Game," the newsperson said. "While it's still uncertain exactly how far Corp 30's involvement goes, this seems to confirm the rumors that gamer Sofi Snow was, in fact, a participant in the attack, along with Corp 24. And with 24's Altered releasing, questions are being raised."

The telescreen flashed an image of Altered.

She shook her head. Would the device start a war? No. But if the Delonese's abductions of Earth's children were ever discovered—*that* would.

She turned down the news in front of her and watched as the screens outside began replaying the morning's publicly broadcasted trial run of Altered on the remaining head FanFight gamers and players—eight each, including Corp 30's who, as of a few minutes ago in the meeting, were now disqualified. She could only imagine Gaines's pleasure that Sofi wasn't among them. Proof that her bombing had saved their operation from discovery. As if Inola hadn't planned on rigging the tests anyway.

Corp 24's spokesperson and queen of i-reality shows, Nadine, displayed her well-known smile while waving the handheld wand over each of the game's contestants, testing their DNA in seconds.

Through the window Inola read the woman's lips. "As you can see, all of the FanFight teams passed with flying colors. But isn't it comforting to know?" The camera angle pulled in as Nadine turned to face the screen full on. "Isn't it comforting to have the *control* in *your* hands? Before you take a new lover, employee, or doctor, make sure you know everything about them. Using Altered."

"This thing's like putting fire in the hands of every Earth

citizen," someone on the car news was saying. "The fallout will be disastrous the first time one of those things gives a false positive."

Good point. She'd give the speaker that.

Inola glanced down and logged back into her handscreen's server. They wouldn't find anything with the wands, though. The young individuals who'd been genetically "altered" by the Delonese had been monitored by a private, select few. And those test subjects were currently unavailable.

She should know. It was her venture she'd cultivated and allowed. And she enforced its secrecy.

An incoming message dinged from the server she'd just opened. Inola set down her drink.

Thought you should know—one of the ambassador shuttles just emerged from the atmospheric shield surrounding Planet Delon.

She frowned. Who is this?

They didn't answer. Just replied: Before anyone could get a lock on it, the shuttle was pulled back in.

Inola tightened her brow further. The text was sent in the same style as the anonymous "tip" she'd received last night that had prompted her to confront Gaines. Meaning? she typed.

It was trying to escape but was prevented. Still searching but scans are useless past the shield.

Inola's stomach constricted. Who was on it? Why was it pulled back?

The sender's response came quick. No idea. But the shuttle had activated its distress signal.

She tapped her screen and asked again, Who is this?

The messaging stopped. She waited. Ten seconds later the

screen went blank and all words disappeared. She swept her thumb over the monitor, searching for the conversation. Nothing. The messages, the info, the traces were gone.

What does that mean? Inola glanced at her clock, then looked up and caught Jerrad's eye. "Did you see those messages that just came through?"

"I did. Do you think the Delonese have figured it out yet, madam?"

Tick, tick, tick, tick . . .

She chewed the inside of her cheek, then took another sip of chardonnay. And peered out the windshield to see the screens displaying another ad for Altered.

Which part? she wondered.

That Sofi and Shilo could save the alien race?

Or that they could utterly destroy it?

5

SOFI

"HELLO, AMBASSADOR MIGUEL AND GIRL-SOFI. NICE OF YOU TO appear."

Sofi closed her eyes and pictured her brother's face. Pictured the sound of his voice. The last time she'd heard him three days ago, in the middle of the World FanFight game that he'd been winning, and that, as the lead gamer controlling his tech from behind the glass, she'd been helping him win.

"You there, Sof?" Shilo's gasping voice had filled her earpiece as he'd kicked and twisted underwater, trying to escape Corp 24's player dragging him down, screaming as Sofi worked like mad to save him. Shi's gaze had swerved to meet her horrified one, holding the same expression she'd seen from him a hundred times through their youth. *Shilo Snow, Corp 30's twelve-year-old star player, wasn't. Finished. Yet.*

And then the bomber's explosion had taken out a quarter of Manhattan's exclusive FanFight arena as Sofi stood on the other side of the giant window of the watery coliseum, watching her brother fight for his life. He'd shoved the bomber off and hurled himself for the surface, just as her entire world exploded into shards of metal and water and bloody bones propelled through a single, wretched pane of glass.

One pane.

That'd been all that had separated them . . .

She opened her eyes, aware that it suddenly felt as if that windowpane were in front of Sofi once again—in the form of fifteen feet of empty air. This time separating her and Miguel from the searching Delonese peacekeepers standing in the space station doorway. While the eyes of Delonese Lead Ambassador Ethos pressed against her and Miguel's backs through a telescreen—seeing, revealing, exposing them toward certain death.

"Don't move an inch," a voice murmured in Sofi's earcom. She frowned. For a second, Vic sounded oddly like Shilo.

She swallowed and cleared him from her head—*definitely not helping right now, Sof*—and gauged the distance to the closest room as the panel behind them spoke again. "Hello, Ambassador Miguel and Girl-Sofi. Nice of you to appear."

Sofi jerked, then tightened her grip on her bag before sliding her other hand to Miguel's to propel him with every fiery muscle in her body. *Ready?* But his fingers pressed into her, holding her in place against that talking wall.

She squeezed his hand. *What is he doing? We have to move.*

He stayed taut and murmured against her hair, "I believe it's a recording."

"Maybe, but those guys aren't," she hissed, tipping her gaze to the five guards still standing at the doorway, framed by the planet's interior of shiny walkways and honeycomb rooms gaping behind them.

"If we go now, we'll get caught."

She swallowed. Was he kidding? If they stayed, they were

going to get caught—so why not take a chance running for it? She eyed the distance to the room again. Ten feet.

Question was, would it lead to another hall or be a dead end?

"Trust me," Miguel whispered.

Sofi stalled. Had he ever asked that of her before?

Before she could decide, Vic muttered into her com, "Wait for it." And again, the voice sounded like Shilo's. Sofi clenched her hands into fists at the sensation. It was just like everything else about this place—it all felt haywire.

The Delonese soldiers stepped into the corridor, and one tilted his head to stare straight into the thin shadow at her. She froze. From her peripheral, she saw his gaze pierce the air, as if he could see her but wasn't sure if she was real. He leaned forward and sniffed the air like a badger. He knew she was here. He could sense it.

What are Miguel and I doing—why aren't we running?

Miguel pressed her hand harder as Sofi's spine rippled like a live feed, every nerve reacting with the need to drag him away from the seven-foot-tall frames blocking the wide doorway. The eerily beautiful and nearly identical beings that aside from the unusual height and large eyes resembled Earth's humans in every way. And right now those unblinking eyes were scanning the space, just like they had that day on the farm.

There's no one here, she murmured internally, imagining her words like a shield, as if she could block their thoughts with her own.

"Don't make eye contact," her earcom said.

Like being trapped in the barn again.

The guard took a step toward her, his eyes narrowing, and immediately she could swear the air pressure thickened. Those tall bodies and thin fingers coming for them.

Cripe. I can't do this—can't breathe.

She needed to gasp, to pull in long draughts. She started to hedge back, chest shaking as she began choking and her vision dimming—

Miguel silently pulled her into himself from behind, and suddenly his heart was there, *beat, beat, beating* against her lungs, breathing with her, breathing for her. "I won't let them take you," she heard him mutter under his breath.

"Focus. You're not finished yet," her earcom said.

She inhaled. Then slowed her breathing.

And blocked out the searching eyes of the aliens.

Tap into what makes your mind work clearer: Technology. Music.

Where's the beat, Sof?

Reaching out mentally, Sofi tuned in to that continued *thud* vibrating against her shoulders, like the bass line of a song, in the form of the playboy ambassador she'd spent the last year and a half loathing. Miguel's heart. Beating life against her frozen one.

From there she moved her mind to the video wall where the pixels were buzzing behind her, working through all their codes and pathways. She let the subtle sound of it skitter across her skin and through her veins, the hazy-lit rhythm becoming both the bass and computer hacks she needed to acquire.

Good. Now, when we came through the rooms earlier, was there any place Vic and I could've used to reaccess the planet's security system?

She looked past the Delonese's faces to try to picture it. But the only access she could recall were the rooms on the planet's icy surface above.

The next second a voice erupted behind the peacekeepers.

Then another emitted on a wall telescreen where hordes of Delonese hovered. Followed by the same voice bursting forth on another wall, then another, as if a recorded track echoed through the hollow chambers along every blank space of the oversize catacomb outside that doorway. "Hello, Ambassador Miguel and Girl-Sofi. Nice of you to appear."

The tall peacekeeper who'd been studying her gave a confused shake of his head, then turned and said something to the others. Sofi's skin prickled, but the peacekeepers straightened, muttered, and flipped around so quickly their boots scraped the black metal floor grate and the team walked out to the corridor.

Miguel loosened his arm and let out a deep exhale that fluttered against her neck as Sofi became aware that her fingernails were pinching his skin. She let go and, without redrawing the guards' attention, slipped for the room ten feet away before checking her handscreen. When Miguel entered, she asked, "How'd you know they wouldn't see us? Did Vic tell you she could shield us like that?"

He was already walking toward the back of the room. "I didn't."

Sofi looked up. "You said to trust you."

"I said I wouldn't let them take you." He halted halfway in his search and began striding back, apparently having discovered what she'd already realized—there was no exit but the door they'd just come through. "What do you mean about Vic shielding us?"

"Using the com. She told us not to move." She tapped the earcom again. "Vic, are you able to see the room next to this one? Because we're not going to make it past the hall."

The AI didn't reply.

Miguel's brow furrowed. "You had Vic on earcom?"

Sofi tapped it again but received no response as she pulled up the last functioning map she'd been able to access on her phone. It didn't show the space station but gave a layout of the ice-planet's surface. If she could figure out where they were in regard to the topical locations, then maybe they could figure a way up into one of the barrack buildings from down here. "Miguel, I think if we—"

"Miguel, you still there?" The tiny holographic version of Vicero abruptly appeared on his handscreen.

"We're here. Thanks for the shielding. But we're—"

"What? Listen, the Delonese have taken back another section of the coding Sofi used to gain control over their systems."

Miguel shifted his gaze back to Sofi, who glanced from him to Vic, only to find the holograph's head cocked as if assimilating data as fast as she could. "They accessed the shuttle containing Claudius, Danya, and all twenty children."

"How?" Sofi edged over to lean in. "We made sure they'd make it beyond the planet's atmospheric field, and it's been in the air over an hour."

"Yeah, but the shuttle is Delon's technology, and they went after it."

Not just after it—they were after the kids. After the proof Miguel'd spent the past year and a half collecting about the abductions. Proof that, while Earth believed Delon was restoring humanity from the devastation of its world wars, the visitors had also been helping themselves to Earth's most precious commodity.

Miguel ran a hand over the back of his neck. Sofi watched his attractive gaze harden, and she pursed her mouth. "What are you saying, Vicero?" Miguel asked softly.

"Not sure yet. But they grabbed enough control to pull it back into their atmospheric shield. And the way they're taking back the rest of their systems, I won't have contact with you much longer either."

Sofi attacked her handscreen again, trying to calm her stomach. "Taking them back? I thought you'd just regained more of their tech."

The AI's tone changed. "I don't understand."

"My earcom. You just gave directions in my com and shielded us."

Vic was shaking her head. "Sof, I haven't had access to either of your coms since ten minutes ago. Why do you think I keep using Miguel's handscreen?"

Sofi froze.

"I haven't been able to access your coms since ten minutes ago."

Prickles of sweat beaded over her skin. That wasn't possible. *Who was talking to me then?*

"You sure it wasn't your suit ghosting?"

Sofi frowned. Glanced down. Stopped. The ghost function. How had she forgotten to turn it back on? *Gad, Sofi.* Except she knew how. The moment she walked into the room she and Shilo had been trapped in, everything else had ceased to exist.

That didn't answer what had shielded them, though.

Tapping her handscreen, she pulled up an interface to adjust the settings on the black slim-suit she was wearing—the same full-body type Shilo used in the FanFight Games. The outfit, along with her body, evaporated into the walls around them, taking Miguel with it, until she could barely make out either of them. Like a trick of the light or eye—as if you weren't certain what you were seeing or whether anything was there at all.

Except for the fact she could feel Miguel as tangibly as her own skin.

"We've got it on now," Miguel answered Vic quietly. His ghostly hand smoothed his shirt and hair, coiffing his looks before he turned to Sofi.

She snorted.

He shrugged. "Sorry. Old habit." Then glanced at her hand-comp. "So, what do we know?"

"Other than you're a pansy?" She allowed a small grin. And reexamined the surface layout on her screen. "I think we can trace—"

"Guys, the shuttle—" Vic's voice glitched.

Miguel tipped the comp.

"They're being—" Vic's holographic image flickered. "Their emergency signal is—"

Miguel looked at Sofi. His expression showed the same instantaneous horror gripping her gut.

She started to move. "We need that tech-room."

"We need that shuttle. Vic, I don't care what it takes, just get us access to it."

The AI's image disappeared just as Sofi reached the door. She enlarged the surface map she'd been working on and hissed at Miguel, "I think we need to get back up to the surface to have a chance at hacking this effectively."

He began to say something, then stopped because he had to know she was right. Down here was a cat's game with thousands of the visitors looking for them. Sofi could feel them drilling into her head with all their noise. Up on the surface there'd only be a few hundred, and Miguel knew the buildings. She winced. But the fact was they'd have to leave Shilo behind . . .

They couldn't help him if she couldn't find him.

She eyed the next closest room, twenty feet down the hall. The Delonese wall vids were still blabbering.

"You'll have to stay within four feet of my suit's ghosting function or you'll become visible. Just like before," she said to Miguel.

They peered into the hall and then, at her nod, darted to that room—in the direction of the elevator they'd come down on, if her instincts were correct. The lights remained steady and low as Sofi headed through the maze of med stations resembling those in the rooms they'd stumbled around in earlier.

Miguel stayed silent as he kept pace, his warmth lingering around her even as the tension poured off him just as perceptibly as it was radiating off of her, especially the farther they made it past the machines. She could feel him. His body. His tattooed arms and chest and neck moving lithely beside her.

It drowned out the awareness of her own heart's nervous patter. She upped her pace and rechecked their bearings. At the back of the room, a thin door stood open and waiting. It led into a second room that was the same as the previous, with another door waiting as well.

Good instinct, Sof.

Only this one had entered had the pods like they'd encountered just before Heller had gone weird. The type that hung like giant vats of blue liquid from the ceilings, beneath low blue lights. Holding lifeless, Delonese beings inside—some full-grown and others the size of fetuses.

Sofi ducked past them and refused to look up.

Except . . .

Except a face caught her eye.

She slowed. "Miguel . . ."

He was already staring at it. The Delonese face pressed to the glass was eerie—not yet alive but identical in every other way to the rest of the race. Its features frozen in time along with its limbs. Like Frankenstein's creation simply waiting for animation.

Sofi's gaze followed Miguel's ghostly arm pointing up at the large vats, to where tiny tanks were attached to the tops, like candy jars. Each one holding what was clearly a type of organ. A heart. A liver. Another that appeared to be a human spleen. They weren't just attached to this vat but to all of them.

Sofi's spine went slick as her heart shriveled in her chest. She tried to speak but the words got lost. Even from here she could tell these parts hadn't just been grown from human cells—they'd come out of humans. And were now being used for—what? She couldn't tell.

But they hadn't simply been extracting DNA.

She reached out a hand and pressed it to the glass—only to jump as an electric jolt surged through her body. With a small cry she yanked away, but not before she swore the alien twitched and an image seared into her brain. The picture of her cells being morphed and mixed with those of the alien, working all the way through its blood and rushing past its heart on up into its mind—with the suggestion of waking it up.

She turned away.

"Sof," Miguel said quietly.

Right. They had to keep going. She shook off the disgust enough to step toward the three closed doors lining the back wall of the room while trying to decide what it would take to destroy this entire planet.

"Sof," Miguel said again. This time more insistent. He wasn't standing near the tanks anymore but in front of what appeared to be a blank wall a few feet away. It took a second to realize it wasn't a wall at all but a thick window. And with Miguel outside of her ghosting perimeter, she could see him staring through the pane.

She joined him and peered through the glass, only to utter a gasp. "What the—?"

The window looked down upon an enormous room the size of a warehouse—and from it, other warehouse rooms branching off. And filling the entire space were the same perfect octagon blue cylinder vats as in this room, lined up in perfect rows, in perfect suspension from the high ceilings, full of thousands upon thousands of adult Delonese bodies, floating in unanimated status. The Delonese had created a lifeless army.

"This is what they're using all the disappearing kids for. They're harvesting them to expand the Delonese species," Miguel muttered.

Sofi wanted to run. To lunge for the doors on the back wall and leave them behind.

Instead, she turned and, clenching her teeth, strode over to the largest vat and lifted her hand. "Like heck they are."

Her fingers curiously felt that same shock again when she touched it. *Strange.* She pressed harder as the reaction from the glass-like siding began burning into her skin. A suspicion formed in her mind that whatever the Delonese had originally done to her was displaying in this bizarre connection. And it was one she could use against them.

Her flesh stung and smelled as if it were charring, but she

kept her palm in place until she felt the splintering. Suddenly that section of the vat cracked and began to leak.

She jumped back just as the base exploded and the tube emptied its adult Delonese contents onto the floor and down the legs of her waterproof suit.

If she couldn't stop their warped crusade fully right now, she'd at least show them someone had seen and was unwilling to stay silent about the sins they were performing here.

Miguel had the same idea apparently—just a different method. He held up his handcomp and was videoing the whole scene. He glanced at Sofi. "As soon as we get the chance, we upload this to Vic."

"And accept the reality that we'll be starting a war that Earth may not survive."

He stared at her. "I assumed we both could live with that."

She nodded. There'd never been a question. Silence for the sake of compliance wasn't something either of them had ever done well. They'd take Delon down one way or another.

Sofi curled her fingers around her aching palm, then frowned. "We need to move," she whispered. Whatever had happened when she'd touched the vat wasn't just confined to her senses—something within her said the Delonese had felt it too—as if it were all connected to the medical room, the systems, and the space station. The soldiers' voices were growing louder from beyond these rooms, clogging her earcom's translator. She turned for the three doors.

"You two there?" Vic's voice erupted through Miguel's hand-screen. "The Delonese have . . ."

Miguel reached to scan the handheld over the second door's sensor. "Say again, Vic."

"The Delonese didn't just . . . They are—"

Silence.

"Vic?"

Sofi ran her comp along the first door's edge. When it wouldn't open, she moved to try the second after Miguel's failed, then the third. She glanced at her screen's surface map, then switched over to the light display showing the Delonese—they were closing in from the hallway through which she and Miguel had come.

Cripe. What were you thinking interfering, Sof?

She dropped to her knees, working faster, typing code into her comp as Miguel tried each door again.

"Did you guys hear me?" Vic's voice suddenly crackled. "They're bringing the whole thing down, kids and all."

Sofi looked up at Miguel as he moved to join her. "What— like they're just going to crash it?" The dread in Miguel's eyes matched the feeling in her gut.

"I'm sorry . . . Can't stop . . . K—"

The signal was gone again.

Sofi tried entering a different code. They had to get to the surface.

The door dinged and swished and Sofi stood. Except it wasn't their door, but one ten feet over that opened.

She started toward it just as a group of Delonese stepped through. Miguel caught her arm and held them both frozen as the aliens took in the shattered vat and the Delonese body on the floor.

"Ambassador Miguel and Girl-Sofi, we are aware you're here," the lead officer said after a moment. "Our sensors have revealed as much. You should know we have taken back full control of the shuttle with your friends on it—so you will show yourself or they will suffer."

Sofi's eyes met Miguel's.

Even ghosted, she saw his thin expression turn from anger over what they'd just seen to fury over the threat to the others. She put her hand on his chest and shook her head. As if to say, *Stay still. Stay silent. As soon as the guards walk far enough, we can lunge through the door. We'll figure out how to save the shuttle and destroy these rooms.*

The Delonese stepped forward and lifted their guns. "Please be aware we will not ask again." Then swung her direction as the door beside her and Miguel softly clicked. The guards scurried closer, cutting off their ability to run back the way they'd come.

Trapped.

Sofi's chest began pounding again, stealing her breath and inflating her fear of being strapped down on one of those beds again. She grabbed Miguel's hand just as he turned his ethereal gaze on her. He smiled.

She shook her head. *No. No, don't.*

She put her hand on his chest, forbidding him, but it was already too late. The look in his eyes matched the pulse of his heartbeat, telling her to brace for something. Telling her he trusted her to figure out the puzzle to this place, and to the whole *diablos* world. Just like she'd figured out the puzzle to him.

The next moment, with a green flash, the door she'd been working on beeped and the seal released. And opened.

The Delonese soldiers narrowed their guns in her direction, lunging forward just as Miguel reached down to brush her cheek and whispered, "I told you I wouldn't let them take you."

He shoved her through the open door and stepped forward five paces, far enough to pull outside of her suit's ghosting function as they yelled—and he casually said, "Eh, *mis amigos*. Nice to see you."

6

MIGUEL

MIGUEL HIT THE GROUND SO FAST HE HARDLY KNEW WHICH ONE of the guards had shoved him. His earcom crackled as his back thumped against the slick, wet surface and the blue fluid from the broken vat sloshed onto him.

They crouched over, demanding, "Ambassador Miguel, you'll inform us of Girl-Sofi's location."

"Ambassador Miguel, you'll inform us of Girl-Sofi's location."

"Amb—"

He waved a hand. "Sí, sí, I hear you, but I can't help you. She ran off looking for her brother." Which was both believable and somewhat true. If that mattered.

Two of them had already rushed through the doorway Sofi'd exited—good gad, he hoped she'd trusted him enough to have kept running.

She knew how to do her thing. The best he could do was give her more time by doing his.

And he knew how to do it quite well.

He peered up at the faces hovering over him and flashed them the wide grin that could "slay a million hearts," according to last week's *Enquiring* magazine. "So, where are we at, boys? Friends? Lovers? Secret admirers? Come now, I won't tell." He lifted an arm, now soaked in that sterile-smelling fluid the lifeless Delonese had been floating in, and sniffed as if in disgust. "At the very least, how about you let me up? This beauty wash is doing nothing for my skin."

The Delonese nearest him gave a snort but glanced at the others before the tallest of the three nodded. "We are only allowed to comply with your request if you behave as Delon-Earth protocol requires, Ambassador."

"Gentlemen, please. I always behave," he muttered, pushing himself to stand, while considering the merciful reality that his *madre* was dead, so she couldn't hear such a lie come from her sweet *hijo*. The woman would probably drag him to the priest right then and there—no matter what these aliens threatened with their guns.

"We have acquired Ambassador Miguel," the tallest Delonese said into his handcom. "Lord Ethos, would you have us bring him now or wait until we've obtained Girl-Sofi?"

Miguel's gut tightened. Their obtaining Sofi was not going to happen—not in his mind, not ever. Not with what it might do to her. What *they* would most certainly do to her.

Calmly, Miguel. You can't save her if your head's fogged. He checked his nerves and went to smooth his hair, then thought better of it. The sterile smell was more than one man could handle, and the thought of that liquid in his hair was appalling even to him. "If Ethos will see me, I'd suggest you take me to him sooner than later."

He casually tilted his gaze toward the large window, through which spanned the warehouse of bodies. "It would appear he and

I have some political business to discuss. At least if he'd like to stay in my good graces."

The lead Delonese's face didn't even flicker an emotion. Just nodded. "Lord Ethos agrees. You will come." Then turned his unblinking eyes on the other two, who promptly fell into alignment on each side of Miguel.

"About your shell of a guy on the floor, by the way," Miguel said just as they reached the med room door. "And you all wonder why your race can't reproduce?"

"I'd urge caution with your words in front of Lord Ethos, Ambassador."

"And I'd caution you against using my people as lab rats."

7

INOLA

TICK. TICK. TICK. TICK.

Inola stood forty stories above her city streets in her air-conditioned Corp 30 office and listened to the clock.

It was an archaic timepiece she'd insisted on keeping, even though it'd meant getting the thing repaired regularly through the years. It'd hung in her daughter Ella's room when Inola had married Ben. And it'd stayed there as Inola had counted down the years and hours until seven-year-old Ella's last diseased breath, only days before Sofi's fourth birthday and months before Shilo was born.

Childhood cancer had been a merciless consumer back then. A ticking time bomb. The fact the disease had all but disappeared might be attributed to Inola—but the clock was a reminder that even the best intentions often come too late when one isn't proactive enough.

A good leader would always be looking ahead, scanning the horizon for what might come and for how to embrace or stop it.

It's what the Delonese lead ambassador, Lord Ethos, had done.

And up until recently, Inola had highly respected him for it.

Any individual who shot his people's planet through a wormhole to land in the Milky Way and park right beside Earth's moon had some clout. And any who did so as a Hail Mary for the sake of rebooting his dying species was her kind of person.

So, if anyone was bound to assist him, it might as well have been someone with a sense of morality. These were kids, for heaven's sake. And in exchange, she got access to some of the greatest medical cures ever seen.

Originally it'd been simple. Look away as Delon took kids to extract a few cells, manipulate others, and send them home healed of asthma, bone disease, and a host of other things. Not to mention each individual's altered DNA she could then collect samples from. In fact, the initial study had shown such promise, Inola had sent her own kids seven years ago, as part of the third group taken.

Until every single child in all three control groups died within the second year, except for Shilo and Sofi—who, with no visible signs of enhancement, were deemed failures. Just living rather than dead.

After that, she had allowed twenty orphans a year, from whom Delon could extract cells without adding any. All those children survived and made it home, with no memories to show for it—and in exchange the Delonese created one health cure a year that Inola's Corporation could sell.

They were doing good work. Merciful work. Giving the Delonese a chance at life and giving humanity the chance not to repeat the Delonese's sterility mistakes.

The only thing was . . .

Seven years of Delon trying to reboot their race hadn't

worked. They were on the cusp, Lead Ambassador Ethos kept saying. But the countdown was on.

They just needed more cells. More subjects. More kids.

More kids. There'd been rumors lately of more kids gone missing . . .

She turned away from the ticking clock—back to the office made entirely of gold titanium walls and bulletproof, floor-to-ceiling windows overlooking the Manhattan hub. Before refocusing on the monitors that Jerrad and his two top-tier intelligence personnel had been silently studying.

She tapped her fingers nervously on the table. "You're telling me there's absolutely nothing showing up about a shuttle issuing a distress alert near Delon?"

The second officer indicated a group of reports scrolling on-screen. "The moment you called from the car, we pulled the feeds from every secure station available. These are from the past two days—and they're as normal as you'd expect."

"I see that. And your meaning?"

"Either the individual messaging you didn't know what he or she was talking about or had access to something we don't." Her tone made clear exactly how impossible she considered this. "You said the messages weren't more specific?" The tech glanced back and forth between Inola and Jerrad.

"Just that one of the shuttles had tried to leave and was pulled back. And its distress signal was activated." Inola pinched the bridge of her nose and tossed a glance at the closed security door before lowering her own voice. "I assume you looked beyond the available feeds?"

The officer gave a nod and respectfully dropped her own voice. "We hacked every defense and satellite we know of, including the United World Corps'. It's not just that there are no reports. It's that there's not even any chatter."

Inola sighed and rubbed her cold hands. "So either the Delonese erased all evidence and intel right after one random person caught it, or . . ."

The two officers looked at her.

Or it didn't happen.

With a click of her tongue, she strode to the window to peer up at the small, pale planet in the cerulean sky. Of course, they could be right. The messages were most likely a hoax, just one of her political enemies messing with her, in light of today's events.

Except . . .

She scanned the bright horizon. "What about Sofi?" She turned. "Could my daughter or that FanFight tech who went with her have done it? The guy, Heller?"

The first officer looked at Jerrad, then back at Inola. "They could've wiped your server messages, yes. At least, Sofi could've. But Heller—"

Inola waved a hand. That's not what she meant. Of course they both could clean codes. Inola had seen it herself last night when she'd had Jerrad pull the online files Gaines hid behind new firewalls—or rather, Gaines had gotten *Heller* to hide, according to the virtual fingerprints uncovered.

"I'm not asking if they're capable with Earth's tech," Inola said. "I'm asking if there's any indication of Sofi using *Delon* technology on a large scale in the past thirty-eight hours." She waited, heart pounding in her chest, aware of what she was really suggesting.

Jerrad bent back over the see-through screens and studied

each one himself. He took a sip of organic coffee, then shook his head and straightened. "We'll keep looking, but I just don't see how. It's like an entirely different language hundreds of years ahead of us. And even with the amount of their tech we use—it's only because they've enabled it." He set his cup down and looked meaningfully at her.

The first officer adjusted her unnecessary fashion glasses. "And if there really was an alert set off from the shuttle, it's far more likely Sofi'd be the victim rather than the perpetrator—if you get me?"

Inola tipped her chin. Yes, she knew what they meant. She and Jerrad also knew *more* than what they meant.

She waved at her handcomp. "In that case, aside from Sofi, who could hack my server that thoroughly?"

"Honestly?" The second officer cleared her throat and side-eyed the others. "Maybe two of the other Corps. Six people in the world, including a few underground gamers."

That's what she thought. Inola looked at Jerrad. "I want the team focused on the planet without drawing attention to themselves, looking for any tidbit they can find. See if there's any crack in the Delonese shield or evidence of data transfers."

"Yes, madam."

"Because, Jerrad"—she softened her tone—"something's going to happen."

"Ma'am, is this to do with Sofi?"

Inola turned to the Second. It had everything to do with Sof—
Boom!

An explosion went off beneath the window. Jerrad lunged for Inola, yanking her away from the glass just as a set of sparks lit up the afternoon sky and all four of the room's occupants hit the floor. Another explosion erupted. Followed by another shower of sparks—this time farther from the pane.

"Fireworks," Jerrad breathed out after a minute. "Blasted tourists."

Inola caught her breath as he released her and helped her up. She straightened her suit jacket as they moved to look down at the street where the crowds were indeed setting off fireworks. Except these weren't just the FanFight kind. This group was full of alien protestors, holding their signs and masks and bullhorns.

"They're preparing to march," the first officer observed. "The Altered invention's got them worked up."

Jerrad leaned into the glass, assessing the gathering, then peered back at the two officers. "Please give us the room."

When the First and Second had shut the door behind them, Jerrad looked at Inola. "I hate to say it, but the fact that Sofi's been labeled a terrorist who's being harbored by the Delonese—"

She was already nodding. "Not my most flattering moment, but it'll pass."

"I'm talking about your safety. I think it'd be best to stay out of the public eye. At least until—"

She laughed. Until what? Until they could unravel this? She sniffed. *Welcome to politics.* She shook her head. "I'm not going to hide, Jerrad. That would only empower the politicians. They feed on weakness like wolves." Inola reached up to smooth her long black hair back into place. "Gaines may want my position, but she's not foolish enough to sacrifice her reputation. That's precisely why she ordered the bombing in the first place—to cover our private business with the Delonese. Her outrageous choice to do it so indiscreetly just proves my point."

"Respectfully, I'm not so sure of that. And there are other ways to remove you."

"What, like assassination?" Inola rolled her eyes. "Even she wouldn't risk the sensitive documents that would release from my life-safe bank. There's too much incrimination."

He tipped his head at the crowds below the window. "And what about them? You're Sofi's mom. If they catch even the slightest hint of your side project, that mob will eat you alive."

Inola couldn't disagree with that.

She studied the sign holders who'd begun heading in the direction of the FanFight Colinade, which stood barely five blocks from her office. In a feat of good old-fashioned human wonder, the contractors had already repaired the coliseum from the explosion. And in another feat of human nature, that same explosion would be all but forgotten today as the Corps tried to distract through continuing the Games.

Feed the citizens on entertainment and they'll not care what you accomplish in secret. Wasn't that the age-old creed of the ruling classes?

Wasn't that the creed she'd lived by?

The tightening in her chest returned as an image passed in front of her eyes—of her children quite possibly fighting on Delon for their very lives. It was only a matter of time. If Shilo was even alive.

Her throat narrowed.

With an inhale she cracked her neck and cleared her voice as an ad across the street suddenly sprang to life. A group of young girls appeared to be pointing up at the FanFight announcement regarding the Games' big finale—the Final Five. The ad was offering suggestions for people to get their votes in for whichever celebrity they'd like to see pitted tomorrow against the player who won tonight. Like everything else, tomorrow's finale contestants were audience chosen.

The ad flipped through faces of past politicians, musicians, and i-reality stars—all of whom had fought and failed in the ultimate match. The only difference was, whichever four celebrities were picked for the final round only participated if they agreed. They always did, of course. The promises of more fame and a slightly easier game were too enticing to decline.

The girls watching the ad suddenly began jumping up and down as nineteen-year-old Ambassador Miguel's face graced the screen, followed by his physique striking different poses across business and entertainment magazines. Titles like "How He Does It" and "Earth's #1 Bachelor—Is He Secretly Celibate?" scrolled beneath them.

She frowned. And studied Miguel's face.

Last night Gaines told her she'd been blackmailing both Ambassadors Alis and Miguel to keep the blame off Corp 30, but to Inola, his behavior had seemed as brazen as ever. It was how he kept the public adoring him, from what she'd seen. Always front and center of their attention.

And now he was on Delon with her daughter.

Where is he in all this?

She eyed the FanFight Colinade in the distance.

Where do I need to be in all this?

Sliding her handscreen into her jacket pocket, she peered up at Jerrad. "Thank you for the warning. But I think I may have something different in mind."

"Miss?"

"I'll be attending the FanFight Game. Please have them bring the car around."

He nodded and turned, but before he could issue the order, a robotic voice chimed across the four comp-screens in the room. "CEO Inola, please hold for a message from Delonese Ambassador Ethos."

SOFI

"BEHIND YOU!"

Without thinking Sofi flattened against the cold honeycomb wall as a group of Delonese guards appeared and rushed past her ghosted body, their footsteps softly muted like hers on the metal surface.

Good catch.

"Now head over fifty steps."

Sofi didn't move. Just panted to catch her breath, then tapped her earcom. "Hello?"

No sound. She waited for a reply, and when it didn't come, whispered louder, "Hellooo."

Nothing.

She frowned. The voice directing her was the same she'd heard earlier, but how could she be hearing Shilo? She was starting to believe it wasn't a voice at all, just her mind. Or more specifically, her old memories. *This is how bad the Delonese jacked you up, Sof. You're hearing your own memories from years ago.*

Just like the memories she'd had the past few days of Shilo. Now she was imagining his voice.

Only thing was—thus far they'd been eerily accurate.

She clenched her jaw and jogged ahead, looking for anything familiar. Ignoring the throbbing in her palm and the guilty knowledge that Miguel had just sacrificed himself for her. Admittedly to an environment he was skilled at, but still . . . She flicked her gaze down to her handscreen, to compare her position to the surface map. The awareness dug in all the deeper that he had simply bought her time.

The only way she could help him now was the same way she could help everyone else stuck in this terror—hack the system, shut it down, and get them all back to Earth.

And then expose wide open Delon's horrific secrets.

Which meant there was no way any of them were making it out of here alive.

She pursed her lips. She was good, but . . .

Fifty steps over, she hit a second near-empty section that appeared much older. The white walls not as white, the lights not as bright, the lab rooms sitting empty. The smell of medical death was still there, though, casting a pall over everything.

"Make a right and follow the catacomb rooms to the end. Take a left at the fork and you'll find another hall."

She shook her head, but obeyed. The voice was right, of course. That path would bring her a few hundred yards from the barracks, if her comp was correct. She found the fork and took a left.

"At the end there's a shaft."

The hall dead-ended into a shaft fitted with a thin black ladder leading upward. She glanced around. They had to be joking.

This thing was beyond old skool for how tech savvy the whole place was.

Didn't matter—she'd take it. Scaling the rungs as fast as she could, Sofi kept her breath even as she headed up the three stories toward an unknown outlet, through what quickly turned into an all-encompassing metal tube of darkness. Kind of like crawling inside a worm.

Great image, Sofi. Gad.

She moved faster.

Something flickered around her, and abruptly a red light was flashing in her eyes. *What the—?* She squinted, and the next second her head hit the ceiling. She flipped her handcomp light on to reveal a square metal hatch barely wider than her body.

She shoved it. *Nothing.* Then tried multiple sides, pushing against the lip around the edges, but the thing wouldn't budge.

Bracing her back against one side of the tube and her legs against the ladder, Sofi shoved one hand against the lid and, with the other, waved her handcomp over what appeared to be a kind of sensor pad.

The lid hissed, squealed, and flipped up, sending a gush of icy air and snowflakes in so quickly it nearly knocked Sofi loose. She gripped her handcomp tighter and climbed the last few rungs, then shoved her head and shoulders through the opening into the outside air of the planet's surface.

The snow around her was thick and so cold it burned to the touch without her fingers leaving an imprint in it. Huh. Sofi turned an almost 360-degree circle to take in the vast surroundings from her little pothole that sat smack in the center of the large fenced-in compound she and the others had snuck through earlier. And beyond that, an entire world of white snow-dusted ground and rich blue skies.

Beautiful. Pristine. The place was a winter wonderland as far as her eyes could see. An ice-entrenched landscape of fog-covered mountains in the distance and, closer in, trees. Nearer still were the rows of barracks inside the enormous fenced-in area that made up the entirety of the capital. And to her left inside that area? The main building she needed. Three stories high and the sides all flat with no frills. Like the design of a cult fortress she'd once seen in Old Canada. With windows scattered here and there and an assembly of massive shuttle bays attached at the end.

The bays.

She looked up for the shuttle—but found nothing besides blue skies and white clouds. Then, with a glance at her suit's ghosting features, stuck her comp in her mouth and slid her hands up to grip the metal lip and hoist herself out.

Two seconds later, a siren went off.

Seriously? She yanked her legs the rest of the way out and slammed the hatch shut behind her while simultaneously gauging the distance between her and the main bay. That's where she needed to be.

Deep breath. Aiming her comp map in the direction of the first barrack, she brought up layers of lights that slashed across the screen, indicating the camera vid placements between her, the rows of army-looking barracks, and the main building. *"Trace that pattern if you want to get to the main building unseen,"* she'd told Miguel earlier.

Her chest winced over what might be happening to him right now.

Stop, Sof. It won't help.

She cracked her neck and took off amid the teeth-chattering cold and that blasted alarm ringing—and covered the yards to the first rectangular barrack in seven seconds flat. When she looked back, there were no footprints. Just like she'd left no fingerprints in the snow. Which was a relief, considering eight guards suddenly appeared and hurried past just as she reached the building's edge.

She lurched back as they surged forward to search the area in front of her. Hunching against the wall, she held her breath to keep it from fogging the air. Then watched as they moved on to check the ground around the hatch.

The wind picked up, slashing her skin, and Sofi gave a soft exhale, followed by a puff of white air. The guards were continuing on to the edge of the clearing to look at something over in the forest. She slid around to the building's metal corner and calculated the next run. She could almost hear the FanFight team asking if she was ready, like they did so many times each round.

A low rumble overhead vibrated the snowy ground under her feet.

The aerial growl was followed by a flash, and abruptly the shuttle was visible overhead. Its reflective surface glinted against the blue atmosphere, catching the bright sunlight, and Sofi's spine about ripped in half. *The kids—Miguel's friends.* Vic had been right. The ship they'd sent up with the Earth's other ambassadors, Danya and Claudius—the latter being Miguel's best friend—and the twenty children, was plowing at high speed through the atmosphere toward the ground.

It's what the guards had been staring at.

Oh. Oh please, no.

She could hear Miguel swearing in her head.

Sofi attacked her handscreen. Her hands desperate. Panicky. "Vic, I'm trying to hack in and redirect it," she said just in case the AI could hear.

The Delonese guards were shouting across the area and abruptly the alarm shut off. One pointed at the far tree line, and they all quickly turned on their heels to hurry back to wherever they'd come from. Leaving Sofi to watch the shuttle fall like a star from the sky, backlit on one side by the distant sun and the other by the giant man in the moon, as the ship sparked and shot off flares that evaporated into the air and snow.

Her handscreen reconnected with the system she'd opened earlier. Her fingers fumbled through the coding, while her mind screamed she wasn't fast enough, couldn't do enough without being plugged in, as she heard the thing dropping . . .

down

down

down.

She felt the sob escape her lips, accompanied by a clouded wisp of horror when she glanced back up. It took everything in her not to rush out and—do what? Stand beneath it? Physically stop it? Her mouth went sour as her helplessness and hatred for the Delonese spiraled.

Please just look away. Oh gad, Sofi, freaking look away.

But the image of that vessel holding all those kids falling from the atmosphere kept her rooted and swiping at her screen furiously, trying to force her way back into the original shuttle's system. If they had to live it in this moment, then she could bleeding well stand here like a ghost and watch it.

Her hands refused to give up trying to crack the firewalls

even though Vic was right: Delon had shut down all access to it. Clenching the comp tighter, she went back to sliding code after code aside as she waited for the explosion to rock the planet and for the ground beneath her to shudder with flesh-infused flames bursting up to rip through the treetops and lick at the sky and landscape. Just like the sense of futility was tearing through her because she could only imagine the fear those little hearts must be feeling.

It kept falling, faster. Heavier.

Along with Claudius and Danya.

Sofi moved back to brace for impact.

She waited.

It didn't come.

When she peered up, the shuttle had slammed to a stop in midair fifty yards in front of her, ten feet off the ground.

Sofi hedged forward, unsure whether to be relieved or to prepare for it to burst into flames. A moment later the shuttle righted itself and swung into proper military formation. Then slowly, meticulously, flew in a straight line toward one of the smaller shuttle bays attached to the far side of the main building.

"Bloody heck," she choked out.

With a loud *swoosh* the warehouse door slid up, the shuttle went in, and the door swished closed behind it. And Sofi eased against the barrack wall to release the tension in her neck before pulling out her handscreen to check for surface life-forms now on the planet. They were there—twenty-four tiny red dots, representing the humans now in the shuttle bay. Surrounded by multiple large groupings of blue dots indicating the Delonese.

They are okay. The kids are going to be okay.

For the next few minutes, anyway.

She peered up at the sky and then took off in the direction of that shuttle bay. Until something lodged in her periphery from the edge of the horizon covered in hillsides and fir-looking trees. A massive fog like she'd seen with Miguel yesterday morning was rolling in. Not in a whisper, but in a cloud moving as a tidal wave across the landscape.

Sofi swung her gaze over. Except this one was different. The color was off and a strange smell permeated the air coming ahead of it, reminding her . . .

The entire left side of her body prickled. It reminded her of the poison gas Shilo faced at last year's FanFight game. And it was headed straight for the compound.

It was headed for her.

Sofi peeked at the surface map again and kept running through the vast white-covered area inside the fences.

Past the open space, past the barracks, through the thin powdered snow in a zigzag pattern to avoid the sensors picking up her movements. The handscreen guided her steps, while her head begged the ghosting feature to hold up against the thickening moisture.

The strange fog was getting closer by the second, slipping down past the trees, through the fence, and over the first barrack, then the second, the third—*Is this why the guards hurried inside?* By the time the yellow cloud hit the fourth row of barracks, she was out of breath and her legs were aching. She reached the side of the wide, four-story main hangar and went for a rounded service door, only to see three blue lights on her handscreen indicating Delonese were on the other side.

She scrambled for another door on a smaller hangar, arriving just as the creamy sheets of mist were licking her heels.

Whether it was poison or not, that chemical smell reminded her of things that made her stomach cringe with the terrors she'd seen it cause. She waved her handheld over the door's scanner and watched in relief as it slid up and open. Some of her tech still worked.

The door zipped shut as the fog crashed against the side of the building. She crouched, breathing and blinking in the bright lights. It took a moment to feel the prick of air on her left heel. When she looked down she found the bootie material still intact, but her skin felt as though it had been eaten away.

Ignoring it, Sofi zeroed in on the space that smelled of metal and sanitizer and was mostly taken up by a giant ship that looked clean on the outside, but something told her the inside was far more well used. The room looked vaguely familiar too.

The cargo hold she and Shilo had sat in for two days. Seven years ago.

She swallowed and refused to let the memory surface—the memory of that trip and those tears. And turned to move into a tiny, thin hall of more white walls and ceilings.

She checked the map. She'd been right—the surface was going to be far easier to navigate than the space station below. Now she just needed to find a guestroom to use. Then start at square one to reach Vic and Ranger, her friend and one of Earth's top techies. Both had helped her hack this station once. They could do it again.

After slipping to the far side of the room, she exited via an open door and entered a hall that was the same as those she'd seen earlier. Metallic walls and gray flooring beneath her feet. She pressed against the side and shuffled along it until she reached the first corner where she stopped and listened.

"*Sofi, the door on your right,*" her earcom blared. "*Can you see it?*"

She frowned and slowed as her handheld lit up with red bubbles.

The kids were on the other side of that wall. But where were the Delonese?

There wasn't a blue light in sight.

Before she could decide whether to enter or keep going, the sensor on the door picked up her presence and abruptly opened to reveal a small hangar. It indeed contained the shuttle of Claudius, Danya, and the kids.

No guards in sight.

With caution she slipped in and kept one eye on her handscreen as she inched forward. No blue dots.

The ship sat in the white space with no movement and no metal clicking or parts opening.

She paused.

A door swished and the shuttle let out a rush of steam, and Sofi about dropped her handscreen as she jumped.

Ambassador Claudius's blond hair, magically still gelled into a peak, popped out and his nice eyes peered around. Sofi blinked. Claudius whispered, "Hello?"

Sofi eyed the perpetually aloof countenance that made the twenty-four-year-old, Euro-born, three-year ambassador one of Earth's preferred when dealing with Delon—due to the ease at which he set everyone. As well as his taste in clothing.

Sofi lowered her suit's ghosting function enough to make her body visible.

"Oh good—you're not murdered. I take it Miguel's with you?" Claudius peered around while straightening his shirt and dusting his cuffs. Then quirked a smile at her. "So, you two biddies going to chat all day, or are we going to figure out how to get off this bloody planet?"

A soft rustle caught Sofi's ear at the same time something behind her caught Claudius's eye. His gaze widened as someone grabbed her and the lights went out.

9

MIGUEL

LEAD AMBASSADOR ETHOS LOOKED UP FROM THE ENORMOUS monitor he was in front of just as the guards ushered Miguel into the small room draped in shadows. The dim was so thick, the telescreen made an actual halo surrounding Ethos as he paced in front of an online audience.

The door slid shut with a *swish*, and the guards resumed their silent positions beside Miguel. "Looks like we caught him in the middle of a call with his madre," he murmured.

Apparently neither found it funny.

Lord Ethos's long silver robe rustled with each step as he paced in the plain gray room. "CEOs Hart and Inola, VP Gaines, and Earth scientists, it's a surprise to see such confident faces. It makes me almost believe the fallout from your Earth drama is being adequately handled."

"We can assure you that it is, Lord Ethos," someone said. Miguel frowned. It sounded like CEO Hart.

"Oh, I highly doubt it's being handled as well as we'd like." Ethos brandished an arm, which was the most expressive aspect of him, seeing as his tan, thin, perfectly smooth face stayed perfectly in place. "Considering I have multiple of your Earth politicians on my planet who are *behaving rather badly*, as you humans call it."

"Ambassador Lord Ethos," Miguel heard Gaines say. "I've seen to the cleanup myself—"

"Yes, the bombing. Although, pardon me, Ms. Gaines, but from my perspective, that explosion only seems to have raised more questions."

"Questions we have put at the feet of Corp 24 and Inola's daughter. Again, we can reassure you it is contained."

"Which brings me to Madam Inola." Ethos stopped to face the screen. It gave his large eyes and skin an eerie green glow. "Allow me to extend my condolences. What a shock and tragedy for you. One child dead. The other a mass murderer who has currently taken refuge on my planet."

"Perhaps we should cut the courtesies, Ambassador. You and I both know she's innocent."

Miguel's brow went up. He was used to CEO Inola sounding angry, but this—this was odd. He edged closer—enough to catch a section of the screen with her face on it. She looked calm as ever, except for the eyes. The glint there . . .

She was afraid. *Interesante.*

A tele to the right of the one holding their faces caught his gaze. It appeared to be measuring Delonese stats against Earth's. *¿Qué diablos?* He squinted and studied the calculations and research diagrams that made little sense to him other than something about them looked odd. He shifted uncomfortably as CEO Inola demanded, "Where are my children, Lord Ethos?"

The lead Delonese's tone dripped with graciousness. Miguel could practically feel it oozing off his short tongue. "If it's the unfairness of the accusation to your child, then I'll admit that's none of my concern. But if you're referring to our business side of things—well then, yes, let's discuss that. It has come to my attention in recent weeks that there appears to be an unusual matter regarding your children, CEO Inola. One we now suspect you've known about for quite some time."

Miguel had inched close enough to the second telescreen that he could also see the expressions on all the faces spanning the monitor. Inola's looked frozen in time.

"It appears . . ." Lord Ethos's unblinking eyes narrowed. "That your children house a very unique brain pattern that's developed over the course of the past seven years—following the one and only time when they were in our care on this planet." He paused and waited. Miguel could practically see the alien's gaze boring into Inola, sucking up every reaction. She gave none as far as he could tell.

"So let me make things very clear. With your daughter's arrival here, we now have in our possession what we believe to be the key we've been looking for. And we will be accessing that brain pattern to apply it immediately."

Miguel froze. An image pressed into his mind of Sofi's fingers connecting with the vat down below holding the lifeless body.

It'd reacted to her. It'd *flinched*.

He tried to keep his breathing calm. His head clear. Even as his thoughts spun to the thousands of Delonese bodies beneath the surface waiting in suspended animation. They weren't just going to study her and reboot their race the way humans did—building generation upon generation. They already had an entire one ready of shells that simply needed filling. They were going to strap her down to some machine like a lab experiment or power source and extract whatever it was they needed to bring that entire new population to life. A population that looked disturbingly like a ready-made army. That's what they wanted her for.

His blood flared as Inola's face turned red on the monitor. "You have no right to do such a thing." Her voice was dangerous now. "We see this as a huge breach in trust, Lord Ethos. Add to that recent reports that you've broken our agreement over the past two years by taking more children than discussed and failing to return them."

"And we will continue to do so. Considering it's taken you this long to notice, one can fairly surmise we have greater need for them than your people do." He lifted his hand to stay her interruption. "Plus"—he actually cracked a smile—"I very much doubt you or your politicians will like the alternative."

"Are you threatening us?"

"We will do what we need in order to restart our race. As nearly every individual on Earth has the natural ability to do at any time. It will be a long process to birth a new generation, so I can only ask you to continue to bear with us as you have already committed."

Miguel peered again at the stat pictures on that second screen. If he didn't know better, he'd say it looked like ones the UWC put together whenever assessing repopulating a new territory as they continued to reclaim Earth's wilder territories.

Except these diagrams looked remarkably *like* Earth.

He slowed. What if they *were* Earth? If Delon was a planet, it made sense they'd be satisfied living on it. But the new knowledge that it was a space station, inside where the near entirety of their population resided . . .

That changed everything.

Why else *had* they come to Earth? And where would they go afterward?

A flicker of disgust ignited. Carving up a ten-year-old memory of coming home and finding his family dead after he'd been unable to save them.

He firmed his jaw. And without further thought, took a quick step forward, leaned in, and blurted out, "Madam Inola, he's lying. There are—"

The guards were on him, yanking him back away from the screen and sliding their cold, thin fingers over his mouth.

"Lord Ethos, Inola, please." CEO Hart was interrupting on-screen. "Now, let's just all calm down. I'm sure none of us intended it to go this far. No one here wants to break trust or talk of threats. We're all reasonable sorts, and I think we can understand that some, er, allowances must be made for us to enjoy the Delonese continued good relations with Earth. I think we can all agree that's what's best. Why don't we put this all behind us and just forget—"

"He has my children, Hart. He's taking *Earth's* children and using them far beyond taking simple cells—"

"Madam Inola is correct," Ethos said smoothly. "Her children are ours, and we will use them and any others as we see necessary. And yes, this is a threat, if you'd prefer to call it such. We will proceed as we see best with your support, or we will proceed in spite of you. But hear this. If your people find out, they will come after you first. Then us. And we are quite capable of defending ourselves—even as we have striven for peace. Thus, my recommendation is that we 'stay the course,' as you humans say. If you do not continue to comply, we will be forced to move against you and, eventually, Earth. Therefore, do not interfere and live. Or resist and lose your freedom. Either way, you may consider yourselves at our mercy."

Ethos clicked the screen off, then turned. And put his unusually long fingers together in a triangle to rest beneath his wide chin. "Ambassador Miguel, now that we've recovered you, what shall we do with *you*?"

10

INOLA

"EITHER WAY, YOU MAY CONSIDER YOURSELVES AT OUR MERCY."

Inola couldn't get Ethos's face or words out of her head. Those cold, unblinking eyes that dared to threaten her and everything they'd accomplished together—after the agreement they'd had, the agreement *she'd* had the foresight to set in place.

And the glimpse she caught of Ambassador Miguel in the background—the brief interruption and expression she swore was trying to tell her something before he was yanked off camera.

She tightened her palms into fists and stood tall on the dais in the middle of the round, thirteen story Fantasy Fighting Games coliseum already packed full of spectators. Lord Ethos's decision went beyond providing for his people. It was dishonorable. More than that—it was impossible.

CEO Hart's and VP Gaines's blatant disregard had been one thing, expected even. But she'd assumed Ethos would be a voice of at least some reason. Instead, the leader of a race supposedly centuries ahead in the qualities she'd admired—those of wisdom, unity, and the value of community—had just wielded positional abuse without even flinching.

The human race had just become servants of amoral masters. And she'd helped it happen.

"Figure it out, Sofi," Inola whispered.

"Madam Inola, they're about to begin," Jerrad said in her earcom.

She blinked. *Yes. Right. Focus.*

Her attention moved back to the crowds just as they broke into a wave, rippling their bodies up and down around the entirety of the ringed amphitheater situated as the energetic heartbeat of Manhattan. Massive. Like an open-air temple to olden-day gods. The audience voices frothed along the thirteen circular stories that rose up like rungs on a ladder toward the heavens, blanketed with golden cabanas, floating eateries, and—from the higher-up cheap seats—epic music pouring through the enormous overhead telescreens.

Her throat went sour at the looks on some of their faces . . .

If the glorified white marble event center sat like a tribute to the great Roman coliseums and their divinities, then, for whatever reason, today the throngs felt like an homage to Rome's bloodlust.

The place was *thirsty.* As if Friday's bombing had incited excitement instead of fear. A week ago the scene would've made her proud. Now it simply felt frail and frivolous after the vid conference with Ethos. Earth was walking a delicate tightrope, and only a few of them had a clue.

The guests screamed. The music soared. And giant red banners spun in long sheets amid the humid breeze, trailing, like blood spilling, past the rows of cabanas, floating eateries, and smoothie cafés down toward the focal point—the arena.

"Corp leaders and highly respected Delonese friends!" The announcer's voice broke through the noise. "As well as friends of friends, friends of mine, and friends with benefits!"

On cue, the audience laughed at the introduction that had become the standard for every round since day one. The announcer's small, wiry build and now red permed hair somehow matched his sport shorts and loose tank top, and he buzzed back and forth on a platform hovering halfway up and midair among the encircling chaos. He looked like the version of himself she'd seen printed on the athlete playing cards the kids still collected.

"Please settle in for a *speciaaalll* game—in which seven players and their teams from Corps 1, 2, 10, 13, 19, 25, and 27 will battle in one explosive episode!" He flashed his charmingly crooked smile across the telescreens and let the excitement build. Then uttered a fake gasp and covered his mouth with a hand that at one time held a personal medal in every extreme skate and snow sport. "Oh—hold on. Did I just use the word *explosive*?"

The crowd hooted as the air sizzled with instant tension.

"So offensive of me. But you know what I say? I say it's *offensive* that someone set off an explosion here and tried to depress our *spiiiiirits*! Can I get a witness?"

The laughter instantly transformed into thunderous approval. Inola shook her head and tapped her nails on the railing of the small, square dais she'd bribed private use of for the occasion. *Nice way of outing the elephant, Favio.* She straightened her spine and lifted her head high. And waited.

"And as proof that our spirits will not be kept down—we have our very own FanFight constituent, mother to a victim of the explosion as well as to one of the possible perpetrators, cancer-curing CEO of Corp 30, Madam Inola! To show the world and its terrorists that *we* have not been depressed by the attack. Rather, we have been strengthened by our unwavering humanity!"

Inola released her brazen smile as he pointed to her standing on the platform beside the UWC CEOs-only cabana. And listened as the crowd roared at a deafening volume. After a moment, she waved, clear-eyed and with that continued smile that said she had nothing to hide other than a mother's grief. *Let the crowd feed on that.*

They ate it up, rising to their feet to cheer the woman who'd come despite the fact that, as far as they knew, she'd permanently lost both her children through no fault of her own, other than perhaps bad parenting.

But who could judge her? Who hadn't been a bad parent? She could almost sense them asking themselves and simultaneously justifying her as she played her part with the confidence of a woman who knew what the people loved and needed. A broken woman who could still stand here in support of others. A mother. A humanitarian who'd gone on to cure cancer after the loss of her first child thirteen years ago. And would go on to help them after this loss of her son and betrayal of her daughter.

She leaned forward farther to wave her gratitude to the announcer and extend love to the tens of thousands of faces circling the playing field. Then stepped back into the shadows of the cabana and allowed the rabid cheering to settle and fade.

Inola's earcom clicked. "I stand corrected," Jerrad said. "Nicely played."

"Thank you, Jerrad. Hopefully that solidifies me even stronger in their minds and buys another level of trust and protection. Please make sure to send Favio the athletic collection of old Olympic medals I committed."

"Already done."

Inola nodded. "Now to find Dr. Y—"

Her voice was drowned out by the sporty announcer shouting again. "So, what do you say we get this party *pumped* up by bringing out our remaining *playaaaas*? Dropping down from those sweet ropes before your very eyes onto platforms hanging midair are the teens here to take it *all*." As he spoke, the final seven FanFight players were lowered by metal ropes from the overhead high beams. Slow enough for the audience to scream for each, as one by one the players' faces and stats were flashed across the telescreens.

Inola's handcomp buzzed in her jacket pocket. She ignored it and said louder in her com, "Let me know when you've located Dr. Yate." Then flicked her gaze over to Ms. Gaines, who sat in the center of Inola's Corp 30 cabana, a quarter of the coliseum over, in perfect eye alignment. The woman had paused from her chatting to stare at her with what looked to be surprise, irritation, and just a hint of fear, if Inola had to guess.

"Madam Inola, you should join us!" yelled the CEOs from Corps 5 and 9 as they walked by, heading into the UWC CEO cabana behind her.

Inola lifted a hand to decline just as the stadium was blasted by Favio's voice rocketing through every inch of it. "FanFight friends, please hold on to your seatmates as the redo of round four in the *United World Corporation Fantasy Fighting Games* officially begins. Today, our players fight until only *one* remains. And tomorrow? That player goes on to the *FanFight Final Five*! The part of the Games where *you* choose which celebrities you want to place in the arena with our winning player. And those celebrities *then decide* if—"

He held out his hand and let the audience join him in yelling, "They'll be fighters or failures!" before he continued. "Will they agree to fight and face death tomorrow? They will if they want to stay in our good favor! So get those votes in today!"

The seven players had unhooked from their ropes onto the platforms, which sat eye level from Inola. All young. All wearing their Corp trade colors on their black slim-suits and masks. All probably listening to instructions being given through their earcoms by their game-heads.

"Now that we've reminded you of what's to come and reintroduced you to your main people for today," the announcer screamed, "let's get these FanFights *staaaaarted*."

A swell of music followed as, below, the vast arena's greenscreen began to shift in the playing field below, morphing through various scenery—everything from cupcake wars to zombies to Atlantis and the avalanche ice world the audience had chosen in past fights. The crowd was deciding which environment the teams would battle in.

"We've located Dr. Yate. He's just entered his space, five cabanas over. Would you like us to send him or—?"

"No, I'll go." Slipping away from the railing, Inola strode behind the cabana rows and out into the sun-drenched walkway where her guards and those of the other CEOs stood looking alert as always. Five spots down, she walked through a thick layer of shimmery curtains into a wide tent decorated in simple yet elegant taste. Two mink-brown couches. A white rug. And a self-manned minibar that served mainly bubbly water with essential oils procured at high cost.

On one of those couches sat the man who'd been both therapist and doctor to Inola's children for the past seven years. Ever since their visit to Delon. "Inola! I've been trying to contact you." Dr. Yate rose and extended a hand. "How are you? How's Sofi? Have you heard from her?"

"I've not. Which is why I'm here."

"I imagine today must've been especially tough for you, my dear. This whole weekend, in fact. I don't envy you, Inola." He smiled sympathetically.

"Thank you, but I'm not here as a patient. Just with a question."

Yate beckoned her to the couch. "In that case, my cabana is secure."

Inola swiped her handscreen anyway to elicit a white noise perimeter, then took a seat before turning and dropping her voice. "Lord Ethos has indicated they've realized Sofi's and Shilo's possibilities and has just made it clear he will not play by the rules. It's also been rumored they took Shilo after the explosion, seizing the opportunity they'd already been looking for to reacquire them."

The therapist stared. "How—?"

"I need to know, what exactly do you think Sofi will do?"

He softened his voice. "Inola. I think the first question is how you could have let this happen. You *know* what Sofi is capable of. Even just being there will trigger memories—"

"I'm quite aware of that."

"Not to mention"—Yate's voice fell even lower—"she may be the key to their rebirth, but she's also a weapon. And now she's been unknowingly handed over to the very—"

Inola uttered a harsh chuckle. "You of all people should know I've no control over my daughter. What's done is done. The question now is—what will she do? Will she step into who she is?"

Yate paused long enough to shift back to professional mode. "We don't even fully understand your children's abilities. Can she be a powerful weapon against them? Yes." He looked down at the arena. "She could bring them to their knees if she wanted. Both of them could. And we both know she would. But if you're asking if she'll figure out how to do it before they figure out how to use her . . ."

He shook his head slowly. "I'm not sure. We've not done enough real-life training. Although I'm inclined to agree with the look on your face—which I'm assuming is that, either way, we should all be afraid your daughter's gone there to get her brother. What she finds there won't be good."

He waited for Inola to absorb this before adding, "But what do you mean Lord Ethos will no longer play by the rules? What is he intending?"

Inola's mind flickered to that look on Ambassador Miguel's face as he tried to say something. As if he was about to say *everything*. The look that said they didn't even know the half of what was about to come down.

"Tell me about Ambassador Miguel. He's up there with Sofi and the other members. Where will his leanings be?"

The doctor's countenance showed surprise, followed by deep thought as he looked out over the Colinade. "Miguel's an interesting one. Two years ago I would've said he's for whatever would best serve him. However, some of his mannerisms and choices, as I've watched him since then, have led me to believe that despite whatever persona he portrays in public, something's changed—an inner transformation that's inclined him toward truth. I believe if he has enough information on this situation, he'll be inclined to protect Sofi and Shilo. Why do you ask?"

"So he'd be able to help them then?"

"I don't know. All I can guess is he'd likely try."

Inola held her breath at that. "And how do we ensure he does?" she finally asked.

The therapist studied Inola. Almost clinical. Calculating. "There's nothing you can do."

"Pardon?"

He laced his fingers in his lap and said quietly, "What Miguel does will be of his own conviction. And what Sofi does or doesn't do is entirely up to Sofi. It will lie in her ability to decide that she is enough and that she doesn't need more to become what she already is. Unfortunately, that's not . . ."

His voice trailed off, but Inola understood. That wasn't something Sofi had ever heard from either of them.

The linen cabana curtains rustled in the breeze and the air turned chilly. Inola nodded. "Thank you, Yate." Then rose and saw herself out.

"Just let me know when you're ready," Jerrad said in her com.

She nodded. She'd done what she came for. She'd stay another minute to keep face, then quietly slip away.

As she strode back toward the CEO cabana, she peered down to find the FanFight's green-screen arena still shifting. *Choosing a scene setting is taking longer than usual.*

Then she glanced back over to where her vice president, Gaines, was chatting away, clearly recovered from Lord Ethos's conference call and Inola's surprise appearance. Looking warm with her swarm of senators and VPs, her expression suggesting she was past greasing the political wheels. The woman was flat-out flaunting.

Gutsy.

Idiotic.

She frowned and let the thought go as the epic music continued to soar, drowning out the audience-gone-wild until the arena below suddenly buzzed and the green-screen locked into its official setting.

"*Annnnnd* the audience has spoken!" the announcer said. "Roman coliseum for the win! Shall we count them down? *Ten, nine, eight . . .*"

"About time the audience voted an old history round," she heard someone in the CEO tent say. "My bet is changed. I guarantee Corp 13's got it in the bag on this."

"I'll take that wager. Where's Hart? How much you offering to be wrong?"

The CEOs laughed again and secured their investments while Inola pursed her lips, watching the arena fill in as the seven players were lowered down into the first section where gladiators and lions were appearing beside a grouping of D&D howlers.

". . . *three, two, one!* And the players are at it—facing the host of gladiators first!"

The teens took off in the arena. The music ended. The crowds screamed out the names of their FanFight favorites. An image of Shilo fighting down there flashed into her mind, followed by him fighting for his life up on Delon—however that looked.

Stop, Inola. If Sofi believed Shilo was alive, then she'd have to hold on to that.

Because Sofi of all people would know.

Inola's handcomp buzzed for the third time in her pocket and she finally slipped it out.

Nice job on the performance in front of the crowd. Very convincing.

Her chest froze. Who is this?

Same as before. Doesn't matter.

"Jerrad, can you hack backward through my handscreen?" she said softly. "The texts are coming through again."

"Got it. Keep them on."

What do you want? she typed.

Nothing . . . yet.

Who are you? What do you want?

But just like three hours ago, the screen blanked. "Did you get that?" she asked.

"Whoever it is knows what they're do—"

Her handscreen buzzed again. She swiped at it but nothing was there. She swiped again and tapped as a feeling of frantic annoyance invaded her calm. Until she suddenly became aware of a presence staring at her.

She looked over to find Hart now in Corp 30's cabana, seated beside Gaines in deep conversation.

He wasn't looking at her. Neither was Gaines. Yet she could still feel a set of eyes drilling into her skin.

A throat cleared behind her.

11

SOFI

THE DARK VEIL DROPPED OFF SOFI'S EYES TO REVEAL SHE WAS now in a large, luxurious room that felt claustrophobic with large pieces of red-and-silver furniture. Mainly of the sitting variety. She squinted as her gaze twitched, as if adjusting to the abrupt brightness.

Delonese Lead Ambassador Ethos stood six inches away. Staring her in the face in a robe so silvery it did something eerie to his skin—making him look shinier. Faker. Much like the rest of the room.

She blinked.

"Aw, Girl-Sofi!" he exclaimed, and stepped back. "I must say, it's no wonder the humans love you. Hunting you was quite the game."

She frowned and pulled back to peer around him at Ambassador Danya standing calmly on the black-and-silver floor above all twenty children she'd helped rescue not two hours ago.

Sofi froze.

They were here. Alive and in this room with Danya, who was

the only Delon citizen to make her permanent home on Earth for the past many years. Oddly, with her high cheekbones and well-practiced blinking eyes, the woman looked more human than Delonese. Sofi swallowed and tried not to appear overly emotional as her lungs burst and broke around her heart at the sight of her and the children. Their faces looked dazed.

She turned to Ethos. "Where're the rest of them? Where are Claudius, Miguel, and my brother?"

"All in good time. All in good time, my dear."

"You may not have much of that, so I suggest you answer my question. Where are they?"

"Oh, come now, we've no need for such measured threats. At least not this early in the round." He flicked a wrist and waved off the peacekeepers who'd stepped toward her. "But please, join Ambassador Danya and the children in making yourself comfortable."

Sofi assessed the floor cushions he was beckoning her to and didn't move.

This wasn't the Ethos she'd been around yesterday. His looks and voice were the same, but his personality was unsettlingly different. More vibrant. Friendlier. *Shinier.* Just like his robe and the richness of the room with its thick black metallic lace hanging from the ceiling and the giant window drawing the eyes out across the fog. It all looked like an electric telescreen that'd been tuned too high.

It made her mind itch.

"No, thank you, I'll stand." She let her gaze follow him before she turned discreetly to the back of the room to inspect the eyes boring into her. Ten tall Delonese stood silent along the wall in robes so silver they reflected the strange designs etched into the heated floor. They were watching. Assessing. Sofi eyed them until one of the aliens shifted his gaze from her forehead to connect with hers. His brow widened and then he tipped his head with a frown.

Huh. Whatever his problem was, it made Sofi's skin just about crawl off her body. She turned away to find the kids situating themselves between her and Ethos, in oddly perfect rows.

That weird smile loomed as he strolled to the center of the window. "Well, suit yourself. We won't be long anyway. My hope is simply to 'clear the air,' as the humans say, by assuring you of our gracious understanding regarding your curiosity about our planet. Although your discovery of the fact that it's a space station is most unfortunate. But we can certainly work with it."

"*Curiosity.* Like harvesting body parts?" Sofi said dryly. She brushed her shoulder against her ear at a slight buzzing that'd picked up. Like a wasp stuck in her head. She pretended to crack her neck just to shake it off. No use. It stayed.

The ambassador's gaze shifted to the kids at his feet. "Body parts? I see nothing of the sort here."

"She's not a fool," Danya whispered. "You know quite well what the girl meant."

"And that is my point." The alien approached Sofi across those silver spiral designs carved into the black flooring and held up his hands in a gesture of innocence. "The only ones anyone has ever seen alive are the children we've cured and sent home. Like Sofi here when she was younger. The fact that a few of my people were secretly using them for anything more than healing their bodies and creating new methods of medicine is only a small part of it. And, of course, a most appalling one, I agree. In the future they'll stick to growing organs strictly from cells."

"A few? You have hundreds down there. Possibly thousands—feeding an army of your own making. And don't tell me those are all grown from harvested cells." Sofi shook her head. Was he saying he didn't know how many there were? Or was he just minimizing the reality of them?

Danya shot her an unreadable expression. Like muted horror.

"Aw, but that is my point." He shrugged. "Who can know? As I said, what's done is done, but we'll not allow it again."

"Yes, that would make more sense," one of the children said in a too-calm voice. "Lord Ethos wouldn't let it happen again."

What? Sofi turned.

The other children were nodding, relief surfacing on their small faces.

They couldn't honestly believe him.

"I can assure you all"—Ethos peered down at the kids—"the culprits for such atrocities have already been caught and dealt with severely. They are no longer with us, and their experiments are being destroyed as we speak."

Sofi actually laughed. *What a crock.* She waved at the kids. "They're not going to trust you."

"Spoken by the girl who, in fact, betrayed Delon's trust just today."

"What trust was that?" Danya's tone showed the same confusion as Sofi felt.

"Girl-Sofi managed to access our security systems. I'm sure I don't need to tell any of us how impossible, let alone unsafe, such an act is."

The ambassador flashed another smile and glanced at the ten Delonese still standing silent along the back wall. And gave a slight nod. Then to the twenty children who were all staring, he clapped his hands quick-like. "Come, shall we leave this stuffy space? For dinner perhaps? Why don't you follow me?"

The room filled with a wave of small voices, begging and interested as the kids clamored to the door where Lord Ethos ushered them all into a narrow hallway. His robe swished around him in a hiss as he strode from the room, like a snake.

She looked back at the ten Delonese who'd quietly slid from their spot along the wall and stood waiting for Sofi to follow their leader. She bit her lip. *Don't lose your nerve. Listen and learn until the time is right, Sof.* Then turned and plowed after Ethos and the kids because she wasn't about to leave them alone with him.

They entered a narrow tunnel made of opaque metal, their footsteps thumping softly as her gaze strayed to Danya. "Is it just me or does this all feel like a false set on one of our i-reality shows?"

Danya offered an odd smile and went to reply when one of the children fell back to wait for Sofi, asking, "How *did* you access their servers, Sofi? Was it really that possible?"

"Don't answer," the voice that sounded like Shilo's said in her head.

She frowned. Of course she wasn't going to answer. Not only because she wasn't inclined to give the Delonese any information, but also because she'd never had to explain it before—and thus had no idea how. Like most gamers, she just knew.

She patted the child on the head, then peered behind her. The ten Delonese were following.

The rest of the kids were already squealing and running through the adjacent area when the small tunnel opened up onto a terrace hovering five stories above the capital's buildings. A crystal-looking dome covered the entire place, sealing in a level of heat that bordered on suffocating, while giving a perfect 360-degree view of the sky above and the surrounding snow-scape below. It was a terrarium in the midst of a cult compound, housing a living garden of glorious vegetation. Most of which were plant types Sofi had never seen. Purple vines, brown flora, and branches hanging off of multicolored trees.

It was both exquisite and a shade off. Again with the overly sharp atmosphere.

"Now that they have a distraction"—Ethos nodded toward the kids—"why don't we proceed?" He indicated a silver-coiled table that held a spread of Earth foods. "Some water perhaps. Or the famed Earth tea Ambassador Miguel has made so popular here."

"I'll ask again—where's Miguel?"

Ethos's response was to pour a cup of tea and hand it to Sofi. She took it but didn't drink. Just used it as something to hold between his face and hers as she sniffed and said, "Because you're violating human rights by keeping us here."

"Oh, come now, Girl-Sofi. It's a matter of logic, really. For security reasons, until we have the information we need, we will be unable to release any of you. Even your corporate nations understand that." Ethos took a sip of his tea and his cheeks did a weird glitching thing across his face. "So it's really your decision." He stopped. And blinked. "How were you able to hack into our space station's security system? Particularly one as incredibly advanced as ours?"

Sofi shrugged. "Maybe you should make your system harder to hack."

Ethos's lips thinned. He pressed them together and ran his long fingers over the table's smooth, silver surface. "You can see how dangerous it would be for my people in the future if some-one outside was able to break into our system again. No, I'm sorry, we cannot have that."

From behind her, Sofi heard a slight throat clearing.

"Thankfully," Ethos added as if on cue, "one of your Earth companions had some rather helpful information." He flicked an unblinking gaze at the opaque door to the left. And took a soft gulp of his still-steaming drink just as Earth's Ambassador Alis and Sofi's game tech, Heller, were brought in by guards.

Sofi's cup fell from her fingers and hit the terrace floor with a sharp *crash*.

Heller? Her mouth went dry as she took in the face of the person who'd been her friend up until this morning.

"Hey, Sof." Heller's eyes and voice were more alive—more wildly colorful than normal. Just like his cheek piercing, which was a strobe-light stud, currently flashing as wild as usual.

She didn't respond, didn't move, didn't do anything to ac-knowledge this person who'd plotted to help murder her brother.

Ethos stepped between them. "Boy-Heller here mentioned Ambassador Miguel solicited help in accessing our system to find the children. Using your friends, Ranger and Vic—both of whom have now been evicted from our systems. But it was your seeming understanding of our technology that enabled it. Who are the others who assisted that knowledge, please?"

Sofi refused to look at Danya.

"Ambassador Danya assisted as well," Alis said.

Sofi hurled mental daggers at her.

Heller moved in. "Sofi, if you'd only listened—"

"You killed our team. Our *friends*, Heller."

"I'm not a killer. I did what I was told. But if you'd let me,

Sof, I would've been able to help and we could've gone home. Everything could've gone back to normal."

"Nothing is normal," Sofi spit out. "None of this—none of them. They are using you, Heller." She swerved her gaze to Ethos.

"Yes, that's it," Ethos said in a smooth tone. "Let those emotions emerge, Sofi. Tell me how they lend to your mental acuity in regard to our technology. How do they help you access it?"

"Just like your mom used you and Shilo," Heller said to Sofi. "Can't you see how doing so is making the world a better place for—"

Sofi lunged at the tech kid's throat. The air around them zapped, and suddenly Ethos was breaking between them as Heller made a desperate grab for her hand.

"Thank you, Boy-Heller, for the benefit of your reaction as well as Girl-Sofi's. So very helpful. Peacekeepers? You may escort him away now."

Sofi jerked away, but not before Heller had slipped a note inside her palm.

The peacekeepers moved for Heller and dragged him out while he yelled, "It wasn't them or us, Sofi. It's about all of us achieving survival."

Ethos beckoned them to the curved window. "Come. See."

The guards pushed them over, to peer below where the yellow fog was still settled far beneath, lurking like a misty ocean around the barrack buildings. The entire tiny city looked half submerged. What were they doing?

Thirty seconds went by before a movement on the ground floor, catty-corner to the window, caught her eye.

Even Alis gasped as suddenly the door at the base of the

building slid up and Heller appeared. His short, dark hair and black slim-suit out of place against the yellow fog.

Sofi's gut filled with horror. *No.* She'd hated Heller for what he'd done, but she didn't wish this on him. She turned to react only to find more guards on either side of her.

Danya uttered a cry, and from Sofi's peripheral she saw as Heller swerved around but was shoved farther into the icy world where he stumbled, then turned to shout. Too late. The fog surged over him and caused him to fall.

Through the mist Sofi watched in terror as he hit his knees first, then his stomach. And even from this far up, she could make out Heller's body choking and shaking. And Sofi was shaking too. She wanted to scream—to rip into Ethos. But the guards stood over her like stone.

And then Heller just stopped moving.

Ethos turned to face her. "Now, Girl-Sofi, I've kindly been patient. But we really need the truth about how you broke into our system. And you will tell us plainly, or this will happen to every one of those children whom my men have just removed from this garden."

12

MIGUEL

WHEN PLANET DELON ARRIVED ELEVEN YEARS AGO, IT APPEARED as a beautiful, silvery globe in the sky, made up of wintry atmosphere and ice-tipped trees.

As a wild, dirt-bike-riding boy, Miguel had been awestruck. He excitedly raced home, wondering what it must be like to live and travel on this white ball of snow that Earth's satellite cameras caught erupting from a wormhole in space.

"¿Qué haces?" his madre said as he grabbed a cold soda beneath her disapproving eye. "No sugar before dinner, Miguel!" But she'd let him keep it anyway as he popped it open and joined *Padre* and his siblings to watch the news screens along with every other human alive—staring wide-eyed as the planet slowly made its way across the sky to settle into orbit on the far side of the moon. They'd held their breath as the reporters showed all the Corporations rushing to contact the visitors with questions of whether they had, in fact, "come in peace."

"Peace and generosity," was the reply, and the world let out a collective sigh. Because for what little information humanity had on them—heck, at least this was hopeful. And for an eight-year-old dreamy-eyed, old-lady-neighbor-terrorizing kid, it was a promise. Of life bigger than he'd known.

Miguel stood in the dim room with the now-dark screen that Ethos was towering in front of in his signature silver robe that made him seem more like an insecure rock musician than the leader of a planet.

This was not the version of a bigger life Miguel had planned.

"All that glitters isn't always good," his padre had once said. The man would never know how right he was.

Ethos turned to him. "Clearly you understand that it is you who chose to come here against our laws. And with that in mind—"

"And yet you and the Council bent those laws in allowing us to come with Sofi rather than turning our shuttle around," Miguel interrupted quietly. "In that way, we are here at your allowance, Lord Ethos, and the fact we stumbled upon unsettling issues is a question upon your people's honor, not ours. I imagine Earth will be just as concerned by what we have to say. Perhaps even more so if it comes to light that you seem to be claiming no knowledge or minimizing crimes going on beneath your very nose."

If a Delonese could flush red, the ambassador would be flaming with the level of anger radiating. Even in the dull lighting, Miguel could see it clearly. Ethos practically sputtered, "As I said, the choice was made by you. We have more than enough right to detain you, as Earth well knows, considering you've brought a top-tier fugitive here. So, while I plan to do everything in my power to return you in the proper time . . ."

A wave of disgust rose up for Ethos, for Inola and Hart—for all of those people he'd seen on the monitor screen who'd been playing with the lives of the very kids he and Claudius had been hell-bent on saving and yet, so far, had never been able to rescue, no matter how much investigation they'd done.

He'd spent over a year searching out these kids—collecting their few memories to figure out their stories—to find what the Delonese were doing to them and what massive human-rights violations were taking place.

And here he'd watched Earth and Delon just have a freaking board meeting, discussing it like the kids were a product?

Images of Earth's protestors bled into his mind. The signs they held up with pics of alien-human hybrids slashed through with blood. Suddenly those calls to violence against the Delonese didn't seem so far-fetched.

"I do hope by the end of our conversation," Ethos continued, "we will be able to smooth over that discovery and come to an . . . *agreement*. As allies. Just as we have always been."

Miguel raised a brow. "Allies who abduct kids for their body parts? Forgive me, Lord Ethos, but you know me better than to think an agreement can be reached on that. Particularly when the evidence in the belly of Delon suggests you're using them for far more than regeneration. One might even be inclined to suspect your sights are set much further than your own repopulation. Perhaps to domination."

Ethos's eyes narrowed and shot to the telescreen that held the stats written in the Delonese language. Then just as quickly relaxed, and the patronizing smile returned. "Yes, I can see how that must look. But let me assure you, you and I *will* come to an arrangement, one way or another." He snapped his fingers, and two seconds later a door behind Miguel opened and Ambassador Claudius strode in.

Miguel caught Claudius's discreet nod as his twenty-four-year-old, Euro-born friend offered his broadest grin beneath a platinum head of hair that contained so much gel, the peak at the front hadn't even moved since yesterday. "Hey, *cuate*. Looks like we ride again, eh?" Claudius glanced at Miguel, then Ethos. Then stopped. And faced the Delonese full on. Two seconds later his face broke into a teasing expression of admiration. "Ethos, friend. That robe. You're a dream in it."

Miguel felt his muscles ease. He exhaled. Claudius could put on a show like nobody's business, and that was a show if he ever saw one. *Nice timing, friend.*

The old alien's robe rustled around his tall, thin frame. "Yes, thank you. I'm quite aware." But his body stood a little taller.

"I'm thinking the silver cape could be all the rage for next season. What say you?" Claudius glanced at Miguel.

"Pardon my fashion distraction," Ethos interjected, "but as you can see, I am privately here, without the eyes of the Council, to offer you, as Earth's ambassadors, a final opportunity to restore relationship with us. Reaching a satisfying agreement will be necessary for everyone to move forward."

That last part . . . Ethos's words were too careful. Calculated. Almost mechanical.

Miguel stared at the alien's facial features.

Having been the youngest Earth ambassador ever also meant having been the Delonese's favorite ambassador ever—which had rendered Miguel a lot more time with them and reading their cues than just about anyone else.

And Ethos's face . . .

There was something in the tightness of his lips. In the way he was breathing.

A flicker of recognition crossed Miguel's mind. He peered closer and watched the Delonese's expression.

Then lifted a brow and leaned back.

"Lord Ethos, considering your people retrieved the shuttle before it hit Earth's radar, my assumption is you don't want your operation discovered. Which suggests a surprising level of fear."

The leader's eyes cracked the slightest bit wider.

Ah.

"Ambassador Miguel, I find your—"

"Which leads one to believe one of two things. Either your people are terrified that, should your appalling actions be discovered by Earth, they'll be forced into a war they've not had the manpower for—or they're afraid of the consequences of said war. Namely, in order for Delon to win, it would have to use weapons on us. And in doing so, risk losing its easiest source of healthy test subjects."

The Delonese lead ambassador stared at him. Then spun and left the room.

"Looks like someone's been drinking the Kool-Aid," Claudius said quietly. He glanced at Miguel. "You think the fear and flattery bought what we need?"

"I think we bought his pride for the moment." Miguel turned and kept his voice low. "But where are the kids?"

"I couldn't stop them. They took them from the shuttle. And . . . Miguel, they have Sofi."

Claudius might just as well have taken a blade and sliced at Miguel's soul. He absorbed the shock over what that meant, while giving a nod as his only external acknowledgment. Between Sofi and the kids—if he thought of them right now, he'd be useless. He needed to find a way to reach Earth. They needed a bigger threat on the table.

He strode over to both telescreens, which had shut off with

Ethos's exit. Miguel slipped his hand in front of them anyway. Nothing. Then touched the second one. The thing stayed blank.

"He'll not let you live, you know," a voice said from the shadows.

Miguel and Claudius both spun to find Ambassador Alis watching from a doorway she'd just slid through.

Claudius snorted. "And so she ascends from hell."

"I made a deal."

"Yes, that was pretty obvious in the whole betrayal of twenty children thing you did a few hours ago." Claudius glared at her as the door closed and she strode to the window the metal shades were still covering.

"I get to resume my duties." She turned and offered a hard smile. "I wonder what it would take for you to do the same."

Miguel frowned at her. His nerves were buzzing. Raw. As if something bigger than this moment was off. And it wasn't just the conversation. It was the look and smell and atmosphere. It was that one telescreen and the warehouses of bodies.

It was the air swishing around his feet that was forming into a fog.

"What the—?" Claudius jumped toward Miguel as the creamy cloud engulfed the floor.

Alis's expression was just as startled. She lunged for the door but Miguel was already there, hitting the scanner, aware his guards were gone as well. Nothing happened. He pressed it again. "Move!"

Alis tried, with the same result—and it didn't matter anyway because that fog was already rising and swirling and entering their throats.

13

INOLA

A FLICKER OF UNEASE HIT INOLA.

She flipped around to see Corp 24's vice president, Zain, standing in the afternoon shadows cast by the CEOs' FanFight tent. "Strange not seeing them here, eh?" He tipped his head down one level where the Delonese's empty, private cabana sat in view, just above the gamer rooms that overlooked the arena— where each team's techs manipulated the virtual components. "The Delonese, I mean. Not my dead players and yours."

She stayed still, not taking her gaze from him as he moseyed toward her, one hand in his pocket, the other smoothing his brown hair flat, while staying close enough to the cabana to stay out of direct public eye.

"In fact, I believe this is the first round our friendly ice visitors have missed in the past three years."

"What do you want?" she murmured.

"Same as you, I suspect." He stopped beside her. "The truth."

She laughed softly. "And who's to say I don't have it?"

He turned and pierced her with his eyes. "Oh, I think you do. Mostly."

Inola raised a brow and assessed him. The man was smarter than she'd given him credit for. "In that case, you should know speaking with me in public is a dangerous idea. For both of us. People will assume we're doing business. So I'd prefer if you—"

"Is it?" He smiled. "Seems to me business deals are being discussed all the time. Take your VP Gaines and Corp 13's CEO Hart, for instance."

She didn't have to look to know they were still deep in conversation. She could sense it—just like she could sense one of the players below was about to be eliminated based on the gasps and yells of the crowd. "Yes, but they've not had a player actually blow up the FanFights, nor a daughter accused of instigating it."

He shrugged. "True. Although the way I see it, it would make sense that two responsible, heartbroken leaders such as ourselves would be discussing our concerns. Especially when we both know we had nothing to do with the bombing."

A scream ripped through the air as one of the players in the arena earned elimination by what sounded to be a lion attack. Inola didn't look.

VP Zain turned away from it. "You know what I find interesting? How Corp 13's player is down there but your kids are not."

Inola kept her expression blank. *What is he getting at? What does he want?* She glanced at her watch. "Forgive me if I'm not following, but I'm actually running late. Perhaps—"

A second scream rang out, and the coliseum's crowd was immediately on their feet. Inola and Zain both swerved to look— and were in time to see a few of the players already starting in on the second portion of the round. Except one of them was being shredded by a howler. The thing was leaning over him about to absorb his life when the beast suddenly disintegrated into the nanobots it was created from. But not before the boy's blood was staining the ground and the med hovers were heading in to rescue him before he bled out.

Zain kept his gaze on the arena. "See, now what I've been trying to figure out is why a mother—even one such as yourself, no offense—would let her daughter take the fall for an explosion she didn't orchestrate. Unless, of course, the girl really did do it. Problem is . . ." He paused. "I don't think she did."

A loud burst of laughter carried through the CEO cabana's linen divider as Inola stared at this man who was as surprising as he was intuitive. How had he drawn these conclusions? Who had he been talking to?

"Not that your belief matters, but for the sake of politeness— why do you think so?" she asked.

The man moved his gaze to Gaines and Hart, who appeared to be wrapping up their conversation. Hart was standing and speaking. Gaines didn't appear too thrilled.

"Because I watched your face."

Inola froze.

"The other night in the session hall," he said. "When your daughter's vid came on the screen, I watched it. The girl was scared and angry, but not guilty. And so were you." He lifted his gaze to the ice-planet shadowing the day-lit moon between slats of the massive telescreens spanning the Colinade. "The thing is, I know what *my* Corp player did. I've studied the evidence." He rubbed his jawline. "But I also know for a fact my Corp had nothing to do with his actions—and, in fact, we were set up.

"But you?" He eyed her. "One of the most powerful CEOs in the world—refusing to defend her daughter? Makes me think that's a coldhearted mom right there." He glanced back over toward CEO Hart who was just leaving Corp 30's cabana. Then down to the empty Delonese spot. "Unless that powerful mom was afraid of something far worse than losing the lives of her children."

Inola felt the blood drain from her face. Gaines and Hart would put a price on his head if they knew this. If Lord Ethos heard this . . . "I'm going to suggest you be very careful with your next few words," she whispered, her skin cold in the suddenly chilly breeze.

Zain turned and assessed her. "I see," he said quietly.

"What do you want?" she hissed.

"I want to know that when all of *this*"—he looked around—"hits the fan, you'll have my back. In the UW Council meetings and with the Delonese. I know you have connections with all of them, and I refuse to get thrown under the bus along with your kids. And I can only hope that, in the meantime, your conscience regarding whatever's going on—which likely affects the rest of us large scale—outweighs your pride."

With a nod he turned and strode from the dais amid the CEOs erupting into fresh howls as they cursed Corp 17's gamers for the dry lightning bolts they'd just coded in on the other teams' players.

Inola watched until he disappeared past the host of security.

"Interesting bloke," Jerrad said in her earcom.

"You got all that?"

"His voice scans say he wasn't lying."

"Did you get anything text-wise off my handscreen?"

"Nope. Your bugger's a genius."

Yeah, they are.

She went to leave the dais when a cheer went up for player 13, and a group began chanting his name. *Matthers.* She sniffed. Just another pawn, like they all were apparently.

Huh. Maybe Zain was right. As pawns they could have each other's backs, or go down in flames. Either way, things *would* hit the fan. Not that her conscience outweighing her pride would change that fact, but—

"Behind you," Jerrad said.

"Your Ms. Gaines tells me you're unhappy with our decision," a voice whined.

Inola's skin crawled. She didn't move as the speaker's hot, clammy breath floated across her neck. Just kept her gaze level as she turned and knocked his arm to walk by him. "CEO Hart, I'm not in the mood right now."

He stepped in front of her. His wet tone took on a chuckle, almost enough to hide the hint of nerves she detected. "Ah, but we've been partners far too long for me to feel threatened by you, Inola." He patted her shoulder, then eased back. "Just checking on you."

"Nothing's changed, if that's your concern."

He peered toward the arena. "And there's the CEO I know. Someone else might be shaken—but you're as steady as they come, my dear." He turned and snapped his fingers for a waiter in the shadows, whom he'd apparently dragged with him. "My usual."

Returning his gaze to Inola, his expression eased into one of contentment. "So, where is she in all this?"

"Sofi? You know as much as I do."

"No one knows their daughter like a mother." His jowls moved when he grinned. "So humor me."

"She's on Delon searching for Shilo, whom she believes was taken there. Beyond that, I'm in the dark."

"Uh-huh." He tipped his head and cracked his neck before looking back down on the players. "You place any bets on the kids down there?"

The handscreen vibrated again. "Never. You know that."

He nodded. "Good, good. Never a wise idea to bet against the player you need most." He turned as his waiter strode up with a cushioned seat and set it down for him before slipping away. Hart sat. "You know, the thing about games, Inola, is that it's not always the best who win. No. It's the player who can outlast the others. See my guy there . . ."

Inola shifted to see the Corp 13 player he was pointing at just standing aside while the other players took down a howler. "He'll win today and move on to the Five tomorrow. Because he knows how to outlast."

The waiter reappeared and handed Hart a napkin, then set a small table in front of him, loaded with two plates overflowing with piles of bird wings and crawfish.

Of all the things to have somehow survived World War III's nuclear holocaust, the river bugs had proven the more hearty. They'd almost seemed to thrive on it. Inola wondered if the things still had radiation, despite all the environmental restoration the Delonese had assisted in. Or at least the ones Hart was slurping on.

One could hope.

Inola's handscreen vibrated in her jacket. She pulled it out and set the white noise perimeter while he tapped at his own. Then glanced at the message. It read:

Ask if he or Gaines poisoned Ambassador Lee.

"Back to your daughter." Hart lifted his napkin to wipe his chin. "I must admit it surprised me to hear Lord Ethos say in the conference vid that Sofi may hold the very value they need. You've been keeping secrets from me, Inola."

She slid the screen behind her back and kept her face still. "I wasn't certain. Neither are they."

"Oh, they seemed quite certain to me."

The screen vibrated. She could practically feel it saying, Ask him.

He looked straight at her. "Have you heard from Sofi or Ambassadors Miguel or Claudius since they've been on the planet?"

"No."

"Was it me or did Miguel look a tad uptight in that call?" Hart waved a bird leg he'd just picked up. "No matter. Alis and the Delonese will take care of things."

"Just like Gaines took care of Ambassador Lee on Friday night so Alis could replace him? Or was that you who poisoned him?"

He coughed mid-swallow and patted his napkin to his face as it turned the slightest shade pale. "Gaines's men, obviously. You and I are the same, Inola. We never get our hands dirty if we can help it. Which is why things don't always get done exactly right. Like that fool, Heller. Kid royally messed it up." He grunted as Inola's spine went cold. "Never send a boy to do an adult's job."

"You heard Lord Ethos, Hart. He will use Earth for his own gain. He changed the rules on us—that doesn't concern you even the slightest?"

"Oh, it concerns me. But think of the good we've done. The cures we're gaining. Your Corp is leading the world in health breakthroughs. And now my Corp is starting to receive some of those benefits too now that the extra security we've provided your Corp has proved financially worthwhile. Soon we'll be leading in technology. Let's not underestimate what we can do with that."

Inola took one last glance at the FanFight arena, which had morphed to the next round—a vampire castle, from the look of it. "Hart, you'll have to excuse me—"

"And tomorrow," he interrupted, "when the ambassadors arrive home, all will be right again in the world. Clear consciences. Tied-up loose ends. Business back to usual. And we'll resume our program. I've already got my company working on a false positive for the Altered invention. Should be ready to release among the public in a few weeks, which means we can begin work on creating our own Altered human hybrids."

Her breath left her lungs. *What did he just say?*

He leaned over his plate and lowered his voice. "Look, we both know we want our relations with the Delonese to succeed. But we're also smart enough to have a backup plan. We can be at their mercy while also equipping ourselves. And to do that, I say we need to be able to compete at their level. If they made Sofi and Shilo into superior humans, then so can we. And on that note—I'd like you to consider making samples of their blood you have on file available to my team. We need to get on this, Inola."

Inola's mind was whirling a mile a second. He couldn't be serious. Except, of course, he was.

She offered a tight smile. "You want to play their game? Sounds inspiring, Hart. I'm glad you're feeling so confident." She pulled out her screen and glanced at it as if she'd just received a note. Which, in fact, she had. It was the same unknown source.

If you want to help your kids, head for the black markets.

She swallowed and blinked.

"Everything okay?"

"Yes, of course." She swiped it shut. "Just a note from the office regarding the new bone-growth hormone we've been working on. I have to go."

"Don't make me nervous, Inola. I'd hate to lose confidence in our relationship."

"Your impotent confidence is not my problem, Hart." She strolled away, barely hiding her disgust as the sound of cracking crawfish followed her off the dais and the announcer's voice reminded people once again to vote on which celebrity, soldier, or politician they'd like to see in tomorrow's bloody fight finale arena.

14

SOFI STARED AT HELLER'S DEAD BODY LYING CRUMPLED BELOW in the creamy fog and soft snow. Her hand crinkled around his note. She felt numb. Distant. Like her mind couldn't keep up with reality. That or her emotions were simply shutting down from the shock. *What have they just done?*

As if in irony, a new tinkle of music struck up. Swells and sweet drops of fancy notes in the fancy forestry room with its fancy human food that stood in sick contrast to the murder Ethos and the others had just orchestrated.

Sofi bit her cheek and looked at the lot of them. The ten silent Delonese didn't even seem bothered. Just moved and shifted around her, staring, studying—the same expressionless faces she'd seen among a hundred others last night as they sang and danced in their beautiful domed hall and chanted about their belief in unity and community.

What a load of cripe. She stared right back. Only to realize they weren't just watching her—they were, along with Ethos, waiting. For what—an answer? A reaction? In that case, she'd give them one.

She lifted her gaze to the tree-lined horizon, then beyond to the moon filling up half the sky. And cleared her throat. "No, I don't think so."

"Pardon?" Lord Ethos frowned.

"My answer is no. To helping you."

"Girl-Sofi, I've just given you an opportunity to save the children. And I shouldn't need to assure you that after them, the ambassadors will be killed as well. I think you'd be wise—"

"To listen," a child's voice interrupted. It was the same girl who'd spoken to her and Danya in the walkway. She looked hollow eyed and nervous. "Lest they do the same to us."

Sofi flinched as an image of Shilo flashed in her mind. What was she thinking? This was a child's life—these were the children she'd been trying to save. How could she not help them?

She glanced from the girl to Ethos, considering how to answer, when she caught the slight flicker across his face. A pleased expression. Gleeful almost.

Her hand squeezed harder around that note.

Oh.

He was using them to get at her. Just like he would be using them for far worse as soon as he got what he wanted.

Because he'd done it with Heller.

She swallowed, ignored the pleading eyes, and shook her head at Ethos.

One of the ten Delonese slid in front of her and peered in her face. "You would sacrifice more of Earth's children then?" He glanced smugly around at the others. "I find that fascinating. If not incongruous."

The music trilled, which gave the odd sense of agreement and made the room's atmosphere feel strangely alive. Overstimulated. Making her nerves hate this place even more.

Sofi kept her words steady, even as her gut ached and crawled and her mind fought to call their bluff. "I think we all know you have no plans to let them go anyway." She shifted back to viewing her friend's lifeless body. "So, in my mind, a quick death would be a flat-out gift of mercy for those children." Her tone almost cut out. She wished it *would* cut out but forced it stronger. "Please feel free to carry on with it."

Ambassador Ethos actually blinked for the second time since she'd been here, and suddenly Sofi's vision grew fuzzy. As if a layer of static slipped over it. She frowned and batted her lashes, and then her eyesight cleared just as Ethos licked his lips with a too-pink tongue.

He nodded at the group of them. "In that case . . . prepare them for the medical procedures," he said under his breath.

At least, she thought he did. She stiffened and waited for Danya or Alis to react, until it occurred to her they were no longer standing nearby. The guards had taken them somewhere while she'd been staring at Heller's corpse. *Cripe.*

"Did you hear me, Girl-Sofi?" Ethos spoke louder. "I said come, let us show you more. I promise, you'll enjoy this."

Ice shot up her skin. "Wait—"

Her voice broke off. As if the music and atmosphere were chemically overriding her mind and making her muscles and throat seize. She glanced down at the little girl. *What have I just done? Those kids. Claudius and Danya.*

Miguel.

"Lord Ethos," she blurted out. "You know I accessed your system with the help of others. What more do you need?"

Too late. The ambassador strode from the room, his silver robe swishing behind him in that uncanny sound of a snake. Followed by the entire group of ten Delonese, with their plastic-like smiles.

A moment later the four guards surrounding her forced her into the bright hall before prodding her into an elevator. Once entered, the thing flipped in a half circle to face the opposite direction, then zoomed them to the ground level.

An elongated second slipped by during which the doors remained closed. Sofi clenched her fingers until her palm flared from the burn she'd gotten on the vat back in the med room as Heller's note itched against her skin. She slid her hand against her waist and discreetly flipped it up to read. She opened her mouth. Shut it.

The metal elevator glided open and a guard jostled her arm, causing the paper to slip to the floor as he shoved her forward into a small shuttle bay like the one they'd been in less than three hours ago.

The message had stated, "We'll all die anyway, just don't make it in vain. The access codes are inside."

Inside what? The note? She started to turn back—to grab for the tiny scrap—but it'd already fluttered farther as the Delonese moved her like a sea.

What did he mean? Inside where? And where'd the little girl go? What was being done to those kids and the ambassadors?

Where was Danya?

Sofi swallowed back a bubble of rising vomit. They weren't getting out of here. They likely weren't even making it past today. They'd all been doomed the moment they'd looked below the planet's surface. And Heller was right.

Now it was simply a game of not letting their deaths be in vain.

"The codes are inside."

She inhaled and looked up. She needed access to one of their portals.

Ahead of her, Ethos and the ten Delonese had entered the clear, glass-looking shuttle single file, their varied suits and tall features, so crisp and perfect, morphing into blobs of monstrous squiggles and lines through the walls.

The next second Sofi's body was moving up the low ramp. She tried to stop, but her muscles seemed to have a mind of their own, and she was through the ship's door seconds before it hissed shut, cutting off any chance of escape for the moment.

The shuttle rumbled to life, and Sofi tried to focus—tried to talk. To ask where they were taking her.

It lifted and swayed, and Sofi felt something edging her brain.

Teasing it.

She tried to take in the faces around her and physical cues and the glass shuttle itself.

Except nothing would work right as her stomach lurched and the smell of Delonese mixed with the movement of the shuttle launched her backward into a memory . . .

HER MENTAL CLOCK SAID IT'D BEEN FOUR DAYS SINCE Papa died and two days since the Delonese had come to her farm and taken her and Shilo. Meaning, two days of darkness, sitting in a rolling, blacked-out, trafficking ship soaked in urine and tears. With no food or water except the metallic moisture Sofi could lick off the icy wall behind her. She sucked in her aching tummy and tried not to wonder where they were ship-ping them to.

Or what would happen to Shilo once they got there.

Poor little man. He could barely stop crying when he'd found her in there, using that weird sixth sense of his. She'd nearly lost her mind trying to locate him, fumbling in the dark and stench among the other kids. And then he just appeared under her arm and asked her to warm him before sobbing his five-year-old self to sleep. His head in her lap. His hair smelling like home.

Which was when Sofi started banging on the hollow-sounding walls and swearing every naughty word her ten-year-old self knew for the Delonese traffickers to release them. They responded by pumping in a gas that nearly knocked the air and lights out of her.

She brushed a hand through her brother's damp hair and covered his shoulders. *Stay with me, Shi.* He moved, then coughed and lifted his head. "Dad?" Then must've remembered where they were because Sofi felt his voice break into silent, fighting-to-be-tough sobs. And it was all she could do not to start sobbing with him.

"It's alright. I'm here." Sofi gripped him and did her best to infuse his body with her heat as his arms constricted around her stomach.

"Sofi, I wanna go home."

"I know, bud. I'm working on it."

"What do you think they're gonna do with us?"

"I don't know. Probably just . . ." She couldn't answer. She didn't have an honest one to give. So she just held Shilo tighter and wondered if Mom was watching the news right now, searching for clues about them. *Please come find us.*

She pressed her nose to his scalp to inhale the scent of farm fields and dirt and sunshine, wishing she could tell him they were back home and this was just one of the games he liked to play. They were superheroes captured by bad guys today.

Shilo shivered and squirmed as the shuttle dropped and took her stomach with it. And the kids whimpered, "What's going on?" "Why've we stopped?" "Where are we?"

Sofi grabbed Shilo tighter and waited.

Fifteen minutes went by and the ship shifted beneath them and settled with a *clunk*. A huge bay door shot open amid icy air and bright lights and people speaking in a foreign language that sent a chill down her spine. She'd heard it on the news the few times Papa had let her watch. It was Delonese.

There they were, stepping closer. And in her still-adjusting vision they looked like big blobs and squiggly lines that began rounding up the kids and shoving them out the door.

"Sofi."

"*Sofi.*"

She blinked and choked and then leaned over to gag as Shilo's face flickered before her, then disappeared.

"*Focus, Sof. You're not even close to finished yet. Figure out what you can use here.*"

She slowed her breathing and waited for the visceral reaction to pass. She could almost feel Miguel's hand on her skin and breath in her hair, reassuring her that she was still here and she was alright. Even as she was aware the silent Delonese surrounding her were staring.

The shuttle shuddered and lifted higher.

Ethos called her over once again to where he stood against the spacious wall of glass.

Sofi narrowed her brow. Then stepped around the other Delonese and strode in front of the lead ambassador. "Where are the ambassadors and the kids?"

"We have sent them to rest for now. But for you . . ." Ethos tipped his head at her as if analyzing a lab rat. "We offer you an encounter with truth."

The quiet hover abruptly dipped, then zoomed low through the massive bay doorway, leaving behind the main building. Out of her peripheral, Sofi could see Heller's frozen body, still lying outside as the poisonous plumes floated up and licked the glass around them. The ten Delonese took this as their cue to stand against the far wall, with those sleek faces still watching her.

The light from the sun hit the ship's glass ceiling, illuminating the interior with cheeriness that was almost laughable. Sofi snorted. *What truth?* And whose truth—because clearly that term was relative here.

"Ah, here we go." Ethos pointed to the ground where the fog was receding the same way it'd come in, leaving the frosted ground clean and sparkling, reflecting off the ship as it flew through the compound, like a glass bubble, past the barracks and trapdoor she'd used, and headed for the tree line.

The farther they got, the more exquisite the scene became. *"Engineered to perfection,"* Sofi recalled the ambassadors once saying. But for someone used to the natural dirt and imperfections of good Old North Carolina land, this was too much engineering.

Like everything else here.

The ambassador narrowed his gaze at her. "Alis informed

me of visions from your brother these past few days. That you claim he's somehow spoken to you. Is this true?"

"Don't answer him."

Sofi blinked. The words were coming from that voice in her ear, like before.

"You will answer," Ethos pressed.

Stretching her neck, Sofi tilted her head to remind herself the reason she couldn't feel her earcom was because it wasn't there.

"The more you say, the more we can help you," Ethos continued, the sunlight glowing off his smooth face that many on Earth had found handsome.

"If you've spoken with my mother, you'll know my memories of this place emerged as nightmares. And in recent days those memories come even when I'm awake," she said, dodging the full answer. Because while she might be losing her mind under the intense scrutiny of Ethos and those unblinking Delonese eyes, she knew good intuition when she sensed it. And if they were going to kill her and the kids, she'd go down without giving anything crucial away.

She turned her gaze to hide her deception. Even as a nudging in the back of her head said there was another option besides death.

A worse option.

The shuttle flew faster while that caution told her she was about to find out.

"Breathe, Sofi," the voice in her ear said.

Are you joking? She mentally cussed the voice out. *Stop talking to me.*

The shuttle rocked, forcing Sofi to steady herself on the window and making the nausea flare. She shoved it down and tried to stay focused, tried to stay clearheaded, tried to stay any blasted way at all that didn't involve her scratching Ambassador Ethos's face off.

The next moment Ethos was pointing out the window. "Below us are the remnants of a city peeking up from the snow. One of many that used to rise high like your Earth ones."

Against her will, Sofi tilted into the curved glass to peer down.

Straight metal lines were laid out in octagonal shapes across a massive area, spread out on the flat plain between the mountains. Whatever had originally stood on the braces was long decayed, but the edges still poked up as far as the eye could see, like bones marking their territory. So why hadn't they seen this on any of the virtual comps yesterday? And how long ago had the city been discarded?

She glanced at the group of Delonese behind them. Had their civilization lived on their surface before they moved below?

"While your people prefer excess," Ethos said, "mine discovered streamlining led to quicker technological advancements. More than that, it created unity."

The shuttle dipped and moved on, going quicker now, toward a deeper valley Sofi had only seen from miles above when first entering the atmosphere on Miguel and Claudius's shuttle. The closer they drew, she noted the swells looked distinctly similar to Old Europe burial mounds. The shuttle flew faster as strange caves with animal statues carved into the valley sides came into view.

"This is our gravity ground. Our mass graves, as your kind would call them," Ethos said. "From our most disastrous planetary war."

"Your people are buried in those?"

"Not here. They were on our original planet. This is a replica—a surface re-creation of what our planet used to be. The entire globe is a visual historical model, if you will."

"More specifically, this is our way of remembering and honoring where and who we've come from."

"And who have you come from?" Sofi asked, her tone steady.

The Delonese ambassador looked at her. And didn't reply.

Right. She glanced about the glass shuttle, then through the ceiling to the planet's thick atmospheric shield barely visible to the eye. How often through the years had she stared up at this globe from Earth, despising it while simultaneously wondering what it looked like and what it was made of?

History, apparently. And more recently, the blood of humans. But maybe what she should've been asking was what exactly the Delonese were made of . . .

She rubbed her neck. "Considering you're using my people to reboot your race, I feel it only appropriate to ask—is Earth your first interaction with another race? Or have you gone through others before us?" She glared into Ethos's eyes. "Have you already tried using others for rebooting the reproduction of your people?"

The ambassador stared at her, unflinching. With a look akin to someone who'd just been grilled about other women on a date, and again said nothing.

Right. Which communicated everything. She wanted to smack him.

How many others had there been? And why hadn't they worked? "In that case, what about your home planet?" Sofi asked. "What about your people still there?"

"We blew it up. So no others would be able to find it or use it."

Sofi actually laughed, though her tone was filled with disgust. "Of course you did."

Ethos swept his hand around the sunlit crystal ship, like he was encompassing his entire people beyond it. "And now we arrive at the crux of the issue." He smiled, and everything about it pricked her spine.

The shuttle dipped.

Or maybe her focus dipped. Because her vision went black along with the shuttle, and the next thing she knew they were inside the planet—flying through its core.

She swung around, then peered back at Ethos.

The alien hadn't moved a muscle. Neither had the other Delonese—as if they'd not even noticed the transition.

What in—? What just happened?

The shuttle slowed and soared alone throughout the layered sections of a black underground city. Black towers of various heights passed by, with rooms and windows—some lit up, some dark. Bulbs around the buildings flickered on, though, as if sensing the shuttle before it approached each section and blossoming into yellow-lit pathways, apartments, and even rooftop areas as well as odd-angled statues of beasts Sofi had no recognition of.

Something was missing here. Something was . . .

Wrong.

She froze. Where were all the Delonese?

"Is this how your home planet looked too?" Sofi asked, her tone careful. "As empty as this one?"

The ship lurched and the image around them abruptly changed—or shoved them forward—into a new section made of solid white.

White buildings, white ground, white lights, white space

surrounded their flying glass bubble. Yet again, if Ethos or the others noticed the intense way the scenery had changed, none acknowledged it.

"Allow me to show you our labs." Ethos indicated the tall white buildings stretching in front of them.

The shuttle jerked, then glitched in the weird skipping-forward movement before reappearing—flying inside one of the buildings of an enormous medical facility.

Again with the white walls. Except these held med machinery. Sofi curled her fingers into fists and refused to look at Ethos lest she follow through on killing him before this fool tour ended and she could figure out a new attack to wreck their system. She'd have to plant a virus to weaken them. One she could control. The problem was, any advantage she'd had was pretty much gone. Unless she took an alien hostage . . .

She lifted a brow and turned to the ten Delonese just as the ambassador started explaining what they did in the labs. She stopped listening. She didn't want to hear any more. Especially with the Delonese members staring again. Their eyes and faces suddenly seemed closer, or larger. Sofi blinked and inhaled as the shuttle air felt heavy and the colors tilted off scale. She quietly bent over and made a slight gagging sound.

SOFI WAS LYING ON THE MED COT—STIFF, LIKE A BUTTER-fly pinned beneath a magnifying glass for people to dissect and analyze whether or not she was okay. Was she okay? It felt like she'd been asking that her entire life.

She wiggled and strained to break the straps, her heart *beat, beat, beating* like wings in time to the music in her head.

"Sofi, leave. Fly! Fly!" she heard Shilo say.

The microscope moved nearer. The Delonese faces peered harder. Their bodies closing in as their hive minds pondered.

Just before they pulled out their knives.

When she blinked again all was as before. She gripped a window brace. This was ridiculous. She was done being calm and playing their head games. She'd had enough of those on her own lately.

Narrowing her gaze, she studied which of the Delonese would be the easiest to take. The one third to the right. Just a hair thinner and shorter than the others. And not quite so confident looking. Question was, how would she do it? She offered him a smile suggesting he'd soon wish he'd never heard of Earth. Or the drama she was capable of inflicting.

A scream outside the shuttle yanked her attention. The sound was followed by another, then combined with laughter and squeals. Children reached up and waved as the ship floated past in this building that seemed to stretch on forever. They were *the* children.

All twenty of them. The kids locked eyes with her and watched with funny expressions, and then she was catching her breath because the shuttle had jerked forward again and was suddenly somehow landing.

The door opened, and Delonese guards were waiting in a short hall where music vibrated through the floors and walls, echoing as the door farther ahead opened and the melody grew louder. And then they were deplaning and walking quickly down that hall—only to step into the same domed room as last night, where the air was light and the aliens were infusing the very atmosphere with perfect harmonies.

"Sofi!"

Claudius and Danya were strolling toward her, arms outstretched, smiles from ear to ear in the vast room of layered balconies, and glittering air, and elegant Delonese everywhere.

And behind them was Miguel.

15

MIGUEL

THE NIGHT MIGUEL MET SOFI, HE'D BEEN AT A PARTY CELE-
brating the successful, newly established Fan Fight Games—which
were the latest in cross virtual and live entertainment created by
the thirty ruling United World Corporations.

"To feed humanity's blood-enthrallment while testing our
Corp inventions," they'd joked behind closed doors.

And as Earth's most popular, wildly misbehaving ambassador, Miguel had been in lavish attendance at the after gala, to
enjoy all the rewards that came with youthful popularity and his
skills of seduction—especially when one had an uncanny ability
to utilize both. He'd used every move to obtain his ambassador
position.

He just hadn't been prepared for the summer storm that was
Sofi Snow.

"Who knew Inola's sixteen-year-old kid was a bloody genius?"
a senator at the glittering party muttered beside him. "Girl and her
team should've won."

"Not just won," said another. "She and her brother should've
creamed them all and claimed the winning title."

"You think someone purposefully gamed the system against them?" Miguel swerved an already curious eye Sofi's direction. And smirked at the pair of old-skool headphones around her neck alongside a tiny owl necklace beneath an expression that declared she despised being there as much as he was enjoying it. *Interesante.* "Forgive me, but I thought gaming was the whole point. However it's accomplished."

"The game-heads, sure, but not the Corps. At least not once the players hit the arena. Trust me, that girl should've won."

Is that so?

"Don't even think about it," Claudius had said as soon as the senators had strolled away. "She's not your type."

Miguel lifted a brow.

"She has morals, Miguel."

Ah. Got it. He'd nodded politely and promptly lost interest.

Not that he disagreed with the senators' assessment of Sofi. He was quite aware her tech brilliance was deemed phenomenal. It's just that he'd assumed everything was always rigged—especially if you were the limelight's current highest bidder. And if she was honestly trying to pretend she was any different . . . He snorted. Then she was a liar. More than that—she was hiding it behind the pretense of morality, which was the worst kind in his experience.

Only thing was . . .

When her mother insisted on introducing them a half hour later, he'd discovered a girl with no interest in the limelight or pretending whatsoever.

Nor in him, for that matter.

It was shocking, really. In the midst of the universe's political games, the star of the underground gaming world had somehow maintained an innocent ideal of becoming what he believed in. And making the person he was more than the puppets the world played. And it intrigued him body and spirit until the point that, over the following month, conviction had altered everything. As if one day he'd been fine, and the next, the entire planet had tilted and he'd lost his grip on the external world he loved and the internal world he loathed. Because the girl with the black eyes and brown limbs—who smelled of sun and fields, and whose heart he broke barely four weeks later, by being so pathetically broken himself—believed in the goodness of people's humanity.

He'd spent the next seventeen months trying to become worthy of that belief.

Because somehow he'd begun to believe it about people too.

And now here she stood in a party room on Delon. This girl who was a summer moon on a winter eve, whom he'd watched walk back into his world and wreck him all over again just three days ago.

And she was not finished yet. With any of it.

Miguel watched the tilt of her head as she lifted her face to this golden glass-domed room that was turning in a slow circle in between the massive day-lit moon above and the white snow-tipped landscape below. Filled with hundreds of white-robed Delonese. And caught the glint in her eye that said she was going to burn this place down.

"Miguel, what do you know of Sofi's tech skills?" Alis asked him.

What? He frowned and swerved to find her beside him, drink in hand. *Where'd she come from?*

A sudden commotion caught his attention as Danya and Claudius loudly greeted Sofi and went to join her and Ethos. He shook his head. He should join her too. He had things to tell her—*concerns, dangers.* But his limbs felt tired. Slow. And his head . . .

"I promised you the truth," Lord Ethos was saying above the ruckus from his place next to Sofi.

Miguel followed his long fingers as he pointed at the Delonese—the ones clustered along the room's balconies, followed by the others cluttered here and there on the varied silver staircases and levels beneath the glass ceiling, surreptitiously watching him and the other humans. To the right, a group was making music while the crowd above kept breaking into song. On the left, some were using their bodies to invent new movements—to complement the people behind them who were doing mathematical equations on tapestries that were beyond anything his brain could fathom.

A scene of perfection.

Except for the reality hidden beneath the planet's surface.

A few yards away, one of them spotted Miguel and raised a glass. Calling for a toast to their favorite ambassador.

"To Miguel!" the group around him cheered, and Alis joined in, nearly sloshing her drink on his day-old suit.

"Reality is not everything it seems." Ethos was still speaking to Sofi, but his gaze had landed on Miguel and Alis. "While you've been assuming the worst intentions, your friends have been enjoying themselves. Even to the point they've come round to our way of thinking."

"And which way is that again?"

"Miguel, join us!" Claudius waved, interrupting Ethos to slip his arm around Sofi's shoulder. Danya laughed at the intrusion, her high cheekbones giving away her Delonese heritage despite an otherwise well-practiced and well-played Earthen persona.

Miguel's skin rippled. Was it his imagination or did Claudius's hand seem to whip through the air too quick? The lights flickered, making Miguel squint and rub the ache from the back of his neck. He shook off the confusion and went to join Sofi—to protect her—to tell her what the Delonese were planning for her, what they were planning for those shells below and possibly for Earth.

Before he could reach her, he was cut off by a group of Delonese. Walking. Dancing. He pushed and wrangled to get past, but they refused to make a way. Almost as if on purpose. A second later they picked up their unity chant—the same as last night. The universe constellations emerged in a flood of colored lights throughout the room. The aliens all moved to stare up at the domed-ceiling stars while blending their voices in the uncanny tone of drones.

He leaned to peer beyond the dome glass and scanned the compound and their position within it, which was five stories up and adjacent to the enormous council chambers—in the very heart of the area's barracks and shuttle bays. And beyond those, the vast forests and icy landscape. Covered with that creamy fog.

That fog.

He stood back. And looked closer at the people in the room.

The matching faces, identical movements, and unblinking eyes. From his experience with them, not one of the Delonese in here was under the age of forty-five—and yet they looked and moved as healthy twenty-year-olds. They were seven-foot-tall replications of perfection.

Pay attention, Miguel. What do you see?

Aliens who look like flawless humans.

"No, what do you sense?" he could almost hear his padre ask.

Miguel studied the atmosphere. The aliens were chanting now. "We are created from technology and born into a product of beauty. We will rise higher through our own experience, community, and personal power."

And yet something in their tones—

Oh.

As a too-tall, tough-skinned, foulmouthed child, he'd experienced it in the dogfights he'd watched. And later, in the eyes of angry patients desperate for a cure from certain Corps. More recently, he'd found it in the faces of those dying over in the black markets.

It's what had made them all good fighters.

When you knew you were dying, you fought harder, without wavering, because survival was all you had. Every time.

And from the flavor of fear prickling his senses in this room . . .

The Delonese were a freaking ticking time bomb.

They were a society who'd overengineered themselves until nature could no longer take its course. And now they were on a clock, counting down to extinction.

He peered at Ethos. This was why they'd shown up to assist Earth eleven years ago.

To prey upon humanity's genetic pool for survival.

The realization dawned—they weren't actually trying to hide the fact they were stealing children. They were hiding their *reason* for stealing them. Because the very need that empowered them to justify the abductions was also their deepest weakness.

They have a weakness.

He shut his eyes and tried to tune out that blasted droning

of identical voices and faces, and focus on how to exploit that weakness.

"And in the end, we will be greater," they were saying. "We will be conquerors of our own truth, our own will, our own death. We will be rulers of destiny."

He sniffed. At least they were motivated. He'd give them that.

"You see where our problem lies, don't you?" Ethos murmured near his ear.

Miguel's eyelids flew open. Ethos stood beside him, waving a hand to encompass the room. "In order for us to exist—and for our races to coexist—we must be willing to assist one another. As we have done for you. You see, in our minds, it is not your lives that are the price, but ours." He stared at Miguel. "And we will do anything necessary to protect them."

Ambassador Ethos switched his gaze over to Claudius and Danya and beckoned them.

When they reached him, Claudius patted Miguel's back. "Lord Ethos is convincing you too, eh?"

Miguel analyzed him. His features, his expression, the droning lilt in his tone. Miguel's throat went dry as the ache reappeared in his spine. He peeked up at Danya. What had they done to him? This was Claudius, but not the version he knew.

"It's a bit to take in, I know." Claudius was grinning appeasement. "The trade-off required—the gifts. But, Miguel, believe me, no one values every life they take more than these people. They honor each one for the gift it might bring them."

Miguel couldn't speak. If he did he'd likely punch Ethos across the chin for whatever he'd done to his best friend.

He shook his head. It wasn't adding up. He needed to get his bearings.

He needed to get back to Sofi.

"You okay there, bud?" Claudius took a sip of a sparkly drink. "You look like a ghost." He stepped closer and peered into Miguel's face. His voice dipping as he asked Ethos, "Will you be able to get it all?"

Miguel frowned.

He turned to force his way to Sofi, but she was already there, fighting to get to him. He grabbed her arm as the silvery air rippled against the glass dome. He could feel the warmth radiating from her slim-suit, followed by her lips so close that her words caught against his skin.

"I hate this place," her mouth whispered. "I'm ready to go home."

16

INOLA

THE HOVERCAR WAS STILL THERE—TWO LANES TO THE RIGHT, seven lengths back. Blue, nondescript, the same that'd been there since she'd left the FanFights twenty minutes ago. Different from her security team's, but still going the same speed and same direction. Maybe it was a coincidence. Maybe not.

Inola took her black hair down from its bun and swiped back to the video on her handscreen. The one she'd secretly recorded in Ms. Gaines's Corp 30 office when she'd gone to confront her last night. Proving once again her intuition was correct.

"I had to, Inola," Ms. Gaines said. *"The other Corps were getting too close. What would they have done had they discovered what we were doing with their kids? With our kids? That we were jacking the games? Corp 24's Altered would've ruined everything."*

Inola's voice broke in. *"So you had them killed, along with my son?"*

"They were going to expose us! All that work we've put into this company to help people—to make them better!" Gaines was practically foaming at the mouth. *"It would've been thrown away."*

Inola looked out the window at the sunset dousing the

147

buildings in pink and gold. Artistic shades rippling off the mirrored skyscrapers and in the sunglasses of myriad passersby. She peered in the rearview mirror again. The hovercar far behind them moved into the lane as soon as Jerrad did.

"I see it, madam," he said, without moving his gaze from the highway. The next moment the car slowed and edged off onto a side street and Inola exhaled. She was just being paranoid.

"*I took care of it, Inola. Don't you see?*" The vid on her screen kept playing. "*We had to delete the evidence! If the Delonese knew we'd let their secret escape, they'd be called into question too. It could rock the entire political system, and people would've lost faith in them and us. If you'd kept your daughter under better control—*"

Inola clicked it off.

If she'd kept her daughter under better control . . .

How many times had that been an issue through the years? "*Sofi, don't make the Corp look bad.*" "*Sofi, stay in boarding school with Shilo until you've learned what real life is.*"

She shook her head. If Sofi was good at anything, it was refusing to be controlled. And while that may have infuriated Inola as a parent, she was grateful for it now. *Tick, tick, tick . . .*

Inola peered down to check her handscreen. She hadn't shut it off since the message had come through, and the blinking text hadn't disappeared this time.

If you want to help your kids, head for the black markets.

Followed by her three: What do you want?

What do you want?

Why are you doing this?

Her stomach knotted and her breathing grew harder. Their message didn't even make sense. What did they know about Sofi and Shilo?

Likely nothing. Which was why the whole thing had gotten under her skin. Her team still hadn't cracked the sender, but they were close.

Her neck stiffened as she checked behind them again through the hovercar's rear window. Jerrad's security team was still there. The blue hover was not. She stretched her shoulders to relieve the tension and melted back against the seat to watch the city skyscrapers and crowds thin as they entered the southeast outskirts of town.

"It's not too late, you know," Jerrad said from the front.

She sniffed and half laughed. "Are we talking for my parenting or for this little escapade?"

"Both. Although . . ." He looked up in the rearview mirror. "If you don't mind my saying—it'll be alright. You've not lost her yet. The Delonese haven't figured everything out, and she's not dead. There's still time."

She blinked. Glanced away. "And yet listening to that vid, I think we both know the truth is I lost Sofi a long time ago."

He made a sound with his throat.

She frowned. "What?"

"How long have I worked for you?"

"Since a year before Ben died."

"And my team watched over your kids during that time with him, and ever since. Even on the farm that day when we stood back because you ordered us to let the Delonese take them, yes?"

"What's your point?"

"Just that if there's one thing I know, it's those two kids love you. Your girl loves you."

"Thanks for the reassurance, Jerrad, but it's not quite that simple." Then, with more humility, "But continue."

He shrugged and rubbed his jaw with his hand missing two fingers. "I just expect it's why she's so angry, and why she's sought some kind of love in the arms of boys, and why she's always trying so hard to get your attention. Not 'cuz she hates you, I can tell you that. You've not lost her, madam." He shook his head and put his attention back on the road. "If anything, she's just been there waiting."

Inola stared.

If anyone else had said those words, she would've ushered them from the car and destroyed their future. Instead, she sat and glared at this man who was, in reality, her oldest friend. And felt her throat swell up with that blasted ache.

His words . . .

A mercy and a correction.

He cocked a cautionary frown and cleared his throat. "It's also not too late to head back to the safety of your Corp 30 office. Because you and I both know this texting hacker is a nut job using the topic of your kids as sick bait. And the idea that we're actually giving cred—"

"I know my kids aren't there, Jerrad, but there's obviously *something* he wants us to see," she said irritably.

"Just not sure it'll be beneficial or *safe* is all. I'd hate to see your intuition misled by the wrong team."

"My intuition cured cancer. I suspect it'll survive this. Besides," she added, gentler, after a moment. "That's what I have you for, right?"

He snorted his final disapproval and let the tension fall where it may as she turned her attention to the shaded buildings and dirty deserted streets.

She hadn't been to this city border section of Old Manhattan in ages. Early on, she'd had to focus on which parts of the city were worth building into her planned, glorified metropolis, and, for every glaring reason in front of her, this hadn't been one of them. In fact, her most recent visit was probably the last time she'd had to pull her kids out of here when they were trying to sell off Sofi's old tech items. All she remembered of that time was that it was fuller then—rowdier. The anti-Delonese protestors and anarchists must've moved uptown for the week's FanFights.

Her screen buzzed, and she flipped on the text-to-voice so Jerrad could hear it too:

Turn right at the side street, then pull into the underground mall. Head straight until you reach the cages. And caution— don't stop.

She glowered. You think? Where am I going? she typed.

To see your kids.

Her patience pricked. Not funny.

Wasn't meant to be.

The side street they'd just turned down sloped and took them and the vehicles following into an old underground parking garage. The hoverlights came on, illuminating the cement surroundings of pier supports and off-shooting tunnels that led to a maze of levels—most of which used to hold shops, but now was more like an underground city with living quarters and trading bays, from what she'd been told.

A man stepped out in front of them, and Inola yelped as the hover swerved around him and kept going. He peered after her with a dazed gaze that said his meals of late had been of the medicated variety.

Maybe Jerrad was right. Perhaps this was a bad idea and the whole thing was from a crazed hacker Gaines had hired. Maybe it was their way of eliminating her.

Except, even the VP knew that if anything happened to Inola, there'd be an automatic release of highly sensitive documents. Documents offensive not just to Gaines, but to many others as well. It was partly how Inola had stayed in business so long.

Everyone needed a layer of protection.

"Madam." Jerrad pointed ahead.

She nodded. And typed, Okay, we're here. Where are my kids? Keep driving.

"I'm becoming less thrilled by the second," Jerrad growled.

"Me too, but just keep going." She slid closer to the left window to peer out on the makeshift mattress booths strewn on the ground against the walls. There were faces now. Peeking out from the hovels and others standing in groups, smoking and hovering over their telescreens or staring at the car.

"What do we have here?" someone yelled out.

"More rich politicians," another hollered. "Hey, you guys are a little early—the FanFights haven't ended yet! It's still down to three players!"

The crowds thickened, and soon the hover wasn't just driving past people watching the FanFights. They were also watching real fights—kids against kids, kids against dogs, men against women—with those surrounding them taking bets and cheering or hissing. Inola began to notice the cages here and there. Lined up along the walls. First they held animals. For food or fights, from the looks of it.

Soon they held people. Inola could barely stomach seeing them, locked in, their faces angry or hopeless. All despising those milling around them. But seeming to despise her hovercar and those of her entourage behind her more.

The farther they drove through the cement city, the harder the expressions and gazes became, and the younger those beside the adults looked.

"You guys looking for some fun?" said a lady dressed as a queen.

"I got you some fun right here! Even give you a discount!" A bald man pulled back the flap of a tent just enough to see inside. Inola looked away and felt her stomach sink into her knees. Oh gad. What was wrong with people? How could they do this to each other?

Explain how that's legal? her handscreen asked.

It's not, she replied.

Right . . . And yet it's allowed by Corp 30 and the CEO who built this city.

That's not my fault.

Then whose fault is it?

She didn't respond. She didn't need to—she didn't owe anyone an answer. Of course she'd known this stuff was here. Everyone did. All societies had their underbelly, and for her part, she regularly sent raids in to deal with them. She'd built houses for some of them, for gad's sake! She couldn't help it that they found their way right back to it.

Even with the FanFight kids—she'd never sent any here. If the others chose to, that truly wasn't her fault.

So where are my kids? she typed.

No response.

"Inola," Jerrad said from the front seat.

She started to glance up just as her screen went blank again, deleting the messages. She snorted. Then cursed as something hit their hovercar's roof with a crash. *What the—?*

"That's it. We're getting you out of here. I don't know if they recognized the car or they're just drunk over the FanFights, but we're done." He accelerated the hover off the ground and above their heads, almost scraping the cement ceiling, and took off.

No argument from her. She took in the crowd that was closing in, yelling about their bets on the FanFights, yelling for the three kids a group had surrounded who were going at it in some kind of knife match. Yelling for the hovercar occupants to come out and play with two sickly children being offered at a low, low price.

They whipped through the under-city, dodging support beams and hanging signs and pipes, and then suddenly were headed up, up, up to burst outside into the evening air.

Inola exhaled the breath she was holding. *So whose fault is it, Inola?*

The security hovers blasted out behind them. They lowered to the street and melted into the thickening traffic. People headed to the markets, she realized after a second. After a day around the arena, they were looking for more entertainment. Other types of entertainment.

"You okay?" Jerrad asked.

"Yes. Take me home, please."

His voice hesitated.

"What?"

"Just wondering if you got what you were expecting, madam."

Reflections of the children's faces back there in those cages, those hovels, those sellers' tents, flashed across her gaze. Faces of children just like hers.

"If you want to help your kids, head to the black markets."

She looked up at the planet. Looked at the city growing larger in her front window, and ground her teeth. *So whose fault is it?*

Maybe there was a reason her daughter wasn't willing to be controlled.

"Yes. I think I got it," she whispered.

The pink sunset faded quickly to purple city lights and flickering ad-lined streets. Between their glow and the cooling evening air, everything gradually eased back to looking normal. Neat. Tight. Packaged up in a bomb that had gotten rid of the evidence so now life could go on as usual—business could go on with FanFights and parties and poverty. And no one the wiser.

No one the wiser except Sofi and her. And those who'd truly lived it and seen what the children had seen. What her *own* children had seen. On Delon and in the markets.

Question was, what were they willing to do about it?

"Madam, in the rearview." Jarred interrupted her thoughts.

Inola checked and saw the security hovers slipping in and out of traffic.

Then frowned and peered closer.

The blue hovercar was back.

17

SOFI

THE DELONESE STOPPED TALKING. CLAUDIUS STOPPED WAVING.
Alis stopped sipping her drink beside Miguel. Sofi braced. For
what—she didn't know yet. But every nerve was trembling as
Miguel stepped between her and Ethos's disconcerting face
and pulled Sofi away to dance, or rather, to hide in a giant room
full of other dancers. They floated through the bodies as his
arm smoothly slid around her waist in calculated performance,
while his fake expression softened. "You look like death. No
offense."

Maybe I am dead, she was beginning to think. And for that
matter, she wasn't sure if Miguel was even real anymore. Was he
a figment of her mind too? She slid a hand to his exposed skin
where the edge of his shirt met his neck and softly pinched it.

He raised a brow and cracked a slip of a questionable smile.

"Making sure you're real."

"You noticed also?" He tipped his chin down. "And what's the
assessment?"

"Your heart beats the same," she whispered.

His gaze landed on hers. On her eyes, her nose, her lips.

And he offered her a careful smile that was all him and not the pretend one he lent the covers of magazines. It was the same one she'd seen another lifetime ago—after everyone left a party he'd hosted and they'd gone for a walk along the rooftops of an old carnival. They'd held hands and talked about the differences of their worlds. His wild life. Her gaming guild. Except now that smile was less certain. Less hopeful and completely devoid of any thought of what he could get from her—only indicative of what he'd failed to give. Even in this moment. As if he could communicate through it everything of the past eighteen months.

"Sofi, the Delonese . . . What they've got down there—what I think they might be planning—I . . ."

She nodded. "I know."

"So, when I make a move, you'll understand—"

The note from Heller fluttered into mind. *"Don't make it in vain. The access codes are inside."* She shook her head.

"Sof, I'm sorry."

"Shh." She put her index finger to Miguel's lips. It wasn't his fault. He didn't need to waste the moment apologizing for this bloody mess. Especially when she was about to ruin it by saying she had a last-ditch plan that involved nabbing the smallest Delonese from the shuttle and holding him hostage as they both went down in a blazing fire of death.

He smiled and pulled his mouth away. "No, I need to say this." Then paused in the middle of the room, between the fifty Delonese bodies swaying to a music that was both ethereal and incredibly irritating. "I'm sorry for what I did to you."

She slowed. Inhaled. Oh.

Oh.

His expression grew serious. She watched his throat move as he swallowed. And somehow knew what the words were he'd left unsaid yesterday.

"I should've been better for you," he whispered. "I should've come looking for you all those months ago."

Her heart shifted in her chest. She knew it because suddenly her ribs were too tight and her lungs couldn't find air.

"Sofi . . ." His voice turned raw. "I should've called."

Three simple words.

Three stupid, simple words.

At a time like this.

Those three words brought down everything that sheltered her heart. As if the wall of ice she'd built that day she'd sat on the floor of her apartment, believing he'd moved on, suddenly shattered back into the pieces she'd thought she'd been. The pieces of herself she'd collected through their rejection, through other boys, through the fake smiles and her hatred of him every time she'd seen him on the tele.

"Every single day for the past eighteen months, I've wanted to say that." He pushed a hand through his hair and his eyes turned dark. "I would've. I *should've*. I just . . ."

She let her eyes hang on his. She went to speak. To agree. To say, yes, he should've and she would've been angry but perhaps she also could've come round and understood that he was different. That he was better. More than better.

Because she now understood.

That he was someone she respected—and that meant more to her than love or lust or romance.

He saw it. She didn't know how, but the glint in his eyes and the tension of his jaw said he saw what she was thinking. He nodded and opened his gaze and, in that moment, offered the only thing he had left that he was in control over.

Himself. He leaned in until his lips brushed her ear and his scent of day-old cologne entwined with her hair, her heart, her lungs. "So this is me calling now."

The music stopped. Her world stopped.

"To tell you I don't deserve you. And if things were different right now, I'd tell you I'm different, but that if you'd have me, I'd be yours."

"Miguel, I—" Before she could say any more words, Miguel's fingers dissipated in hers and she was left gripping air. The room flickered, suddenly bright with that blasted overelectrified telescreen sensation.

"We don't have more time," Ethos said from somewhere. "We need the information now."

What? Where'd—? Sofi turned to see what Ethos was doing—and found the entire room stalled and staring at her. The Delonese. Claudius. Danya. Sofi spun back to find Miguel—to find where they'd taken him, what they were going to do to him—when a rather tall twelve-year-old boy with deep eyes and sun-kissed brown skin, who probably smelled like an Old North Carolina summer, stepped out from behind Danya and lifted a finger to his lips.

Sofi's heart melted and froze, and cracked wide open as every particle in the room disintegrated.

She stared at his face.

The aliens kept chanting.

Her lungs stopped breathing and the room began glitching.

Shilo?

18

MIGUEL

THE LAST THING MIGUEL KNEW WAS IT ALL TURNED SLIPPERY—
the room, his head, his heart. As if the world was sliding from
his grasp and dripping from his veins as he was sinking, sinking,
sinking. He reached up to stop them, and to save her. "Sofi." But
his mind kept falling back in time, through images flashing.

His childhood.

His brothers and sisters, madre, padre, aunts and uncles.
All relishing the muggy heat as they laughed and called him
"good boy" and sipped their *cervezas* in lawn chairs on the grass
beneath wide Los Angeles magnolia trees. He remembered the
fiesta for his cousin—right before the city had been bombed and
an earthquake took most of it off the map.

His mind flickered forward to their deaths—to another
bomb—this time in Old Colorado during World War IV, when
he'd come home at nine years old to find their bodies strewn
through the rubble. He'd barely had time to grieve before being
swept up by Corp 19 as a personal "assistant" to an underling.
Rubbing shoulders with the elite. Learning what they wanted,

what they loved, how they lived, and what he could attain if he flattered and fawned enough.

Until he'd learned enough to flip the game over and, within a few years, have the world flatter and fawn over him.

His mind skipped to his first kiss with a girl whose name he couldn't recall. And his last kiss—with Sofi, eighteen months ago.

He lifted a hand to rub his neck where that ache just kept growing. *Why is it flaring? What is wrong with my spine?* But then more memories rushed in, like a vidscreen on fast-forward. Flooding their colors and noise until his nerves felt raw and his brain hurt and he could hear himself swearing and calling Sofi's name.

Ambassador Ethos was suddenly there, in the dark with him. "We have a system of peace and simplicity," the alien said. "A way of life we've lived far longer than your planet has even existed. We've learned from our wars and mistakes centuries ago. Whereas, let me show you your world today."

The lead ambassador held up a handscreen and brushed his fingers over it. A video popped up showing a newsfeed from Earth on which Nadine was speaking. Even with the sound off, Miguel could determine the gist of her message. A real-time stream scanned the rioters frothing over Corp 24's Altered device. Picketers had switched from marching with signs to throwing mini explosives up in the air and into store windows where Delonese products were sold.

Miguel's head felt heavy. He massaged his burning neck again and tried to focus as Ethos swiped the screen, pulling up a homemade vid from someone at one of the black markets. The fact that the lead ambassador had access to someone's handheld enough to tap in and watch along with them was disturbing in itself. But the images of what was happening to those children—let alone the fact that the individual filming was doing nothing to intervene—made his skin flare. They brought up memories of what had been done to him as a preteen after his parents passed.

The alien shut off the handheld and looked down at Miguel with giant black eyes. "Your people seem to have little value for each other aside from squandering their neighbors for selfish perversion, as we've just seen. In contrast, not only do we value your people enough to use them—we use them for good. Nothing is wasted when we dismantle them—"

Miguel let his fist fly this time and landed it on Ethos's cheek, only to discover the Delonese's face dissolve in midair along with the rest of his body.

¿Qué? Miguel tried to figure out where he went, but his vision started flickering faster. Flinging him like a slingshot from experience to experience. His first UW meeting as Earth's youngest ambassador at seventeen. Followed by the first time he saw a child in the crowd with that vacant stare. Like the faces of others in the black markets—children who'd been sold and used by regular humans and left scraping to survive like dogs. Except most people treated their dogs better.

His neck and spine were *throb, throb, throbbing.* He ground his teeth as the pain transported him into new places, new scenes. As if his life were a book and he was falling from page to page. Like a dream where you try to run or scream but your body won't cooperate.

He began to shake, his muscles jerking—clenching in reaction to the mental overload. The Delonese were ripping out parts of him.

He watched the scenes fly away and his head screamed to slow it down.

Slow it down, Miguel. Focus. Hold on to one.

He reached out to grab the next scene that came up. And locked eyes with it—with her.

Sofi.

They'd known each other for three weeks and he'd flown her to the only drive-in left in Old America. They sat on top of the hovercar and watched the screen and fading sun as the couples in cars around them kissed.

"TELL ME YOUR FAVORITE MEMORY," SOFI WHISPERED.

He winked. "You sure you know what you're asking? I have a lot."

"Nope. Not allowed," she said in her very serious, life-is-worth-something tone. "You only get one."

Fine. He opened his mouth to tell her about the places he'd traveled and the famous people he'd met. About the adventures cliff diving and rock climbing . . . Then stopped.

And told her instead of the one time his padre had said he was proud of him. They'd been sitting on the hood of an old Ford truck, not unlike where he and Sofi were sitting now. Listening to mariachi music and watching the ranch hands farm the orange tree fields. And for no reason whatsoever Padre had put his arm around Miguel's shoulders and said, "I'm proud of you, *hijo.* You'll be a good man."

Miguel's voice clouded and his throat turned warm. He looked away.

He had brought Sofi here to try to convince her to sleep with him, but that no longer interested him.

Because rather than looking at her with hunger, he'd just bared his soul as a friend. And he couldn't recall the last time he'd had a female version of one of those.

"Now you tell me yours," he whispered.

"The day Shilo was born," she said in her simple voice. "Ella had died a few months before, and Mom and Papa were smiling. My family was my home."

Sofi leaned over and put her hand on his chest, right above his heart, and placed her head there too. She gave him a soft peck before tapping his heart. "Your father was right. You're a good person in here, Miguel. Whether you believe it or not."

He barely spoke for the rest of the night, even when he flew her home.

Just inhaled the gift she'd deposited, in the raw spaces she'd excavated.

The gift of believing he was someone more.

Until . . .

It all began dripping away . . .

Her voice. The setting sun.

The sweet taste of her soft kiss.

Miguel frowned. *What is happening?*

His mind was black again—and that fog rose, surrounded by the presence of Ethos.

Something in his mind was changing—*leaving*—as if bit by bit pieces of his soul were being carved out and tossed away. What in—? What were they doing to him? His very chest was ripping open. The pain unbearable. It was all spinning around. Sofi's voice, her face, their friendship.

The Delonese crooned—their voices swirling faster through

the dark. Their unity chant ringing in his ears, drowning him in its verses before birthing him anew from its promises.

Until it all froze. Midair. Midsip. Midsong.

And she was standing there in front of him in the black void. Bitter tears lacing her cheeks. She was crying. Why was she crying?

He shook his head, but pieces of his memory were missing. He'd known her once. This girl staring at him.

And suddenly he was crying too—because that place in him she'd altered was disappearing.

Which was when he picked up swearing at them because he needed to remember. He swore and kept her face in focus until it was gone and there was nothing to yell about anymore.

In fact, he couldn't remember why he'd needed to in the first place.

And then the darkness lifted. His vision cleared. And he was back in the beautiful domed hall—where the famous Delonese opera singer was belting out her song and the aliens were dancing, and Claudius and Danya were grinning beside him while Alis was laughing.

Alis. He frowned. There was something she'd done. Something he was supposed to recall. But then her voice called out for more tea and asked Miguel what he thought about the Council meeting that morning and turning up the unit productions with Delon. And it suddenly occurred to him that everything was alright after all.

"Have you seen Sofi around?" Alis leaned over to ask after he'd nodded his support of pushing the vote through.

Miguel frowned. "Sofi who?"

Alis's voice was smooth. "Sofi Snow. Corp 30's game-head."

Miguel felt his brow widen. *The girl who bombed her brother? Why would she be here?* "Wasn't she just on Earth's terrorist most-wanted list?" Poor kid. He couldn't imagine what anyone had done to make her want to harm her own family member by blowing him up like that.

19

INOLA

INOLA CHANGED INTO HER NIGHTCLOTHES AND THEN DOUBLE-checked her handcomp. No more of the messages. No more on Delon or the ambassadors.

Nothing more on the blue car. Yet.

Good.

She logged into her private server and pulled up the internal in-box of the attorney general. Then strode into the plush, gray living room of the fiftieth-story suite she occupied on the far end of the city, where one side of windows looked across the skyscrapers and business blocks, and the other gave a wide view of the dark, unlit water.

In the background the tele was playing vids of her kids. Old ones she hadn't watched—hadn't even thought of—in forever. But something about today—the mood, the fights, the stupid black-market jaunt—had made it seem appropriate. She'd put the vid on when she arrived home and went to take a shower. And for a moment it'd felt like being back eleven years ago just before everything had changed. She'd driven home for a visit with them and their father and found them playing out in the fields.

Shilo's voice was squealing, and Sofi was chasing him. *"Watch us, Mama! Watch us!"*

"I'm watching!" Inola had laughed and the vid jiggled as she'd chased after them with it.

Now Inola turned away from the tele, picked hot tea from the wall dispenser amid the soft glow of the cream wall lights, and let their voices simmer in her mind. Those voices she'd missed out on too often over too many years because she'd been so busy saving the world.

But maybe the greatest thing wasn't always to be the savior or victor. Maybe it was to care for the others who one day might be saviors or victors or leaders.

She turned to look out over the city. *So whose fault is it, CEO Inola?* Maybe saving the world was simply showing love and mercy to others in the belief that love would penetrate the hearts of those touched—and illuminate inside their skin until it altered every belief and view and ability they had—to become a campaign of love that overrode the hate and fear and darkness.

Loving our fellow man.

Maybe that's what she'd been too busy missing . . .

With a last glance out the window in the direction of the black markets, Inola shut the sound to the recordings off and went to her wide desk beneath the giant painting of Ella and took a seat. With the private in-box of the attorney general staring back at her.

She set down her tea. And began to make a video, detailing every aspect of her involvement in the Delonese project. Since day one.

How she, Inola Snow, had taken it upon herself to assist the Delonese in rebooting their race—in the form of letting them take cells from Earth children, to grow in labs. And in turn she'd ensured those labs helped humanity.

How it'd started with Delon taking five orphans eight years ago to extract a few cells, inject a few of their own, and send them back to Earth—dropping them in cornfields for Inola's people to find while keeping it random enough to prevent others from connecting her Corp with them.

How she'd started a school to protect and assess them. And how they did the same with a second batch of five children six months later, and then a third test group that included her own kids, taken from her farm, the day following Ben's death. She'd honored his wishes until then. After that, she honored her own.

How both her kids had been cured of ailments.

And then how the deaths had begun. The test-subject kids simply keeled over one by one within a matter of months. All except for Sofi and Shilo, who, failing to exhibit any unique traits over the next few years, had been considered failed too.

And how from there on out, she'd revised the program to allow the Delonese twenty kids a year for cell extraction only, with the condition they return them for her to monitor. In exchange, her company experienced years of medical success— and the children had been none the wiser thanks to the memory erasures. And how if it meant reversing the centuries' worth of DNA modifications that had rendered the aliens sterile, then it also meant they could prevent humans from repeating the same mistake.

Until her two children began displaying unexplainable symptoms. An ability to mentally connect with each other. To understand and manipulate Delonese technology. It's partly why she'd started the FanFights—to prevent their own curiosity from catching Delonese attention. And to see just how far they could go using the nanobots and coding.

Except, then rumors reached her ears that the Delonese were taking far more than the allotted twenty a year, and some of those kids weren't making it back.

And how that'd all led to Gaines's bombing, due to Altered.

And the cover-ups.

She explained every bit of it. In detail. All the way through today's vid conversation with Lord Ethos.

There. It was all out in the open, spilling from her lips on the privacy of the vid. The same info she'd sent in one form or another to her life bank.

But this vid—she placed it in the attorney general's box.

The *Send* button blinked at her.

She clicked *Hold*.

Closing the doc, she looked over to find the home vids had ended and the living room lights had come up, sending their glow across the white couches and gray carpet as the screen dimmed. She picked up her tea and flipped on the telenews to scan the latest on the FanFights and was promptly met by an advertisement for Altered.

Nadine, Corp 24's goodwill ambassador, was on the telescreen.

Inola leaned back and studied the woman, chewing over how she'd practically been attacked by her outside Inola's own office yesterday.

Her brow dipped. What did Nadine know of all this? Inola assessed the tilt of her head, the level of trust in her eyes, her stance, her body language, with new interest. What was her connection with Ambassador Miguel—and was she in current contact with him?

The ad suddenly panned out in an apparent repeat of the morning's test run of the product on the FanFight players. Inola leaned in as, in the background, she noticed Hart and Gaines.

She'd forgotten they'd been tested as well—at Nadine's challenge, since they'd both so publicly opposed it. She sniffed and let a small smile play around her mouth. Sliding her fingers over her handscreen, she pulled up the secure number she kept for undocumented searches and sought out the i-reality star's contact info. She assigned Nadine's name to it. Then tucked it away in her private docs.

The next moment the ad finished and the screen flashed its announcement hailing the FanFights end segment that had gone down in literal flames of fire and torches and a splendid amount of blood. The epic music soared as the screen panned in a circle to show the enormous crowd on its feet screaming for the victor, the victims, and all of the gamers.

Matthers, Corp 13's player appeared on the winner's platform of the corporate players' rounds, arms raised in triumph, as the announcer interviewed him about the last level and how it felt to have won it all. Followed by the camera moving to CEO Hart, who was being interviewed by Nadine.

Inola turned up the sound.

"How does it feel to have your Corp come out with first place, CEO Hart?"

"Good. Wonderful." The gentleman's smile was magnanimous. "Of course, we knew he'd win. The whole team really—the gamers, the player, the audience voting in support of us—it's just really been a wonderful experience all around."

"And yet you, me, and everyone else here knows that if that explosion hadn't gone off, your team wouldn't have won. How does that make you feel? That your players succeeded at the loss of actual lives?"

Inola laughed out loud. Yes, she'd definitely have to contact this girl. She'd obviously written her off way too quickly when Nadine was in her face with that camera yesterday. She wasn't afraid to oppose sides.

Hart's neck reddened but beyond that he refused to look ruffled. His smile stayed as poised as his tone. "Well, we can all agree, the loss of those lives was just tremendously unfortunate. A true blow to the gaming and FanFight community, to be sure." He looked straight into the camera. "Which is why I'm relieved the UW is going after the culprits. Sofi Snow—I'm sure you've heard she's now been labeled as the mastermind behind it. And Corp 24. Very sad. But we—"

"Corp 24? I'm assuming this is all new intel, because the public's not been officially informed Corp 24 was legally confirmed to blame, nor that Ms. Snow was the mastermind. Simply that they were under suspicion. Could you explain further, please?"

"Well, obviously, we can't say for certain yet. But I think when it's all said and done, those will be the ones who must take responsibility for the bombing and murders. I mean, it's only a matter of time—"

Inola shook her head and controlled her hand from typing out a very uncouth message to him at this moment. *Keep it clean, Inola. Give Sofi more time. Give us all more time.*

"So you being the winner by default is still good enough for you then?" Nadine interrupted. She turned to the camera. "In that case, I guess it'll have to be good enough for the rest of us. Thanks very much, CEO Hart. And now if you'll excuse us—" She moved away from him to the edge of her interview hover so the viewer could get a full shot of the arena and stadium behind her. "I believe the audience has finished voting on the Final Five."

She pointed up to the overhead telescreens that were counting down the final minute of the votes.

The music was chiming, script scrolling at the bottom in a similar countdown fashion as Nadine's face came back on with that smooth-lipped smile that had earned her the position of most fetching i-reality star.

"What a great interview with CEO Hart. And now that the Corp 13 team has officially conquered the third biannual FanFights, their player goes on to the final phase tomorrow. The final round will decide who is the Final Five FanFight champion for these Games!" Behind her, the audience burst into approval as, like an echo of Nadine, the announcer, Favio, said the same.

Nadine waited for them to calm before continuing. "For those of you who need a refresher—this is the leg of our Games where a player can walk away or choose to compete for the chance of doubling their winnings! And as we expected, Corp 13 has informed us their team will compete! As well, the audience was tasked with picking any four citizens from around the world to pit against this player and his gamers in the ultimate battle of life and death. These players can agree or disagree to join—because the gloves come off and survival isn't guaranteed. In fact"—she leaned into the camera—"rumored reports are this season's finale is specifically about survival, so the stakes will be higher, as will the chance of death. *But who can say no to all of you?* So let's see who our audience has chosen!

"The audience-voted FanFight Final Five players—pulled from anyone—are as follows." Nadine turned to look at the screen behind her as the names and faces were put up one at a time. "Corp 13's player, Matthers Smith. Followed by the Icelandic Ambassador Alis." Nadine's voice sounded surprised.

Inola paused midsip of her tea. Really?

Her photo faded and a new one emerged. "Herron Zain, Corp . . ." The i-reality star's tone dipped. "Corporation 24's vice president and interim CEO."

Nadine cleared her throat. "Now, let me remind everyone that these suggestions can still decline—voted in or not. No one's ever turned it down before, but there's always a first!"

She laughed halfheartedly, then looked at the next photo. And stalled before she said, "Inola Snow, president and CEO of Corp 30."

Inola stared in shock. In horror. *What?*

"And to everyone texting in asking if the United World Corporations' recent ban prohibiting Corps 24 and 30 from the Games stretches this far—according to the law experts now flooding my screen, both VP Zain and CEO Inola are considered individuals rather than attached to their Corporations for this level, just like any other superstar's appearance. So the UWC will have to counter the wish of the masses if they want that ban upheld."

Inola blinked and shook her head as if she'd heard wrong. There must be a mistake—or at least a mistake in Nadine's wording. She glanced at the pic on-screen. It was of Inola. And the announcer in the background was saying the same thing.

Oh gad. What was the audience doing? What had they *done*?

This was beyond gaming. This was . . .

"And . . ." The photo changed to the final frame, and the i-reality star hesitated as if unsure of what she was seeing. Then a soft whisper—"Me. Nadine." She blinked and looked up at the camera, her face pale.

This was a culling.

ⴺ◻

SOFI

SOFI STARTED FORWARD WITH A CRY. *SHILO.*

She went to grab him and run from this crazy Delonese-filled room, but before she could, he put up a hand.

Sofi frowned. *What? Why?*

Something bumped her, and suddenly Alis was peering in her face. "Anything wrong?"

Sofi blinked and stared at the lady's lovely bald head and wide eyes and false smile. She opened her mouth to reply. Then glanced back at her brother.

"Don't," Shilo said.

Alis followed her gaze to where Shilo stood and scanned the area around him. Her features didn't alter—didn't register him at all.

Sofi frowned. Oh.

It was the same as earlier—the voice she kept hearing in her eircom and head. Guiding her. It'd been *his* voice. And now it'd morphed into full-on visions of him. And here she thought she'd survived alright. When, in fact, she'd been gradually going insane.

"Listen, Sof."

That or this was another game the Delonese were playing in her mind, or perhaps her heart was playing all on its own, but either way . . .

"Sof."

Everything inside her ached to respond. His voice and twelve-year-old face were too real, too familiar, too close to where she was standing. She wanted to go home to their southern farm and August skies and hide him from this giant cracked-up universe.

Instead, she peeled her gaze away and ignored the flaring homesickness. *You're not real.*

"Just listen to me," he said.

She couldn't. Not if she wanted to hang on to that sanity for what still needed to be done.

She turned back to Miguel—only to find the expression on his face blank.

"Ambassador Miguel." Alis had turned to smile at him. "Ethos and I were just discussing how Sofi here broke into their systems yesterday."

Miguel's empty stare broke. He smirked and eyed her. "Did she now?" He winked. "One might wonder if her abilities are so skilled in *other* arenas as well."

Sofi slowed and frowned, then peered around to see who was listening. What had he heard? Who had caught on to them that he was now suddenly playing along with Alis's game?

"We talking about gaming the systems?" Claudius said, striding up. "We're all ears, girl."

"Some of us more than others." Miguel chuckled.

Sofi shook her head. What was going on?

"Yes, won't you share with us?"

She didn't know, she started to tell them. She just knew Shilo's heartbeat was growing louder and louder—hammering in her ears, in her teeth, in the back of her head. And Miguel . . .

What was wrong with him?

He'd shifted his rapt attention onto Claudius and Danya. The perfect picture of ease.

"Sofi, you need to focus—"

She turned back to Shilo beneath the hazy lights and domed ceiling, except he wasn't there. She swerved in a circle, searching between the swaying bodies and faces.

A movement pulled her attention. The ten Delonese had moved closer. All watching. Waiting.

"Can you see it, Sofi?" Shilo said.

See what? What did they want?

She blinked and her brother had reappeared. He tipped his head toward Ethos, who was now staring at her with a look of deep concern. Ethos's face went grainy, then cleared.

"Can you see it?"

Who? Ethos?

Sofi pinched her arm as hard as she could and only succeeded in drawing strange looks from Claudius and Miguel. The latter of whom she stared at a moment, then strode over to him. "Can I talk to you a minute?"

He glanced around. "I'm not sure I'll be good company at the moment, what with all the noise in here, but far be it from me to turn down a lady's—"

"Miguel, what's going on?" she hissed.

"Not quite following, love. We're just here having a party."

No.

She tried not to notice the way his smile looked stuck in place.

The way his eyes had stopped blinking . . .

No, no, no, no. "Don't." She shook her head. "Don't do this. Don't you dare leave me alone here too. Why are you acting like this? Who's listening?"

The frown he gave her would've been heartbreaking enough if it hadn't been followed by a gentle look of pity. Both of which were genuine. She'd seen them before. Even more than that—she knew them because she knew him.

"Miguel, please, I can't do this alone." Her voice broke. "I need your help. The *kids* need your help." She reached out and touched his arm.

He covered her hand with his and grinned. "I'm beginning to think you had a little too much to drink, yes?"

"I don't know what they did to you, but I need you to remember."

"Remember this party? I can do that."

"Girl-Sofi, we're running out of time. We need to know how you understood our codes."

She pulled back. Bit her lip. And with a last small smile, pressed her hand to Miguel's heart. Willing him to remember himself.

To remember her.

"How did you know the technical language?" Alis asked.

"Who helped you?" another challenged.

The voices were everywhere now. Ethos's louder than the rest. He looked up at the ten Delonese watching. "Dig deeper. Don't stop until you've found the answer," he said to them. Then his face flickered and reappeared full force as streams of data ran across his cheeks and through her vision. They were data from Delonese comp codes.

A recollection emerged in Sofi's mind of deciphering the

code yesterday in the room with Vic and Heller. Then creating work-arounds in their own language that were similar to the tech she'd used in the FanFight Games. It had always just made sense. The images blended into another memory, then another, until they all turned into electrical pulses and numbers that were gathering around her and trailing through the room's atmosphere, the Delonese bodies, and overly bright colors that were suddenly fading to gray.

"Can you see it?" Shilo asked again in her head.

She gritted her teeth. Like a word on the tip of her tongue that she couldn't quite grab, the images were there. Turning and taunting. They flooded her vision—the numbers, characters, codes, reaching up to a frenzied pitch.

She blinked. And looked at Ethos's face. It faded to the color of his robe.

"It's what I've been trying to show you, Sofi," Shilo said aloud in a voice that echoed light through the dark room.

Ethos's eyes widened and he gasped.

Sofi paused and stared. Then swung back to her brother. Had Ethos heard Shilo too?

"Good morning, Ethos."

"Impossible," the alien whispered. Then peered back at Sofi. "What've you done? What—?"

Her vision glitched as a set of numbers and algorithms ran across Ethos's face, like a comp-screen. She peered closer to read them. These were codes and calculations she could unravel. Like sifting through musical notes . . .

Ethos turned to the ten Delonese. "Finish wiping Ambassador Miguel's memory and cut hers open if you have to. But get what we need. Don't let her wake, and if she does? Kill her."

Sofi tipped her head and looked past the numbers to Ambassador Ethos's eyes and cheeks and chin.

Then reached up to wrap her hand around his throat.

"Now you see it," Shilo whispered.

The very breath of life.

The break between virtual and reality.

The realization of what she was.

The wall machine Sofi was hooked up to suddenly beeped, and a cry of pain ripped from her chest, and her head and neck jerked forward just as a vibration shook the ground and a chasm of light opened beneath Shilo and tore through the room.

The dancing bodies and domed space evaporated. The numbers and images evaporated. Miguel evaporated.

The system controlling her mind turned off.

Sofi opened her eyes.

And sat up in the Delonese med room with a single, thin cord attached to her body. With those ten Delonese medics staring at her from their position along the wall.

21

MIGUEL

BLINK . . .

Blink . . .

Blink . . .

"*Ambassador Miguel's main memory cleared,*" a robotic voice said. "*The past one year and nineteen months have been extracted along with certain experiences deemed to be problematic. Exactly 2 percent of his history has been erased and will now be replaced with the requested override. New memories will be based upon surrounding years and will continue his status as Earth ambassador. Please wait for the process to finish.*

"*Reboot beginning . . .*"

22

INOLA

"PUT ME ON-SCREEN WITH AMBASSADOR ETHOS, AND REQUEST Jerrad bring the car back around."

"Madam Inola, a one-on-one teleconference with him is highly unsanctioned—"

"I'm aware of that," Inola snapped at the security tech's face filling her telescreen. "Don't tell me how to do my job. Just pull him up."

"Yes, ma'am."

She turned and poured herself a drink, downed it, and went to her large walk-in closet to find a change of clothes. Flats, slacks, and a gold-embroidered sweater. Understated yet classy enough.

"Madam, the hovercar's out front," Jerrad said over the tele-com as Inola emerged from the dressing room.

"Thank you." She strode out to stand in front of the living room's screen and tapped her foot while she waited for Ethos in what she'd decided would be her own sort of Hail Mary. A last-ditch effort to do what she could—to control what she

185

could—before she dramatically moved her pieces in a game that had already been set in motion by all parties playing.

When the connection lit up and the vid flipped on, Ethos's eyes filled the tele.

For a second it looked like he was on a shuttle. Was he already on his way back to Earth? "CEO Inola, what a surprise." Curiously, nothing in his expression revealed the least bit of shock.

"Ambassador Ethos, thank you for seeing me."

"Of course. It's not every day—or *ever*, in fact—I'm summoned to a one-on-one private meeting. Nor is it a habit I would normally agree to. But I suspect this is of a more sensitive nature regarding our previously mutually supportive relationship."

"Have you seen the news?"

"I was just watching, in fact." He leaned forward. "Interesting developments for you. I must say, you humans have a creative passion for your political games—even taking them to the FanFight arena apparently. Reminds me of your gladiator types a few millennia ago. But if you are calling me up to grumble—"

She actually laughed. "Don't insult me. My political drama is not your problem." She tipped her chin while keeping her gaze narrow on him. "However, the fact that you still have my child, or both of them, is."

His lips parted. Closed. "CEO Inola, I believe *I'm* the one who's just been insulted here. Are we to repeat the earlier conversation?"

A text beeped through on her handscreen in front of her.

You are on the world stage tomorrow, it appears.

She swiped it off.

It flicked back on through its own accord.

They don't intend you to survive.

She glanced back to Ethos. It was the same sick person who'd sent her driving to the black markets.

I might be willing to help.

She froze.

Ambassador Ethos inched forward again, until his face was quite near the screen-cam. "Madam, this conversation is tiresome. We've already spoken of it—and I've given my answer. I'll ask that you be efficient with my time."

"I'm here to humbly ask you to reconsider."

Lord Ethos's impatient sigh was as audible as his annoyance. "I'll state again that you offered them to us originally, madam. We cured Girl-Sofi's asthma and Boy-Shilo's bone disease that would've killed him eventually, in exchange for more test subjects. Yet, when your children displayed unique abilities resulting from our Delonese interference, you kept them from us. And now you seek to complain?"

She sniffed. "My children are gifted—that's nothing unusual."

"Ah, then why else put them in the Games, if not to keep them under your eye and off our radar?" He licked his lips. "When we checked into their history of losing in the Games—imagine our surprise at finding large sums of money paid to outside forces to cause them to do so." He stared at her. "Now, what kind of mother pays others to ensure her children come in third and fourth place? Perhaps one who knows their abilities exceed what is considered normal. Perhaps one whose daughter was somehow able to access our highly flawless security system from a simple guestroom on our planet.

"Girl-Sofi and Boy-Shilo aren't just skilled, their brains are on an entirely different level. And speaking as one leader to another, on that item you should be immensely proud."

Sofi had hacked them? Inola refused to smirk. Or swallow. Or blink. Or show that her hands were trembling with the emotions flooding her.

Tick, tick, tick.

"I doubt even you have any idea what your children are capable of. We believe their minds can actually commune with our replicated cells and, in effect, switch them on. So I'll ask *you* to reconsider your offense with us." Ethos slid back and spread his hands. "Instead, be grateful that your children are the honored ones. The closest we've come to regenerating a race. You would rob that from us? Two humans for an entire species? I'll suggest again that you fall in line, madam, before it's necessary to force you."

"Those humans are my children."

"How very small-minded that sounds. You of all humans understand sacrificing a few for the greater good. Unfortunately, your clarity is clouded by your relationship to them. I will remind you—much of what resides inside them already belongs to us. And I am quickly growing impatient with this regurgitated conversation. It's the last time I'll have it with you."

She flattened her tone. "Then let me be clear once again—if you do not return my children in full health, I will be forced to publicly expose the practices our group has been participating in."

He cocked his head in the cushioned seat as the bright lights gave him a yellow glow. "Your ability to disperse sensitive information is overshadowed by our technological superiority. You can either stay in compliance or force our hand in exposing a fake story about you for the sake of protecting our people's futures. Frankly, as your people say, I'm comfortable with either."

"I respect the offer, but those of us who've been around a few generations know better than to trust our secrets only to technology. So let me guarantee—whether I'm alive or dead, the information on our business dealings *will* be released if my children are not."

His gaze narrowed. "I believe I was quite clear before that anything you raise against us will start a war with us. You know how that will end."

"Perhaps. But are you willing to risk that? You wiped my children's memories once—you can do it again. Return them to me within two days and we'll carry on. If not, I believe you'll have more on your hands and reputation than your people are in the mood to hassle with."

"So that is where we stand then." He pursed his lips and waited for her to nod. "You play a dangerous game threatening us, Madam Inola."

"And yet I have every confidence I'll win."

He stayed thoughtful for a full minute. Or more likely silently infuriated. Then, eventually, lifted his hands. "In that case, I have a proposition. It amuses me that you've been chosen for the FanFight's Final Five tomorrow." He paused. "We truly only need one of your children. So agree to fight in it, and you can consider it done. I'm currently heading to Earth as we speak while wrapping up a . . . situation. Be in that arena tomorrow, and I'll release one of them."

He was a worm lying through his perfect teeth. She could see it. Taste it. But before she could address it, the screen went black.

And she knew what she would do.

Because she could never live with herself if she was wrong.

She strode out without waiting for the security tech to inform her that the call had been discontinued.

Fifty floors down, she stepped out of the elevator and into the parking garage, where Jerrad had the hover waiting with the door open.

He looked flushed. *Angry.*

"I take it you saw the news." She climbed in.

"I did."

"Good. Please take me to the i-reality star Nadine. I believe she's currently at home." She turned to peer out the window as he pulled the hovercar out of the garage, where it dipped and emerged onto the city-lit streets.

"I can, but—"

"The sooner the better. And, Jerrad—"

He flipped around in his seat. "Inola, you're not honestly considering—"

"I am."

He stomped on the brake and stayed facing her. "As your head of security I forbid it."

She scowled. "You forget your place, Jerrad."

"I know exactly where my place is, if you'll pardon my saying so, madam. It's the same place I've stood for the past eight years, and I'll be blasted if I'll move from it now and allow you to walk into a ridiculous game."

"We both know this has nothing to do with the Games," she said quietly. "We're not fools. Gaines has been fighting for my position, and now she'll aim to get it in the most *ridiculous* way, as you say."

He turned back to the road but lifted his gaze to glare at her in the mirror. And began to drive. "Why not refuse it? You have that option. Even the fans will understand."

Inola chuckled. "As much as humankind adores playing savior to chosen causes, we just as passionately love seeing the powerful fall." She shook her head. "No, they will relish this. It's a smart move on Gaines's and Hart's parts. If I decline, I'll be labeled a coward, and that'll destroy me enough in the public eye to undermine my position anyway. In that way, you have to admit it's rather poetic of them. Take me down the same way as my children, and in front of a worldwide audience. But, Jerrad, if I succeed? I'll have the entire human race behind me—not just to secure my continued position, but to command the respect of the other Corps to do what needs to be done regarding the Delonese. And no one would bat an eye."

Jerrad chewed the inside of his cheek. "It's true you'd be untouchable." He pulled up his handscreen and glanced at her again.

"Then help me win."

He glowered once more before finally nodding. "So we make sure you succeed then."

He began verbally giving instructions to his handscreen. Probably pulling in favors to find behind-the-scenes info, arena changes, and all of Corp 30's latest game gear along with having them assemble the backup gaming team.

Which reminded her . . .

She swiped at her own screen for that last text message sent. The person said they could help her. How? When? Except, as she already knew, nothing was left of it.

Inola went back to looking out the window to the flashing

ads and buildings lighting up the dim. The protestors were standing on the street corners, even this late in the evening. Sipping from old coffee cups and waving those signs. One had a pic of Delonese Ambassador Ethos's head photoshopped onto a baby's body and read, "Mommy, why don't I look like you?"

She snorted and glanced back at her head officer. "By the way . . . in case anything happens, there's a copy of my life-save files in my box at the Old North Carolina farmhouse, in the basement."

"Inola—"

"Just in case."

"It won't come to that. I've already got our people on tomorrow's sport. For now the question is, what are you going to do here?" He tipped his head to the window. They were on the street in front of Nadine's house.

"Give her the exclusive i-reality episode of a lifetime."

He nodded and waited a second too long before peering back up at her through the mirror. When he did, there was a mist over his eyes. And without hesitation he said, "You know I would take your place in the arena tomor—"

Something smacked the hover roof right above Inola's head. The car's security siren went off with a loud wail, which would attract the peacekeepers in about 30.2 seconds.

The window beside Jerrad was hit next.

"What the—?"

The front window and side door were shot out at the same time, and a second later Jerrad's blood spattered onto the backseat.

23

SOFI

SOFI WAS IN A WHITE ROOM.

She hated white.

Ceiling, floor, hoverbeds, and machines. Even the suits of the ten Delonese medics standing against the wall were white. She squinted. They were staring at her. The same tan faces, same eyes, same ten individuals she'd seen everywhere else for the past five hours.

Or rather, fake everywhere else.

The room had a low vibration coming through the walls along with a soft tinkle of music, like the hum of an engine. Where was Ethos?

And Shilo?

"Where's my brother?" she whispered.

They stared with wider eyes than should be possible. She didn't have to be an expert on their emotionless expressions to know the one they displayed now was fear.

They were scared.

They should be.

"I asked you, where is Shilo?" She went to slide off the cot, then screeched when a fiery pain jabbed the back of her neck. Her hands flew up and found some type of electrical cord with five connectors branching off like fingers implanted into her skull.

Oh gad. Her stomach lurched at the agony shooting down to her spine.

The Delonese jumped into motion, hurrying to her like bees. "Shh, it's just a dream. Lie back down."

"You won't feel a thing."

Two of them held syringes in their hands, and another a silver scalpel.

Three Delonese males went for her legs. Like heck they were going to strap her down. Sofi reacted and kicked and writhed. They clamped onto her limbs and whispered with their soothing tongues.

She screamed and arched off the table—and suddenly her brain was skimming over it all, through the past few hazy hours of a forest room, and an unreal shuttle ride, and dancing, and laughing kids until it landed on her last clear memory.

Claudius emerging from the ship in the shuttle bay with his still-fancy hair, asking if they were ready to finish this thing or not, just after she'd escaped the poison fog.

The soldiers had been standing behind her.

Wearing ghosting suits too.

After that . . . her heart dropped. They'd taken the entire group—her memories were flooding back now. How they'd stuck Sofi on this bed amid her screaming, plugging her into in a virtual reality that mirrored and interacted with those of the children and others. Intended to evoke emotion and elicit information.

More than that—they'd been testing her brain's ability to awaken others.

Sofi's stomach turned.

The glitching room and faces—and the conversations with Ethos and Miguel. Had all taken place on a mental plane. It was like a FanFight Game, but on a twisted-mind scale.

Oh gad. Miguel. What have they done with him?

She kicked out and broke the needles off those syringes and sent the scalpel flying. "Where are Miguel and my brother? What'd you do with them?"

"We're fixing Ambassador Miguel to resume his Earth role," two of them droned. "It will look natural. No need to be alarmed. You have your usefulness."

"Fix?" She was having a hard time breathing. The fire in her head was licking her lungs now. How many others had they "fixed" through the years?

The cord's fingers connecting to her brain stem and skull were making her woozy.

She sagged back and shut her eyes as the bodies bustled and poked and prodded around her—holding down her legs and arms and talking in those sick tones as that cord held her neck to a machine in the wall.

The cord.

They'd been testing her *mind*. Meaning she was hooked up to a portal, like a freaking human comp-screen. A comp-screen . . .

I can access their data.

She pushed her thoughts backward through the cable, uttering a scream at the ensuing pain. She didn't care—just pressed farther, weaving her way mentally into the system of algorithms and wiring until she hit a circuit board that blasted her mind with a display of the power codes. Her body jolted at the shock.

She clenched her teeth and scanned it and, without over-thinking the fact it was the weirdest thing she'd ever done, mentally adjusted the data stream as she would on a virtual-reality screen.

Abruptly the lights went out. The cord hissed and clicked, then dropped its wiry fingers from her skull and neck and retracted into the wall. Like a snake recoiling from its prey. Sofi's head dropped forward, lighter, clearer. She blinked.

And looked up.

The Delonese gasped and stepped back, and Sofi rolled off the bed as the door timer went off.

Whir! The alarm turned on.

Dodging, she ran for the door and slid through it before the timer clicked and the thing dropped back down to seal in place behind her. Then mentally imagined locking it.

She paused and tried not to vomit all over the floor. That cerebral hack of their system was a mind jack.

Crud.

Now what.

She licked her lips.

"Shilo, you there?"

She went for her handheld—*Vic?*—only to discover it missing.

Focus, Sof. She scanned the hallway and prepared to run, then slowed, stalled—and shut her eyes. Intuition telling her the answer was different. Just like she'd said to Miguel. Just like Heller's note stated.

It was underneath the surface.

C'mon, Sof.

Tick, tick, tick . . .

Her brain felt like a freaking clock, with all the pieces ready to assemble. The memories. The mind game. The Delonese tech.

She just couldn't grab the bigger picture.

"Don't make it all in vain. The codes are inside." Opening her eyes, she stared at the small white hall, shut out the yelling Delonese stuck in the room behind her, and searched for whatever she was supposed to be seeing from the nonexistent brother in her head. *Where's the beat, Sof?*

She listened for the thrumming she'd heard earlier—like the sounds of a shuttle. Then noted the alarm still whirring, followed by the *pulse, pulse, pulsing* of the systems she'd entered through the cord's fingers at the base of her head.

The components trickled back in place like musical notes. Numbers. Symbols. She let the imaginary strains descend and let her mind dance to the bass beats, thudding each code stream into place as if it were a numerical rhythm.

The data she'd accessed through the spinal portal was still there—not just in her brain, but in the walls around her. But broader. More expansive. As if she could reach out to the rest of the core. Assembling. Reassembling.

Tick.

Tick.

Tick . . .

Her mind exploded with a visual of a massive internal system. Too much—too intense—her body reacted to the surge and threw her against the wall. She hit with a *thump* and dropped to the floor, those streams of data still flying in front of her eyes.

It was the entire Delonese hard drive.

Tock . . .

And she was staring at every detail of it.

Oh gad. She could mentally access and read their codes.

Sofi slipped a hand to her mouth and stared. Her brain—her mind—how was this possible? Was this what they'd done to her?

Was this what her mother had been trying to hide, and Ethos trying to access?

Sofi couldn't just evoke a response from a lifeless shell of a Delonese.

She chuckled aloud. Her mind could *see* their complex system as if it were just floating there in her head. More than that—she could comprehend it without even being hooked up to a comp.

She imagined accessing their system, then began analyzing and worming her way into files—as if sorting a set of songs on her playlist—into the very bowels of the Delonese hardware. Reaching out with her mind and wrapping new streams of code through their system, like a tree stretching its branches and roots all at once. It was beautiful really. And brilliant.

She accessed the virtual log and scrolled through the telescreen images. Tuning in to the conversation links to get her bearings. Until she realized she wasn't on Delon.

She was on a shuttle. And it was two hours from Earth.

What the—?

Where was everyone else?

She scrolled over today's vid logs. *"I don't care what the benefits or challenges are, Lord Ethos,"* the Delonese Council chairperson was saying on-screen. *"The reality is, Girl-Sofi was able to hack into our system from one of our guestrooms—using the help of a tech kid and an AI. And that alone makes her an imminent death sentence to this planet."* The Delonese encircling him were nodding in agreement. *"Until we know what has allowed her to even minimally understand how to access our tech, we think it wisest to continue to have her and all other live humans separated from this space station. We cannot risk her breaking in again."*

She sped forward.

"Lord Chairperson," Ethos's voice was saying over a com, *"they are showing remarkable abilities. Ones we cannot begin to downplay the nature of. I've been informed the same ingenuity shown with our systems has also begun stimulating the hive minds from this distance. Our medical team is working on her and the others now."* She heard him shift in his seat. *"We will continue on course Earth, where I will stay to see that the situations there are adequately dealt with regarding Corps 30, 24, and 13. When we feel it is sufficiently so, I will deposit the ambassadors back in their positions. Then I will return with this shuttle, the children, and Girl-Sofi. At which point I will expect to share good news with the Council."*

"Very good, Lord Ethos. You have our full support to proceed."

She shook her head. And reached out through the shuttle's tech systems all the way through space to the planet's internal pathways. Her mind stretched past the firewalls like slicing through water and down into its core.

She focused first on the viruses she'd uploaded to the Delonese system yesterday, then called up the map of human sensors, same as she would've on her handscreen. And yanked them open to splay out over the ship.

A display of red dots lit up behind three doors in the next hall from where she was standing. Her lungs expanded.

Mapping the controls with her thoughts, she mentally accessed the fastest routes to reach them. Then opened her eyes, blinked, and took off at a run.

She rounded the first corner on the shuttle, only to be jerked backward into a wall again as her brain suddenly exploded with buzzing.

Blasted aliens. She pulled herself up. It was as if the place had come alive and woken the hive, and the data streams were moving faster than her neural pathways could attempt. They were coming after her.

She tried to resist with her mind and shut down their coded attacks, but there was too much data to hold all at once. Sofi gave up, erected a new mental firewall, then physically headed for the second hall and the first door that, if her cerebral image was correct, held Miguel inside.

24

MIGUEL

SOMEONE WAS CALLING HIS NAME.

A woman.

She had a nice voice, Miguel decided. Inviting him to join her in saving the world or some such thing. He frowned. Why did the world need saving? It was perfect. The Delonese had made it so—had promised so. Just like they'd promised to help him advance their future together through his exciting new UW Corp initiatives.

"Miguel," the girl said, and the way she said it almost made him wish the world did, in fact, need saving just so he could take the sadness from her tone. But at least he could wake up for her. Tell her it was really quite alright.

He opened his eyes.

Then offered a smile to a girl with a kind face, brown skin like a summer sunset, and long, dark hair flying everywhere. With black eyes full of an anger so pure, he wondered if he'd encountered it before.

Wait, was she someone he'd angered in his past?

The next moment his spine split open as his neck and head caught fire and a blast of ice shot into the back of his skull.

It was like a freaking fire hose. Visions. Images. Pictures and conversations, pouring out over him, weaving their way into his skin and nerves and neural connections. The fresh scenes of someone else's life suddenly coming back as his own. They were from *his* life. His scenes. His conversations.

He glanced up at the girl with the wild eyes. This was his friend.

The downloads were simultaneously terrible and intoxicating. As if the gaps he didn't know existed just got filled in and so much richer. And the feelings of a thousand memories exploded all at once, fresh and raw, as if he was experiencing them again for the first time.

Then, like a spigot, it shut off. And he smiled up at the girl. "Have I ever told you I love how much you smell like Earth?"

"Not that I can recall, no. Have I ever told you how much I hate the smell of Delon?" She leaned against him and disconnected something at the back of his neck.

He clenched his jaw and shut his eyes and tried not to unleash a slew of inappropriate words as the thing hissed and recoiled and just about made his nerves claw through his skin.

His head flopped forward at the same moment the glitching stopped. He blinked. The haze around his eyes disappeared along with the pain in his neck. *Cripe.* He looked up at Sofi and blinked. And saw her more clearly than perhaps he'd ever seen her in the entire last two years.

This woman with the dark eyes and a light in her soul that, eighteen months ago, had beckoned him home. It was still beckoning. Leading the way in bravery and beauty. And the abilities through which she'd clearly done her thing—and done it well.

Whatever the *diablos* "it" was. "What just happened?"

"According to their comp logs, after the soldiers grabbed you in the blue vat room filled with lifeless Delonse, they took you to meet with Ethos."

He rolled his shoulders, then ran a hand through his hair. "Yeah, I remember that. It's just after that—"

He shook his head to clear the haze that had followed. "There was a fog."

Sofi slid her hand on his arm. "Apparently he didn't much like your lack of adherence in that room and decided to hook you and Claudius up to their med system to wipe and reshape your memories." She slowed, and her voice softened. "Just like he's done with Earth's kids for the past eight years."

He pursed his lips and stared at her. And stayed listening.

"When they grabbed the rest of us, they did the same," she said quietly. "It's the glitching and Shi's voice that finally gave it away and woke me up. I disconnected and came to find you."

He opened his mouth. Shut it. "That's a lot to take in." Then leveled a slight grin. "And you figured all that out? How?"

She smiled. "Miguel, I can't just hack them with a comp-screen. I can access them. With my *mind*. I can mentally access their system."

His brow went up. He rubbed a hand over his neck and his grin widened. "Of course you can." Then he glanced at the door and frowned. "So, does that mean you're able to stop Ethos?"

"I think so. I've actually not tried yet." Her smile turned sheepish.

He nodded as his expression grew serious. *So, was any of it real?* he wanted to ask. *Inquire later, Miguel.*

He shut his eyes to make sure the glitching was still gone before moving to—

The sweetest pair of lips in the world pressed softly into his.

His eyes fluttered open but the mouth had already slipped away, and she was pulling him up with her. "According to the records I accessed, our conversations were real," she said shyly. "Just—you know—in case you're wondering. Not our physical movements, but the words and emotions were. Which should make it easier to find the others."

The others. Right. Images flashed. The faces of his friends and the children Ethos was attempting to . . . He frowned. "Where *is* Ethos?"

"In the main cabin." She stopped and looked at him. "We're on a ship. Headed for Earth."

25

INOLA

"JERRAD! NO—PLEASE, NO!"

Inola could hardly see through the smoke and fear. And the tears. She was weeping. She couldn't stop weeping. She ducked low into the seat and grabbed the stun gun from her bag. Then tossed it aside and tugged out the tech-gun from Jerrad's jacket hanging open on his lifeless body. And tried not to vomit on the seat. *Her friend!*

She slid toward the opposite door and felt the handle as the hover's sirens kept wailing and voices were shouting and a red laser dot suddenly flickered through the car. Someone was waiting for her head to appear.

For the first time in her life she wished she was trained at killing more than just political careers. The person deserved to die. To suffer horrifically for this. She slid down to flatten against the floor and rubbed a hand over her eyes to clear the stinging smoke and tears. What had she done? She'd gotten him killed!

Voices. Someone yelled. More laser dots—hundreds—filled the car. *Cripe.*

Inola heard a bump against the door and then someone was

opening it. She lifted the gun, but they said in a hushed tone, "Don't shoot, we're here to help." Without waiting, the young man grabbed her arm and pulled her out—straight into the open door of a blue hover.

Shots exploded, and he jumped in and slammed it shut. "Go, go, go!" he yelled at the car. A second later it was speeding from the scene, self-swerving around the corner before turning on its lights and heading into the heart of downtown traffic.

The guy crawled off Inola, who was now screaming and calling Jerrad's name.

"Lady, lady—it's okay! You're okay!"

"We left Jerrad."

"Yeah, well, he wasn't okay, and you'd be dead if we'd tried to grab him. But here." The guy handed her a tissue and waited for her to catch her breath and stop shrieking about Jerrad.

It took her a minute. To become rational again. To realize his point was valid—even if that didn't change the shock or the horror. Or the fact that Jerrad was gone.

And that someone had just tried to kill her.

She frowned and sat up. "Who are you?"

The faces of a twentysomething-year-old kid with a red beanie and a beard, who looked like a tech geek if she ever saw one, and Nadine both stared back at her from the opposite backseat.

The guy rubbed his chin, then stuck his hand out. "Ranger."

She didn't take it—just nodded warily. Then turned to the star. The girl who'd just traumatized their world with her announcement and whom Inola'd been on her way to see. Inola set the gun beside her but kept her hand on it. "To what do I owe this saving? How much money do you both want?"

"Let's call it monitoring more than saving. And no on the money." He said the last part as if he found it humorous.

She bit her lip. The blue car that'd been following her was his. "I see." So he was the one. "You've also been sending me bizarre messages?"

The guy leaned back and tapped his handscreen, which looked similar to the hand-built kind Sofi preferred. "Look, let's not get any weird ideas here. I'm not into people's moms or anything. And, in fact, I can't actually recall ever truly rescuing anyone in my life."

Nadine chuckled dryly.

"Well, looks like you pulled it off," Inola felt obliged to say. "So what did he want?"

He took a thoughtful look at her. "I'm friends with your daughter. The same people who set her up murdered my girl-friend with the bomb. When I intercepted your vid for Sofi last night—"

Inola's hand eased off the gun. "Your girlfriend was in the FanFight explosion."

"One of the Ns," he said in a tone indicating he'd no wish to talk about it.

She should've known. She'd seen the triplets but rarely spo-ken to them. But, of course, they had real lives with people they loved. "I'm sorry," she murmured. Then lifted her chin. She'd take it—whatever he was planning. "What are you going to do to me?"

He frowned. "To you? No." Ranger shook his head. "To them." He ran a hand over his beanie and cleared his throat as the hover downshifted and slowed. "Having intercepted a num-ber of rather intriguing conversations between you and your gal, Gaines, CEO Hart, and then tonight, you and Ambassador Ethos, I figured Nadine here could splice something together. Maybe cause a few waves. Expose a few lies. Considering I can't help Sofi up there, might as well make a few lives hell down here."

She turned to Nadine, who was smoothing her strawberry-blonde hair up into a ponytail.

The i-reality star shrugged her delicately tattooed shoulders. "I'm always in for a good story." She tightened her jaw. "Especially if it involves someone trying to take me down or selling little kids."

Inola went back to assessing Ranger, her leader-of-a-corporation skills kicking in. Finally. "And what do you want out of this?"

"I want you to admit what you've all been doing is wrong, that the way the UWC's running the world—how you're running this city—is wrong. Y'all are destroying people's lives." When Inola remained silent, he dropped his tone. "And I want you to destroy Gaines and Hart's plans by letting me help you both survive tomorrow so we can expose them along with that Delonese, Ethos. Talk about a sick b—" He stalled, his expression seeming to take into account he was cursing in front of a mom. "Because I'm pretty sure their plan is to kill you both."

"Although, if she's not up for entering," Nadine said, batting her eyes toward Inola, "you could just get mama-CEO here out of the country."

Inola sniffed. "Not unless I want a host of Delonese and bounty hunters pursuing me the rest of my life. Thanks, but I'd like to face the United World Corps full on as it skewers me."

The hover stopped in a parking garage, and Ranger ran a

scan with his handheld, checking for sensors or people, then opened the door and slid out. "Sofi keeps a stash of her FanFight gear here. We'll try a few suits out, and then I'll rig up some tech to connect me to them. That way, while your Corp gamer teams will be assisting you through the virtual-reality aspects, I'll be able to run backup control. Meaning they shouldn't be able to override anything."

"You know our Corps already have gear we can use." Nadine's hair wisps breezed across her temple in the chilly wind. Much softer than she appeared on the tele, Inola thought. Much humbler and more normal than while in the public eye. She pulled up her coat hood.

Inola decided to like her. Even if her suggestion was a shade naive. Look how someone had just taken out her head of Corp security in a matter of seconds.

"No offense, lady, but your Corp 24 tech isn't on the same level as mine or Mama Inola's. And Inola here will likely have hers manhandled by some of Gaines's thugs. Meaning without me you're both going to be hurting. And without you?" He paused and grinned at them both. "I won't have an opportunity to do my girl, Sofi, a public favor and stick it to the UW Council." He turned without awaiting a reply and, with a casual cluck of his tongue, led them to a black door set into a black wall with black lights flickering off it.

"When we're finished, you're welcome to camp here or get your security teams to take you back to your Corps—if you trust them to do so. I can show you both which ones I've tapped and know are clean. Like your guy Jerrad," he said with a glance at Inola. "He was a good one."

Inola swallowed and nodded. "He was."

Music thumped through the walls from inside the black building, making the thumping grief in Inola's throat all the heavier.

The sign on the door said "Mom's Basement."

26

SOFI

SOFI AND MIGUEL ARRIVED AT THE SHUTTLE'S NEXT ROOM together, and she half expected another med group of Delonese to be inside.

Instead, it was eerily quiet. Like a white-walled ghost town the size of a small apartment complex. In fact, the whole *ship* was eerily quiet. Except for those bloody sirens going off.

She kept expecting peacekeeping soldiers to come running, but from the maps she'd pulled up, it appeared Sofi had accidentally managed to seal all the rooms on the shuttle when she'd locked the one she'd escaped from. Including the flight deck where she'd identified Ethos and Alis had been, according to the internal vidscreens. Except now that space showed up empty.

The moment she and Miguel slipped into the med space, the lights came on—and her heart leaped up her throat.

Ambassadors Danya and Claudius were there, lying on med beds. Cords in their neck just like she and Miguel had unhooked from.

But the others, the kids—their bodies, their feet, their faces—were covered in sheets from head to toe. White. Cold.

Like a morgue.

Miguel slid his hand to her back and she looked away as something in her chest fractured. Like a chunk of ice falling off a glacier. Oh gad, what had they done to them?

"Sof, let's just start with Danya and then make our way down?"

She nodded and strode to Danya's side, slipped fingers onto her arm, and noted that she didn't move, just like Miguel hadn't. And yet Sofi could see her lids twitching.

What nightmares was Ethos neurologically feeding Danya?

Sofi shut her eyes to block out the kids, the sirens, and how freaking freezing it was in the room and in her breast. And let her mind dive back into the vessel's tech systems.

Her entire body jerked at the shock. She would've thought a few tries in she'd be able to maneuver it better. Instead, each time felt like higher doses of information flooding her mental pathways, overloading them with chemical reactions. The Delonese were lashing out against her system intrusion again. It felt like spikes around her, as if they were trying to decide what the hacker was and whether to flush it or weaponize it.

Sofi pulled back from the planet's mainframe and focused on the information the shuttle contained.

She found the memories. The ones the machines had stolen and stored. The ones of the Delonese Danya, who, according to her files, had become far more human than the Delonese were comfortable with, and of her husband, Salim, and their two small adopted children. She saw Danya's memories of their wedding. The look on Salim's face, and the expression in Danya's mirror as she was getting prepared. And whatever Sofi had thought she'd known about the woman—she became acutely aware she knew nothing at all.

The woman was in love. With her husband, her life, her kids. She was in love with humanity and the life she'd gotten to live on Earth thus far. More than the life she'd led before on Delon.

It felt intrusive, looking in on her world like this. Sofi shut it out, but not before deciding that if they survived this, Danya was a woman worth knowing. Not for her position, but for the very good depths of her soul. Which was odd, considering Sofi hadn't even wondered whether Delonese had souls or not.

She tweaked the data streams and finished the upload along with a few of the ship's informational vids, just like she'd seen in the hall. Then opened her eyes and waited.

Five seconds later, Danya uttered a gasp, her eyelids flew open, and the cord in her neck released as Sofi exhaled.

She left Danya to Miguel and moved on to Claudius—this time keeping his memories private. She didn't want to know. Didn't want to see. Not because of his history but because of Miguel's. She'd lived the last year and a half assuming the worst, and she'd hated him for it. She didn't want to relive the years before that in vivid detail. So she simply redirected the codes and waited until he woke, memories back intact. Then moved on.

To the children covered in those white sheets.

Behind her, Miguel was helping Danya and Claudius. Explaining. Adjusting.

She placed her hand on the first sheet and carefully lifted enough to see a young girl's face. Five years old perhaps. Pale. With blue lips and eyelids and a cheek that kept twitching. It was the child who'd spoken to her in the hall and again in the Delonese garden room.

Sofi felt her pulse. It was there. She exhaled and suddenly noticed there was no cord at the base of the skull. Just a round blue dot behind the ear.

Gently Sofi poked it. The girl's lashes fluttered.

Sofi gripped it between three fingers and tore it off as a memory shot through her head of doing the same to herself one day in the Delonese labs at the age of twelve. The medics had been terrified and furious from the expressions in her recollection. *Good.*

The child's eyelids flickered again, then opened. "Sofi," she breathed. "I've been waiting for you."

Sofi smiled in confusion. "You have?"

The girl nodded forcefully. "Shilo told me you'd come. He said so in my head."

Sofi glanced around the room. "He did?" *How? Is he here?*

"But—" The child suddenly appeared about to cry. "Ambassador Ethos said things in my head too. Things to ask you that I didn't like."

Sofi's chest clenched. She leaned over and embraced the child. "Shh. See Claudius and Danya there? He did that to them too. And we're going to keep him from ever doing it again."

She hoped.

She beckoned them over, then hurriedly rose and patted the girl's head before moving on to the next sheeted child. And tried to keep her hands and heart steady.

Danya came behind to join the girl as Sofi went on to the next and the next and the next. Checking their pulses, pulling their blue feeds off.

She'd gotten through fifteen before she heard a soft gasp of awe. She swerved around to find one of the boys staring up at Miguel. His eyes huge. Round in recognition of who this most famous man on Earth was. "I saw you before," the boy whispered. "When you got us from that room. And you're sometimes on the tele. I know, because my friend's mom likes you," he added sheepishly.

"Well, she clearly has good taste." Miguel squatted on the floor and, within moments, had six kids crawling on him.

"Speaking of taste, what do you kids think of my outfit?" Claudius interrupted. "Too much? Too little?" Sofi glanced back again to find he'd wrapped a sheet around himself like a diaper, and the children burst into chuckles.

"Just setting us all at ease," he said at Sofi's appraising eye.

"No, no. It suits you." To which the kids started giggling all over again.

"Where are we going?" one of them asked.

"Are we actually going back to Earth this time?" said an older boy.

"See that girl there?" Miguel pointed at Sofi. "She's pretty smart. Like, really smart. I bet she even knows how to fly a ship and get us home."

Sofi frowned. Could she in fact fly this ship? She raised her brow. Huh. She actually hadn't thought of that.

She couldn't think of that now. She continued down the row, waking the rest of the kids.

It wasn't until she reached the end of the room that the awareness dawned. Shilo wasn't there.

She spun around and glanced at all their faces. Their beds. Their big eyes. And felt the panic begin to set in. It took a millisecond to dive back into the shuttle's mainframe and rescan the three levels of hallways and blocks of rooms searching for any other dots or firewalls. Then rescan again.

Her chest couldn't get enough air. Her lungs deflated too quickly. The map showed the human dots in this room. That was it. They were *all here*.

She stopped. She couldn't breathe. *Shilo. Isn't. Here.*

This wasn't how it was supposed to be. He was supposed to—

Hands wrapped around her shoulders, pulling her into a body that smelled softly of cologne even after all this time. Miguel's fingers brushed her cheek as if amid the crowded room and voices he knew what she was thinking.

"He's here, Sof. You know that."

"He's not. Miguel, I've searched my head, I've gone over the ship repeatedly, and there's no one else." She peered up into his face, her voice barely more than a whisper on the verge of breaking, as the keening grief and fear rose inside her. Threatening to tear her apart.

His eyes studied her. Strode over her cheeks and chin and grief-stricken gaze. And simply said, "Then look again."

She stalled. If he never spoke one word to Sofi again, or even went back to a life he'd previously lived, she'd still die a million deaths to defend him in this moment. For this gift.

He believed her.

She wasn't crazy.

She kept her gaze on his face as she opened her mind and, instead of invading the ship's portals, listened to them. To the wires, the electric nerves, the *beat, beat, beats* that represented each individual the tech security was tracking.

The heartbeats. Unified. Beating in sync. Like drones in a hive.

Except for one.

It was the faster, stronger beat of a heart being concealed by a slim-suit in ghosting mode.

Her eyes warmed and widened. She grabbed his arm and tore from the room—barely remembering to mentally force door codes to open for the hall, and then again for the one three sections down. It slid up in silence.

The lights flickered on.

And Sofi burst into tears.

27

SOFI

SOFI STOOD BESIDE SHILO'S HOVERBED AND HELD HER BROTH-
er's hand as she released the cord of wiry fingers from his skull.

He didn't move. Didn't seem to breathe. Didn't blink.

They waited. Sofi moved her hand up his arm, to his chest,
and tried to find his heartbeat as her fingers trembled in nerv-
ousness against his black slim-suit.

When her fingers began to shake harder, Miguel slipped his
hand over hers. And she swore she could feel his chest clenching
with the same awareness—that something was very wrong.

Shilo wasn't waking.

"Miguel—"

The next second one eyelid popped up and a giant smirk slid
across the kid's face. "Admit it, you thought I was dead for a sec."

Sofi shrieked.

Then punched his arm before falling on him laughing and
weeping and telling him off with some very strong words that
their mother would've been appalled by.

He sat up and tackled her with his awkwardly long twelve-
year-old arms. His black eyes and brown skin and grin flashed

just as golden as Sofi's in the yellow lighting. "About time you figured it out. Thought I'd be using a cane by the time your brain kicked in."

"I knew you were communicating with me." Her smile shone through her tears. "You had me thinking I was hearing your ghost! You could've at least explained a little clearer."

He shook his head and tugged her arm to pull himself closer. "It didn't work like that. It took me forever to figure out what was going on—let alone how to find and connect with you. At first all I could do was send you images. Then when you reached the planet I could use a few words, but it was hard."

"You shielded me and Miguel when those guards were looking for us. I heard your voice."

Shilo smirked. "Nah, you shielded yourself when you tapped into the coding in that wall vid. I just guided you." He leaned his head on her shoulder. "But it was like a haze, Sof. Like I was swimming in numbers and time and they kept asking me questions about you and me—and how our brains work."

Sofi peered up at Miguel, whose eyes seemed suddenly quite misty. She swallowed and laid her cheek on her brother's head. "And what'd you tell them?"

"That I had no freaking idea and they could go to—"

"Language, dude."

"Says the person who just cussed me out for playing a joke."

"That wasn't a joke, it was sick. And—"

"But, Sofi, I like the way our brains work." Shilo's young face grew serious. "I like that I could reach out to you and know that you heard me." He rubbed his cheek with his fist. "I don't know what they did to us as kids, but I'm not scared of it anymore. Because it helped you find me."

28

MIGUEL

WHEN MIGUEL WAS FIVE, HIS OLDER NEIGHBOR INFORMED HIM that only wusses cried and real men were stoic.

At the time he'd had no idea what *stoic* meant, but he'd gone with it because older neighbor boys were suave. More than that, he'd touted it—to the point he became the preeminent stoic non-cryer who had mad skills over all the other wusses. A trait that came in handy during his early years after being taken in by the politicians.

At least that'd been true up until this moment. Now? Now he was standing in a room, with the woman he respected, as a tear slid down his cheek and off his chin and onto his rather soiled dress shirt. And surprisingly, he felt not one bit wussy or stoic. He simply felt . . . emotion.

Miguel stepped back, only to be seized in a hug from that awkward twelve-year-old boy, who looked strikingly like his sister. "No offense, but you used to be kind of a jerk. Good on you for fixing that, dude."

Miguel actually had no idea what to say to that. So he simply patted Shilo's back and said, "Me too, kid."

"Excuse me." One of the children stood timidly in the doorway, waiting. "Claudius said you might need to see this."

Right. They were still on a shuttle. In space. With Ethos. *Diablos.* His head was still hazy.

The child led them out into the hall where a number of walls were flashing on like enormous telescreens, displaying a feed from Earth.

"This is being streamed right now," Danya said softly.

Sofi's face appeared on-screen and, beneath it, the banner "Imminent Terrorist Threat #1," while the voice-over declared, "According to Delonese Lead Ambassador Ethos, the Earth ambassadors Alis, Miguel, Claudius, and Danya are still in the process of negotiations on a new trade deal—and are in high spirits as to the successful outcome of continued support in the Delonese and UWC relationship."

"Where *is* Ethos?" Claudius asked with a "hey dude, glad you're alive" nod at Shilo.

Miguel glanced at Sofi. She was already shaking her head. "I've internally checked everywhere on the ship. Even pulled back all ghosting mechanisms—"

"He took a small shuttle," Shilo said. "I just scanned for it and a small pod left a half hour—"

"*You* can mentally access our tech too?" Danya lifted a brow.

"Not as well as Sofi. But it's like I can hear her thoughts. When she's tapped in, I can piggyback and look around."

Danya stared at them both with the sharp edge of a smile. "They're going to hate you both." Then grew serious. "More than that, they're going to—"

"Try to kill us." Sofi nodded, then shrugged. "They've already reacted to my intrusion of their system, but I don't think they've figured out how it's happening yet. So, best of luck to them."

The wallscreens lining the hall flashed to more vids of protestors, with rioters holding signs on different streets throughout the world. Miguel barely caught a glimpse of each scene before it moved on—but enough to see they weren't protesting Sofi. They were demanding the Altered device be released for mass use.

It flipped to a new topic, showing excited faces awaiting the final FanFights. Many already lined up outside of the Colinade, holding their places to get in.

Miguel peered at the time on the screen—it was morning in Old Manhattan. The fights were set to begin in nine hours. The banner scrolling across the screen's base blipped on and began announcing a countdown.

"With the announcement only five hours ago of this year's voted-in contenders, the Fantasy Final Five is already making big waves," the voice-over said. "Seen here are pics of our most important and jaw-drop-surprising contestants ever—Corp 13's winning player, Matthers Smith; Corp 24's vice president and interim CEO, Herron Zain; Icelandic Region Ambassador Alis; Corp 24's i-reality star Nadine; and in the biggest shock of the day, Corp 30's very own highly respected CEO, Inola Snow."

"What?" Sofi turned, disbelief etched across her face.

"Are they joking?" Shilo frowned. "They can't do that." He glanced at Miguel. "Can they? I mean, she's like a major world CEO. And she's my mom. They can't just force her in like that." His tone was angry.

Miguel stared at the screen. At the faces of those they'd chosen.

"This was no vote," Sofi said. "This is an elimination."

A smart one, Miguel thought. *And a sick one.*

"We're simply waiting for Ambassador Alis to show now," the news announcer continued. "Although, according to Lord Ethos's last vid communication, it seems she may not make it for the event. In which case for the first time ever, the Fantasy Five will be fighting as the Fantasy Four. And we can only hope it doesn't make for a much shorter game."

"Hey, guys?" Claudius suddenly called out. His tone odd. Strained.

Miguel could see his friend standing at the door of a connecting room but not what he was staring at inside it. But whatever it was, Claudius's face had gone white.

He swerved his gaze over onto Miguel's.

Miguel frowned and strode over as the others hurried to follow. The kids instantly curious.

Claudius held up a hand. "Hey, kids, I don't think—"

Miguel stepped into the room.

Oh. Oh crud.

Alis and Heller were lying on cots where they'd been plugged in.

Her bald head. Pale skin edging the soft dress suit she'd been wearing at the meeting yesterday morning. Her eyes staring up at the ceiling. Blank. Cold.

Heller looked exactly as he had in the shuttle on the way up to Delon. Except now his lips and skin had a blue tint, and his face was frozen in an expression of pain. His cheek piercing still blinked with myriad colors.

¿Qué?

One of the kids let out a cry and the rest came crowding in. Miguel grabbed the three closest and turned them away, sending them to Danya and Shilo, who pulled them all over to look out the shuttle hall's massive window. "Shh, it's alright," Danya whispered. "Everything will be alright."

"She's barely cold," Sofi murmured, leaning down to place her hand on the body. Then moved over to Heller. "He's likely been dead since yesterday. I saw it happen in my mind. They virtually sent him into a poisonous fog—although it appears that was an elaborate mental simulation. They've both been suffocated."

Miguel caught the grieved lilt in her tone and moved toward her just as her voice hardened and she swung her gaze his way. "What I don't understand is—what exactly is Ethos doing? He had to know the alarms went off on this shuttle. How is disappearing to Earth going to help anything? Let alone leaving Alis and Heller here *dead* while the rest of us are *alive*."

"I'm thinking we check the shuttle's bridge," Miguel said quietly. He led them back out into the hall and listened as Sofi slid the door shut behind them. Sealing Alis and Heller in so the kids wouldn't see.

"He's cleaning up," Danya said from her space at the window where she held an armful of children. "He knows the alarms went off, but this ship and his peacekeepers are fully capable of maintaining control. Or they should be. Which means he knows you hacked into our systems and their firewalls kicked you back out but has no idea that you're able to read and assimilate into them. That's likely what's confused Delon too." She peered back and forth between Sofi and Shilo. "He believes their tests of you were yielding the results he wanted—that he was accessing *your* minds. Instead, you were accessing ours."

"But what does that mean for us?" Claudius glanced between

Miguel and Sofi. "Are we stuck here in space until he returns, or are you gonna get on trying to fly this ship?"

Miguel watched the siblings eye each other.

"What do you think?" Shilo said. "Maybe if we get into the system and—"

Sofi sniffed. "I think we've never flown a ship before."

Shilo shrugged. And grinned. "How hard can it be?"

INOLA

INOLA HAD NEVER BEEN TO A RAVE BEFORE.

Not that this was a rave, but maybe it was and she didn't know. And whatever they called this, it was how she'd imagine a rave to be.

Loud. Colorful. Dark. With a giant guy in a black trench coat and tie-dyed hair guarding the door.

The giant nodded to her and she nodded back before Ranger led them down a dark hallway with speakers overhead blaring a tune she'd heard more than once when Shilo had his headphones up too high. Usually during one of her monthly drop-ins when she stopped by his and Sofi's apartment to check on the nanny and their lives.

If she'd known they were hanging out at these kinds of clubs, she would've dropped by far more frequently. Or so she wanted to tell herself.

At the end of the black-lit hall, the space opened into a large room filled to the brim with teens all talking and walking or huddled around the tables and wall teles. And toward the back there appeared to be some kind of oxygen bar.

"So we'll hydrate you first"—Ranger turned to yell—"then get you settled." He waited for them to nod, then waved his hand toward a row of blue tables flickering oddly beneath the rainbow-colored strobe lights.

Inola pulled her coat tighter, despite the blood soaked into it, and hurried after him, past the group of kids, who couldn't be much older than Shilo, wearing mullets and neck piercings. And past a huddle of girls all dressed up as some type of anime animals with oversize eyes.

"I take it you've never been here before?" Nadine shouted in her ear, not even hiding her amusement as Inola tried not to stare.

Inola kept her chin up, scanning the room for anyone ready to knife them.

"You're the most dangerous thing here, you know," Nadine said, this time closer to Inola's ear.

Inola nodded and slid into the seat Ranger had pulled out and quickly said yes to whatever oxygen drink thing he offered, then glanced up, only to catch sight of herself in a wall mirror.

Oh.

Nadine had a point.

Bloodied clothes, messed-up hair, tear-smeared face. Inola looked like one of the people she'd seen down at the black markets.

Between that and the fact that she was the person who sent kids like these to Delon for testing . . .

Inola swallowed. Nadine hadn't just been jesting.

Pressing back her shoulders, Inola smoothed her fingers over her face and hair in a way that fit her status. Or rather, fit Shilo and Sofi's status—since that seemed more appropriate here. She watched the waiter with the twinkle-light skull apron as he brought over a basket of fries, tortilla wedges, and some type of fizzing drinks—and abruptly Ranger disappeared to go do something. Nadine pecked. Inola took a few sips to be polite.

The thought of Jerrad still lying out in the street made it all she could do not to get up and go find the restroom. She couldn't get the image out of her mind. Or his last words out of her heart.

Or the grief from her lungs.

She blinked and refused the tears access. Not now. Not in front of this crowd who had gradually begun to turn their eyes her way.

"Is that—?"

"I think so."

"What's her mom doing here?"

The room grew even more interested the moment Nadine pulled back her hood.

"It's Nadine."

"I dare you to ask to be on her show."

"I dare you to ask Sofi's mom if you can be CEO."

Inola swept her hair off her forehead and stared right back at them the same way she did the politicians. If they were going to recognize her, she at least had to own it.

Except these kids were no politicians. They had colored hair and tattoos like Ambassador Miguel, but unlike him they wore garage clothes and kitten ears and vid-game controllers that appeared to have been grafted into their skin.

She inched closer to Nadine. How often did her kids hang out here? Two weeks ago Inola would've forbidden it. Now? "Dude, check it out—they're here with Ranger!"

Three seconds later most of the room was crowding their

table as Ranger took a seat beside her. "Hey, Range, are you help-ing them tomorrow?"

"Doing what I can."

"You gonna use Sofi's gear stashed here?"

"You know it."

Inola eyed this Ranger friend of Sofi's. The way he spoke and the way they admired him—he was far more important than she'd realized. A new rush of gratitude swept over her for this guy who'd taken it upon himself to rescue her and watch out for her daughter. Especially if he knew what Sofi knew about Inola. Maybe it meant that Sofi could find a way to forgive her.

The kids stayed clustered round and studied them. She over-heard one say, "It's a lost cause, man. Corp 13's Matthers is going to clean their clocks tomorrow. You know how he plays."

Ranger sniffed and set down his drink. "That may be, but if you'll excuse me, I'm gonna pull our s—" He looked at Inola. "*Stuff* together for them to try on. Be right back."

The moment he left again, Inola's voice froze. Unlike Nadine, who simply smiled and answered an endless stream of questions about her shows, her travels, and her latest skin-care products.

Inola thought to join in, but what would she say—"Hi. Thanks for being friends with my kids"? "I hope they don't do drugs with you"? As if they could even hear half of it over the pulsing music.

She was saved by the halt of said music and a strobing flash across the wall telescreens. The next second an image came on, of Sofi and Shilo. It was followed by a vid. Pics of them in the Games, but even more pics of them behind the scenes. Funny video clips Inola had never seen. Some with their friends. A lot training for FanFight routines.

Even some from events held here in this place—birthday parties and a few holidays. It was as if someone had scoured the online world for every important moment from the past five years and put them together just for her.

Something told her they hadn't though—not just for her. The care invested in this montage said it'd been made a while ago as a part of what these kids did together. What they did *for* each other.

The vids were celebrations of the lives they all led.

Inola watched the last few images float by to the type of music Sofi and Shilo loved. And suddenly found herself wiping her eyes just as the lights came up, and the room full of faces, young and old alike, smiled at her. As if they had just given her both a gift and a thank-you. For Sofi and Shilo being part of this loud, strange gaming-room world that clearly valued them.

This time when the tears fell, Inola didn't even swipe at them as she stared at these humans.

These people had been her kids' true family when Inola had failed.

A swell of gratitude rose in her chest—even amid the grief and fear suffocating her lungs. Gratitude for this place and these tender hands that had been there when she hadn't. That had helped and celebrated her children into becoming the people they were.

The people she'd not been able to see them as.

Even if Inola hadn't always agreed with Sofi's choices, she understood now more than ever why she'd made them. Why she'd wanted attention. And how much farther she would have run if these people hadn't been there.

Oh gad. Inola wanted to hug every last one of them.

"Nadine? Inola?" Ranger appeared from a red hallway. "I've made up cots for you both to sleep on. If you'll follow me, we'll get your gear all tested and laid out, and I'll introduce you to a tech friend of mine named Vic. Then I suggest you both get as much rest as possible."

Nadine smiled and hugged a group of girls, and Inola stood to say a quiet "thank you" to the entire room. Then went to follow Ranger, only to be stopped by a teen barely older than her son. The boy glanced up at her with sincerity. "No need to worry, CEO Mama. No one will get in here tonight. We'll keep you safe."

Inola blinked back a new rush of warmth from her eyes and simply offered her hand in thanks to him. To them. For all of it.

3 0

SOFI

"OKAY, I'VE GOT ACCESS TO VIC. I'M PUTTING HER ON-SCREEN."

Two seconds later a holographic head of Claudius's favorite Artificial Intelligence appeared on one of the wall comps in the shuttle's flight bridge.

"About time—I've been wracking my sources trying to reconnect with you guys."

"Oh, is that Vic?" Claudius asked casually. "Hey, girl."

"Claudius, you bleeding idiot! You had me scared—"

The shuttle swerved and flipped.

"Shi, what are you doing?" Sofi yelled. "You're—"

Shilo's chuckle rang out beside her, the most charming, disarming, and irritating sound she'd grown up with and missed the last few days.

He spun the shuttle back over. "What? It's not like it affects anything."

"You don't know that!"

"Fine." He leveled it out to be completely even, then kept a steady pace with a look on his face that mimicked a grandmother.

Mentally she sent Shi an image of her rolling her eyes. "I realize you've had more practice at this tech thing, but I'm still finding my way around in the system. And Delon is trying everything to gain back control of this shuttle."

"Fair enough."

The next moment she mentally dove in and reengaged the fail-safe controls for the ship to effectively fly itself. Because disconnecting it from Delon and understanding the basics of toggling the shuttle had been one thing—and both had taken a few hours to learn. But making it through Earth's atmospheric shield to then land safely? She and Shi would kill them all. "Don't touch," she said to him.

She looked at Miguel. Now for coordinates. "Any preference on where we land?"

A shadow crossed his face as he flicked a glance toward the hall where the kids still were. Then ran a hand through his hair as his lips tightened. "I'd say they need a medical center, Sof. Probably the UWC."

Behind him, Claudius nodded. Then snorted. "Let the politicians' doctors figure out how to deal with our little bit of drama."

"Vic, can you give us coordinates to input for that?" Sofi was already sliding her fingers through sections of the console comp. When the AI didn't reply, Sofi glanced up to see her still glaring at Claudius. "Sooner than later?"

Miguel peered her way again. "Sof, are you guys able to ghost this shuttle from Earth's radar?"

"Apparently we already are. Ethos likes his privacy."

He nodded. "In that case, Vic, what are the chances of you

having game-level handscreens and comps waiting for us when we get to that med center?" Miguel had been studying the news channels all covering the FanFights. Trying to learn what they could about the situation.

"You got it, boss man. By the way, I'm getting paid overtime for this, yes?"

"I'll trade you. This for Claudius."

"What? Hey, I—"

"Done. Claudius, you start tomorrow."

"As what?"

The AI grinned and even Sofi chuckled. Then pointed them toward the flight-bridge window, which was quickly filling with Earth's atmospheric blush. "Um, guys, you might want to brace yourselves—" But they'd already entered. Fiery flashes were burning past the window, with hardly a jolt or bump.

"Must be an upgraded model," Shilo murmured in Sofi's head.

"Sof, maybe keep the shuttle cloaked as is, so you don't draw attention," Vicero said.

"Hadn't planned on figuring out how to change it," Sofi answered, her voice higher than usual. "You guys might really want to buckle up."

They were coming in fast. Too fast. Earth was looming bigger and bigger in front of the window.

The shuttle suddenly shuddered, then slowed. Just not enough.

They screamed through a puff of clouds and she thought she saw a few birds fly past, and then they were staring down at the ocean. And to the side of them—land.

"Manhattan," Shilo said.

"Welcome home," Sofi said.

"Stop talking and focus on not killing us," Claudius exclaimed. "Because have you seen me?" He splayed a hand down his two-day-old suit. "There is no way in heck I'm going to my grave wearing this."

31

MIGUEL

"SOFI, WHERE ARE WE GOING? DON'T LEAVE."

From the corner of his eye, Miguel saw Sofi kneel beside a little girl as he and Claudius and Danya rounded up the others. It was the first child she'd woken a few hours ago.

"We won't be gone long. We just have to finish something we started." Sofi took the girl's tiny fingers in her own. "But when we get back, I'll take you for dessert. How does that sound?"

"But . . ." The girl looked around. "I'm scared. I don't want to go to more doctors."

Miguel's heart about shriveled in his chest. He set down the boy he was holding so he could grab more hands as Sofi pointed up at the sky overhead, where the invisible shuttle they'd just stepped off hovered. "Do you see the plane?"

"No." The girl shook her head.

"But do you know it's there?"

The girl nodded.

"How do you know it's there?"

"Because we were in it. It helped us. And I can feel it."

"Exactly." Sofi picked up the child and moved toward Miguel

and the door they were now heading for. "Just like I've been with you and helped you. And just like Shilo did too. We'll still be with you—even if you don't see us."

"But how?"

Miguel caught Sofi's soft smile as he yanked open the med-roof door of the United World Corporations Manhattan branch hospital they'd landed on. She pointed at Claudius and Danya. "Do you see them? They're going to stay with you. They won't let you out of their sight. Not for anyone."

"Promise?"

"Promise," Danya said over her shoulder as she hurried them down the hall where medics began appearing with expressions of shock and panic. "Ambassador Danya, Miguel and Claudius, what a surprise. How'd—what are you—?"

"How may we help you?" one finally blurted.

"They need to see the emergency doctors immediately. Put them at the front of your patient line," Danya said just as one of the children grabbed her leg and began to cry.

"No more doctors, please," the little one whimpered.

"What is going on?" a doctor asked, rounding the corner.

Miguel strode forward. "Ambassadors Claudius and Danya are here to explain and assist you. Take the children's names, take their stories, take videos, and make sure they're physically seen to. And you will do it in the most unfrightening way possible," he added. "They've been through enough." He ignored the UW woman's shocked expression and looked at Claudius. "You got it from here?"

His friend's only response was to nod with a "Go do it," before carrying the two kids clinging to his neck into the exclusive presidential suite patients' room while saying to the quickly growing assembly of med personnel, "Look, I know it's a lot to process right now, but we'll walk you through it."

A trail of the rest of the children followed, with Miguel and Shilo bringing up the tail.

"And, sir." Miguel turned back to a nurse at the door. "I've ordered my own security team to escort them while in here. No one—and I mean no one—is to have access to these kids other than myself, these ambassadors here, or my team. Is that understood?"

The nurse nodded—probably more in shock than clarity.

"Good." Miguel strode from the room and grabbed Sofi's hand. "You ready?"

She nodded as one of the doctor's voices echoed into the hall: "So, tell me again what exactly is going on with these children?"

Miguel didn't wait for Claudius's response. Just took a last glance at the kids before heading to the elevator with Sofi and Shilo. When they reached the bottom floor, they strode out to find the hover Vic had sent. And in its backseat, the backpack of handscreens and earcoms Vic had arranged for.

Miguel handed them their coms. "Vic should already be on. Sofi, do you want to pull up Ranger?"

"I still don't see why we don't show up at the FanFights in the shuttle," Shilo said, taking his.

Sofi was already adjusting her slim-suit to reconnect it with their tech. "Because that thing is hinky to fly—and I'd rather not draw attention until we've assessed the situation from the ground."

Shilo snorted. "Says the girl who just showed up in an air-ship over Manhattan in the middle of the FanFight Games."

32

INOLA

"CORP HEADS, DELONESE LEADERS, PEACEKEEPERS, MEDIA, AND highly respected friends." The announcer's voice rang out across the Colinade levels and echoed up from the vast arena Inola was standing over. "As well as friends of friends, friends of mine, and friends with *benefits*."

As if to accentuate his words, the long, thin red tendril banners snapped in the breeze along the thirteen Colinade levels.

Unfortunately for Favio, the audience's response was as thin as his voice. Muted. Hesitant. As if this bizarre scenario, with its unconventional selection of players, was thrilling, yes, but also suddenly a tad uncomfortable as they faced the reality of seeing the contestants standing midair on their platforms. Inola licked her lips and kept her head high as she stared out at the faces she'd tirelessly served for the past twelve years. Had she been perfect? No. Had she unintentionally betrayed some? Yes.

But she'd been there. And she'd tried to do right by them, even when she'd missed it.

"Welcome to the event you've all been waiting for," the announcer continued with a little more flourish. "The culmination of every FanFight week. *The Fantasy Fighting Games' Final Five!*" His voice rose forcibly as if to incite more excitement. "The part of the Games in which the final player—the last of thirty contenders to survive the arena—faces off against four brand-new *challeng-errrrs!* Are we ready for it?" he suddenly screamed, effectively breaking the tension.

This time the audience responded with shouts of their own, followed by applause.

The announcer smiled wide into the camera lens. "I thought so. Especially since those challengers are of *your* choosing—from professionals to i-reality victors!" His tone dropped low, into a confidential style, as he leaned forward and flashed his crooked smile. "And for the first time ever in our short FanFight history, you've requested the unthinkable. Two Corporation CEO leaders plus an ambassador who, as you know, isn't even on this planet, and last but not least, everyone's favorite i-reality star—Nadine!"

He cocked an eyebrow at the camera. "I mean, leave it to you all to push the envelope on what's acceptable."

Hysterical applause charged the crowd with a visceral sense of approval. As if endorsement had been given that they had done their duty after all, and that they were simply upping the value on entertainment.

The telescreens zoomed in on Favio again as he smiled and said, "You're welcome, World." Earning himself a whole new burst of laughter and another snap of those red banners.

"Speaking of pushing it—my researchers just submitted a set of stats that say the probability of surviving this game is only 20 percent. Which leaves me to question—what challenges have you all chosen?"

Another entertained roar.

On the platform beside Inola, Nadine suddenly shifted, and for a moment Inola worried the poor thing might faint. Until someone started a wave in the crowd, and almost the entire coliseum of ten thousand people swirled in one smooth, circular swell of colorful hands and faces. Only those in the upper stands looked put off. Which would make sense. Inola had sent a few of those invites herself this morning.

"Unfortunately, Ambassador Alis is unable to be with us today. So I vote she owes us for next time, what do you say? Yes? Yes! Perfect! And now to get on with the Games. Allow me to introduce you to your four FanFight *contenderrrrs!*"

Pop! Pop! Pop! Inola jumped as the lights beneath her platform ignited in fire. She grabbed one of the side ropes for support, forgetting she also had one currently secured to her vest.

Behind her, Corp 13's teen player uttered a soft chuckle. Inola ignored it and searched for Ranger's face behind the glass down below, in the tech area, Room 5. *There.* She gave a slight exhale of relief to see him behind the glass, staring intently. He raised a discreet thumbs-up to her, then to Nadine.

Inola nodded. "Don't let us down, kid. This only works if I win."

"That moment you realize your life is in the hands of a geek who literally spends his days in a place called Mom's Basement," Nadine murmured.

"Hey, don't knock the hired help, babe." Ranger snickered through their earcoms. "And I've got this. We've tapped an AI named Vic, and I've got a host of worldwide gamers already hacking in. Just try to stay alive and don't lose your spine while we disable the opponents. We'll do the rest."

Inola was tempted to smile her gratitude but couldn't. Her hands were shaking. She stared down at them as the epic music blasted through the Colinade. She'd not shaken that way since her first time addressing the United World Council as Corp 30's freshly elected CEO. And yet, here she was, never more out of place in her life. The irony of which was almost humorous, considering she'd helped create it.

The announcer was going over their names and histories. She waved and tried to appear as if she wore this skintight slim-suit of her son's with the same confidence she'd expected of him through the years. Then purposefully swung her gaze up to CEO Hart and, beside him, Gaines. Both of whom were coyly not even facing the arena as they entertained guests in her Corp 30 cabana. Including Ambassador Alis's Icelandic Region counterpart, Senator Finn. From their body language she'd bet anything he was the individual they'd chosen to try to weasel in for Corp 24's soon-to-be-vacant CEO seat.

Inola narrowed her gaze.

Already at home. Already blatant in their victory.

Her gaze moved on to Lord Ethos's still-empty cabana. *Where are my kids, Ambassador?*

There was a cough and she peered over at Corp 24's VP, Zain—standing on the platform to her left. Poor guy. He actually looked brave and excited—like he might have a fighting chance to win. He peeked over and tried to wink, but the light in his eye wavered, giving away his admission of what they both knew. That they were alive now. But one slipup or missed observation and they wouldn't be.

However the accidents were preplanned to take her and the others out—if successful, the perpetrators would be seamless and above suspicion.

Her eyes moved to Ambassador Ethos, who'd finally appeared.

He offered her a broad smile as he and three other Delonese entered their cabana.

Inola tightened her lips and nodded.

Well, they'd managed to do what no one else had dared in the past fifteen years. She'd give them that.

They'd managed to outmaneuver her.

Almost.

"You'll release that vid to the attorney general before Nadine's interview goes live?" she muttered to Ranger.

"Loaded and waiting."

She looked back at Ethos. *Where are my kids, you fool?* "And you and your friends will keep scanning for Sofi and Shilo?"

Whatever his answer was, the soaring music drowned it out as the crowd's cheering echoed off the arena walls. The massive green-screen below her and the other three contestants rumbled, and suddenly the mirrored top that covered the field slipped away to reveal their first fight scenario.

Inola froze. They had to be kidding.

It was the exact same water landscape as when the bomb exploded here last week.

The same drone sharks. Same danger. Same crystal-clear water.

She peered down ever so slightly to the FanFight gamer rooms. Was that tech, Ranger, seeing this?

"Well, that's kind of poetic," Nadine said.

"Kind of appropriate," murmured the Corp 13 player.

A rustle from the platform on Inola's left side yanked her attention up. Zain had hunched over. Inola frowned. No one had touched him. He'd just been standing there. "VP Zain? Are you okay?"

He wasn't. She didn't need a doctor to tell her that the slight fringe of yellow foam around his lips wasn't from stress. Someone had gotten to him.

It didn't matter—there wasn't time. The music had blared and stopped, and Zain pushed himself back up.

The announcer and audience were counting down to the drop.

Inola braced as her earcom buzzed while Ranger adjusted it. "Ranger, Zain is down," she whispered.

"We know," a girl said in her com. "We're going to try to help him."

Inola stalled.

Then frowned. That voice.

"Hello?" she whispered again.

"Hey, Mom."

An involuntary cry slipped from Inola's lips at her daughter's voice.

"And, Mom, I found Shilo—he's safe and here too."

Inola swung around to find them, to see them. Across the arena. Through the stands.

There they were. Sofi flashed a handscreen thirty feet in front of her. And Shilo—

"I'm four to the right of Ambassador Ethos's cabana."

"Does he know?" Inola's eyes hazed over, tears blinding her vision as his messy brown head waggled in watery view.

"Not a clue. We're monitoring the tech around him."

She straightened and swallowed. And smiled. "Sofi, how'd you guys get here?"

Tick, tick, tick, tick . . .

"Mom, did you know Shilo and I can control *all* of their technology?"

TOCK.

33

SOFI

SOFI INHALED AND WATCHED HER MOM STANDING ON THE black platform midair, fighting to regain control of her emotions alongside Nadine and the two others from 24 and 13 as the kid from 13 looked elated. Of course he did. There was no way he couldn't win.

A twinge of an ache filled her, for her mom who'd been a corporate goddess. Who'd cured cancer and created lives as well as ruined them. Who'd given her own children over to a cause—only to have that cause become bigger than she'd fathomed.

She stood looking so frail. So human. And the expression on her face said she was bravely terrified. Sofi swore her own ice-crusted heart chipped just a smidge.

"Sofi, did Ethos bring you, or did you come in spite of him?"

"He didn't bring us. But he'll wish he killed us."

"Good."

She scowled and glanced over at Ethos with his attendants—in his Delonese cabana seven spaces over from her. Then winced as a spike of heat stabbed through her skull. *Cripe. What the—?*

Delon had identified her neurological fingerprints. They knew she was the hacker, and she was on Earth about to expose their secrets.

And they were not happy.

"*Fourteen . . .*" The crowd was counting to the drop with the announcer. "*Thirteen . . .*"

"Sofi, focus," Shilo said. "Deal with that later."

Right. Sofi cleared her mind, only to feel her stomach roll as she re-eyed her mom's surroundings. She'd never watched it live from this perspective before—from in the stands just above the gamer quarters. It was weirdly magnificent, with a full view of all thirteen levels, the telescreens, and the entire arena. Including her mom, who was about to drop into the pool of shark-infested water.

"Mom, you don't have to do this."

"I think it's a little late to back out now," her mom said with a nervous chuckle.

Sofi moved her gaze to scan the telescreens.

Her frown deepened.

Something about this whole thing . . .

"*Ten . . .*"

It wasn't just who was fighting, but the way the audience was behaving.

The faces. The discomfort she'd seen that'd morphed into raging excitement and thirst begging for—what? Did they know they'd not just get entertainment today, but were bound to get some blood on their hands? At least Corp 24's.

Gaines and Hart knew, and they were in the Corp 30 cabana practically soaking in it.

A run of close-up shots kept flashing from screen to screen of the stands higher up—the cheap seats where the occupants didn't look nearly so pleased. Some looked angry. Frustrated. As if this fight was giving them voice to resist the aliens or politics or the companies that simultaneously provided for the poor while keeping them down. Sofi peered closer at their faces, only to realize she recognized many from the black markets.

She swerved her gaze to her mother. Had she allowed them in? Had she *invited* them? "Range," she said quietly. "What's with the upper levels?"

"Inola and Nadine thought if they were going to make a showing, it'd do the world good to see the nameless faces the world has forgotten. Vic sent out the invites."

"Seven . . ."

Sofi's throat swelled. The response from the cabana crowd ricocheted off the gaming windows, swift and loud, cheering—as if to drown out the voices seated above them. To shut down their complaints and anger.

Sofi stared. She'd thought the aliens would be the death of everyone on Earth. But something told her she just might be wrong. She glanced at her mother, then Gaines and Hart again.

Maybe humans would.

"Good grief, Sof, focus," Shilo said in her head.

Clenching her jaw, she shook it off and caught his eye. Then recentered on her mom. "Got it. I'm here."

Slipping on a pair of earbuds she'd found in Ranger's bag, she swiped on her scrapp music from her handscreen. Then lifted her thoughts and spread them until they bumped into Shilo's. "Ready?"

"Two . . ."

"I've got Mom. You're good," Shilo thought back.

She nodded and mentally set to work slipping her way into

the tech-firewalls below and the Delonese nanobots they utilized. And opened up a portal to all four gamer systems.

The countdown ended.

The black platforms dropped.

34

MIGUEL

THE AUDIENCE'S ROAR SHOOK THE MARBLE BENEATH MIGUEL'S feet.

CEO Inola hit the water the same moment as Nadine and Zain, landing in a fifty-foot tank of shark-infested water.

Anyone else bothered at how sick the irony in that setting is? Claudius messaged from his station with the kids at the UW Med Center. Man, even I wouldn't have voted for that.

It's why the audience chose it. The horror and inappropriate taste of it only made it all the more exciting. Miguel's eyes rescanned Sofi's and Shilo's surroundings.

A commotion erupted in the pool, and Miguel dropped his gaze to where the Corp 13 kid, Matthers, was already halfway to the bottom. The three adults hadn't even gotten their bearings.

Matthers sliced a shark with his blade, drawing blood to attract the other drones, then kicked and swam faster.

A roar went up from the audience. It's why they loved the finals. Seeing the leaders and superstars who were masters of their own arenas put to the test on a more even playing field was part of the entertainment. It brought the rich and famous down a few notches—made them more human. And more beatable.

"Gross," muttered Vic in Miguel's com.

Shilo stood beside Miguel now, issuing instructions into Inola's earcom. "Mom, head for the bottom, but move to your left. Watch the tail on that one—it'll sting. Ranger, I think Zain and Nadine should just shadow each other and follow Mom's and Matther's lead. If they fight for the—"

Sofi took over. "Vic, add weight to Mom's suit and get her down there faster. Then have two of the game-team zero in on Matther's boots. I hacked the code so they should be able to turn on the air in them and get him to float. Have the rest attack the scenery programs. I can get them in only so far before my brain can't balance it all. Shi and I are still trying to keep the Delonese channels stable."

Miguel peered over at Ethos. According to Sofi and Shi, the tech interference they'd run meant he'd have no idea they were here until they wanted him to.

"Careful, guys," Vic suddenly said. "Watch the landscape." Another roar of the crowd and the fight scene was suddenly changing. Miguel ran a hand across his neck. This was new. They rarely altered a scenario midlevel. But two of the gamers had chosen to morph the setting—and the voting audience had allowed it.

The scene became a rocky landscape set at eye level from where he was standing, pushing the players up out of the water and splaying them out on dry land.

He watched them flail and lie flat on their backs, attempting to ditch their breathing gear and catch up with their wits. Even Matthers seemed thrown off.

"Cripe!" Shilo said.

"Language," Sofi uttered.

Except Miguel was thinking the same as his gaze caught the massive spider that scuttled up over one of the rock crevices. The thing had to be twenty feet tall and, even Miguel had to admit, gorgeously impressive.

Dude, that thing is awesome, Claudius texted.

Also, how're Sof and Shilo doing?

Keeping their mom alive so far, Miguel swiped back.

"Claudius, unless you're sharing tech tips, stop distracting us," Vic said.

A scream ripped through the air and for a second Miguel thought it was a player—until it happened again.

The sound erupted from the spider.

"Yeah, that's not creepy," Shilo said. "Okay, so, Mom—"

Zain suddenly stumbled, then fell. Miguel leaned forward, swerving his gaze from Zain to Ethos to Hart and Gaines.

"C'mon, move," Ranger said in the earcoms. "Get up, guy."

"Mom, if you reach down into your suit, I've created a virtual knife," Sofi said. "Grab it and slip under the spider's stomach when it goes after—"

The spider was on Zain before Inola could get over there. Twenty feet in front of Miguel, a dribble of foam ran from the VP's lips just before the stinger plunged into him. The audience screamed. Miguel frowned. The guy was already done for before he'd even stepped into the arena.

Inola slipped her hand to her side and retrieved the blade.

"One of us is down, two to go," Nadine muttered.

"Nadine, move!" Ranger yelled.

A cry rang out from her lips as a crossbow arrow plunged

into her arm. Another whizzed by Inola, who dropped to the ground in preparation to knife that spider. It landed square in Matther's back and elicited a cry.

Miguel peered over to see who'd shot them. "Sofi, it's Gaines's men. At the base level. Security," he said louder into the com. "Take them out."

The spider scuttled toward the players at full speed, stinger prepared.

"Okay, you know what? Forget this," Sofi said in his com. "This is over. Watch my back, Shi and Vic."

Miguel watched Sofi swing over the side of the arena and start running for her mom, Nadine, and Matthers.

35

INOLA

WHAT THE—?

Matthers?

Inola swung around to see where the arrows were launching from, but it all blended together. The faces. The crowd. The voices.

She turned back to the kid. This wasn't supposed to happen. He was Corp 13's—the one supposed to lose but not by being killed.

Another screech from the audience and the spider was descending toward Nadine. Inola looked around, rose, and, terror flooding her veins, headed toward the giant black arachnid with the blood-red belly.

A commotion went up in the stands to Inola's right. A number of audience members erupted, and Inola glanced over to see Sofi running across the landscape toward her and Nadine.

She was gripping a blade of her own.

The beast let out that eerie scream and attacked Nadine. The i-reality star attempted to duck and roll but got caught on its spindly leg just as the stinger bore down. Suddenly Sofi was there with her blade skating beneath the spider's belly, slicing it open from front to back.

The animal disintegrated into thin air and Sofi stood, dusted herself off, and looked toward Inola, who let out a choking sound. The girl she'd loved, even when she didn't know how to love better, had come.

Sofi turned to the audience and murmured to Shilo in their earcoms, "Wanna hook me up?"

Abruptly, her face and voice were being blasted over the loudspeakers and telescreens. "We're done here. This isn't a game today—this is a murder match." Sofi spread her hands and slowly turned in a circle. "And these aren't real players like the FanFight gamers. These are ill-equipped people being tossed in for *your* entertainment. Except this time there are already deadly consequences." She pointed at the curled-up dead body of Zain.

A shocked hush fell over the audience. Showing their surprise at the confirmation that Zain was actually dead, but even more so at seeing Sofi, the number one terrorist in the world, standing in front of them. Lecturing them on murder.

"You want to see a fight?" Sofi continued. "Then I'm here. And I've just fought one of the biggest battles against Delon on behalf of you all. So stop wasting my time with . . . *this*." She spun around with an expression of disgust. "And get on to doing something worthy of your spines."

Inola swallowed and stared up at the stands full of people who were suddenly gasping.

"What?"

"What'd she say?"

"A battle with Delon? What kind of battle? Check the news!"

Inola stared into Corp 30's cabana, at the faces that appeared frozen in time. As it slowly dawned on her that, out of every-thing, this was the one thing their political finagling had perhaps not counted on—the thing she and Gaines and Hart and the Delonese had not understood in all of their technology and science and regenerative experimentations. You could control technology and agendas and public impression, but you couldn't control human conviction to interrupt a game—let alone an entire planet apparently—to care for their fellow man. Especially in the face of a messed-up world.

It was the thing that separated humans from AI, flesh from prosthetics, Sofi from the genetic replications they'd sought to create.

Inola nodded at Sofi, then turned to the wounded kid as the crowd in the stands began clapping and the announcer cleared his throat. "Gamer Sofi Snow, everyone. Apparently back from the ice-planet."

The applause turned to thunder, until the entire stadium was echoing the fierceness of Sofi's impassioned face.

And for a moment Inola felt it. The pride of a mother who knows she's had many failings, and yet knows she's also succeeded. Because her children have outgrown her and out-performed her in all the areas it truly matters.

Compassion. Even in the midst of her hatred for Inola, Sofi had maintained compassion.

And *that* was her greatest weapon.

A person could change history with that kind of thing.

Inola looked over just as someone yelled, "Nice speech, except you're a traitor!" from the direction of Corp 30's cabana.

Sofi swung around and laughed.

"I'm not the traitor. Not by a long shot."

Time's up, something whispered inside.

Her daughter was about to undo everything. Including Inola herself, along with her position, her power, and her career.

And for the first time in her life, Inola wouldn't stop her. She'd watch her daughter rise as she herself surrendered.

Sofi raised her hands and pointed to the stands. "But I'm about to introduce you all to some."

36

SOFI

SOFI POINTED UP TO THE SCREEN.

"Do you have that video ready, Ranger?" she heard her mom say.

"You know it, Mama CEO."

"Play it."

The next moment the face of i-reality star Nadine flashed across every tele in the Colinade. "Ever wonder what your Corps are up to behind the scenes?" Her smile flickered just as catty as ever. "Well, let me show you."

Sofi turned toward her mom. "Mom—?"

"It's fine. I'll be fine."

But it wasn't fine. Something moved in Sofi's mind. An image—a force—a feeling that jolted her nerves like electrical wires. She glanced up at Delon. It looked the same, but every neuron said the planet was shifting inside. She could sense it— as if it had assessed the data regarding her hacking, and Ethos's reading of the situation, and made a decision. Its system was gearing up. The thing was weaponizing.

An alarm began blaring in her head at the same moment she

caught the look in Ethos's eyes as he edged from the shadows, moving toward Inola with his wide, unblinking gaze. *Ah, cripe. Stop him, Sof.*

"*Shi, see Ethos?*"

"*I'm coming.*"

"*No, just head off his tech options. I've got Mom and the others.*" Maybe if she stopped Ethos, she'd stall the planet too.

"Mom and Nadine, get Matthers and head for Miguel," she said aloud in the coms. "Miguel, can you grab them?" She looked around for the knife she'd used only to realize it was sitting back by the now nonexistent spider. *Too far.* "*Don't, Ethos,*" Sofi said, using her mind to try to reach the alien telepathically.

If he heard her, he wasn't listening. He was simply staring at her mother with a look that said, from one leader to another, he considered her betrayal of him the highest level of offense.

Sofi branched her thoughts out and felt around, as if pressing with one's skin into the dark until it brushed against something that triggered goose bumps. In this case she mentally stretched for the closest Delonese technology she could control.

A spear.

On the sidelines twenty feet from Sofi, left by one of the gamers for Matthers. Keeping her gaze on Ethos, Sofi wrapped her thoughts around the weapon and flipped it up, then centered it thirty feet in the air above her, mentally holding it pointed upward at the Delonese lead ambassador.

"*I'll not say it again, Ethos. Don't do this,*" she said in her head again.

"Sofi, to your right!"

Ranger? She swung to see what he was yelling about in her earcom—

Another crossbow arrow. It skimmed her arm, then crumbled. Sofi winced.

"*Sorry. It was only partly Delonese,*" Shi said.

But Ethos's hand was already moving. Sofi saw Miguel leap for him, but even from here she could see he'd be too late.

Sofi let her spear launch. And in her mind's eye the pace was slow. Like swimming. At the same time her senses felt the ice-planet above prickle and react—an image flashing into mind of weapons being raised. The glittering piece of silver leaving Ethos's hand suddenly curved a different direction. A closer direction.

It curved for her.

Sofi blinked, and out of the corner of her eye caught her mom's expression.

Perhaps it was the glint in her mother's gaze, or simply that she knew her mother's heart far better than she'd ever realized— that the love inside the woman was the same love and blood that ran through Sofi and Shilo. Even if it'd not always been easy to find or well shown.

Sofi started to swerve.

Her mother stepped in front of her. Sofi reached out and shoved her mom away, only to see Shilo running to intercept.

While Sofi'd been watching Lord Ethos and the others, so had Shilo. And he'd already been on his way.

"*No,*" she said to him through her mind. "*Don't you dare—*"

Sofi's spear hit Ethos. She heard the thump into his chest— straight and true.

Followed by the faint sound of her brother's cry beside her.

She glanced over to find blood pouring everywhere. On Shilo's hands and knees as he went to catch his mom, his fingers already pressing in around where Ethos's blade had buried into her chest. Ignoring the arrow that'd just swiped his calf. Their mother crumpled to the sand.

"Wait a minute, folks." The announcer came on, interrupting Nadine's vid. "What's happening in the arena? What's going on here?"

A second arrow swiped Sofi's arm and landed in the dirt, barely missing her brother.

She looked over to find Ms. Gaines's thugs—the ones who'd attacked her and Miguel back at his house three nights ago—standing beneath the overhang by an empty game room.

"Vic," Miguel was yelling in the earcom, "I told my security to take those guys down. Why are they still—?"

"They did! Gaines must've had more in place."

The lead was crouched with his arm still midair. Security was rushing in again, yanking them down. Others were going for Lord Ethos while even more headed for her. But it was too late.

She was too late. She had been a second too slow in shoving Inola aside. Her mom's face widened as Sofi dropped to the ground beside her. Beneath Shilo's shadow as he leaned over, saying, "Mom, no. Mom, please don't go."

But the blood kept flowing. Like flowers blooming in red patterns on her mother's suit, only to *drip, drip, drip* to the sand and become rivulets around where her body fell.

The announcer kept blabbing. "We're getting a report confirming what you and I are all seeing with our eyes! If you're wondering if that's Shilo Snow we're seeing down there—in fact, it is! Back from the dead apparently. Inola's own child stepped into the arena to protect his mother, but something appears to have gone horribly wrong. As you can see, he and his sister are both hovering on the ground with what looks like blood from possibly fatal wounds. The question is—were those wounds inflicted due to the plotting of her own children or—"

The vast crowd was screaming, rising from their seats and cabana couches and stepping into the fading sunlight. In excitement. In burgeoning awareness of what had just happened. The video above him had just been explaining who'd been behind the bombing—and they were ready for a fight.

Their voices picked up a united, supportive cry. "Shilo! Shilo! Shilo!"

But the look on her brother's face said he'd stopped listening to anything but the slowing patter of their mother's heartbeat.

Tick.

Tick.

Tick . . .

She was gone.

With Shilo bent over the body of the only mother they'd ever known.

Sofi gripped his chest and pulled him tight.

Shilo peered up and simply uttered, "Why?"

37

MIGUEL

THE PLACE BROKE INTO CHAOS. THE CROWDS SCREAMING—THEIR delighted thrills at the twists the event had taken were now turning to cries of betrayal and dissent. They'd seen what happened—and the teles were already giving split-screen slow-motion replays of a daughter and mother and son all running to save one another, as Nadine's interview finished up in the background.

Cameras had caught Ethos flinging his blade—apparently forgetting that nothing was beneath the eye of technology. Even in a private cabana with the curtains mostly closed.

And that was enough for the anti-Delonese rioters.

Ethos's tent was now surrounded by a swarm of security, fighting off a stampede of citizens. Except something told Miguel it was already too late. The spear's aim had been true. The Delonese ambassador wouldn't make it out of here alive.

Miguel turned to find Sofi in the arena, kneeling beside Shilo in the blood as the crowd picked up her and her family's names.

He started for her, Sofi's lashes fluttering as she slipped her hand around Shilo's shoulder and held it there. Embracing her brother, who was too young for any of this.

Because at the end of it all—despite the years of rejection and pain—this was still their mother.

Miguel reached their side with no idea what to say—what to do—how to fix any of this.

So he did nothing except push away the officers and med personnel, asking them to give them room. Then kneeled and held her up as she held Shilo.

38

SOFI

SHILO WAS RIGHT—WHY? WHY TO ANY OF IT?

Sofi's arm tightened around her brother while he curled over and laid his head on Mom's chest. This sweet, Earth-scented, sweaty twelve-year-old boy who was Sofi's person—who'd belonged to her and she to him more than any other.

She felt his body shake as he began to weep uncontrollably. Then break into a hundred little-boy pieces. Because his question of "why" had been a bit more than his young heart could understand.

Her throat swelled up and her chest went cold.

Until a movement beside her—and suddenly Miguel's strong hands were on her shoulders. He said nothing. Just sat with her. And whatever it was inside that had always been fine, that had always needed to be fine—for Shi. For her mother. For herself—wasn't fine anymore.

The space around her heart broke.

And then broke again. Over and over again, cracking wide open.

For this life and Shilo. For the memories and years of night-mares and visions that had nearly destroyed her. For the children who weren't as lucky as they were—who'd been used and thrown away and no one would ever know their names. She wept for her past. For what had been. For what could've been.

For the dad they'd loved and lost. The mother they'd needed and hardly known. The half sister she couldn't even remember.

Sofi wept for herself.

The person she'd tried to become when left on her own, and the boys and choices she'd used in hopes of becoming better. For the girl she'd been before Miguel's silly rejection confirmed what her mother had always shown—that Sofi was never worthy enough.

Sofi wept because all the codes and data sequences and information streams in the world could not fix this.

She heard Hart's voice bellowing somewhere over the chaos. And Ms. Gaines's right behind him. The lower sections stampeding to leave. Or stay. Or join them on the rock slab scenery—she couldn't tell. She didn't care.

She hated them all as she sat there holding a brother she couldn't help because she couldn't even help herself.

Humanity. The Delonese. There was no difference between them. They all killed their own, and the only time they cared was when others did it to them. Ethos had been right.

You're not finished yet.

She shut her eyes and let her heartbeat take over all sound. As if the only music worth hearing now was that of reality—the refrain of one life still surviving while another died for nothing more than political games.

And it would all eventually end up the same.

The hate came slow. Matching the sensation of the Delonese planet that'd been nudging her subconcious. As if their atmosphere up there was thickening. Edging into her veins like a trickle, then a flood. The anger of the entire space station as it finished moving its weapons into position. The desire to destroy these people who always, eventually, destroyed each other anyway. She let it weave through her head and work like a portal. With it came the sensation of having a piece of control. Even if it was slight, she was still stronger than those who'd done this.

With a flicker of relief, she reached out and wrapped her mind through and around every bit of Delonese metal in this stadium. In the weapons used, the support beams, the telescreens and expensive handscreens. She invaded them with her cerebral eye and watched their tech pathways and access codes one by one light up and come alive.

"*Sofi,*" Ambassador Danya said inside her head.

"Don't talk to me," she said through gritted teeth, and pushed farther out, to the satellites and space-walks. And then to Delon.

Their weapons. They were aimed at Earth.

Running through systems, she edged along the firewalls to find her way in. It took her all the time in the world and yet no time at all. Scanning, sorting, unraveling the streams that made up their technological glory. Playing with it as one would a puzzle to see just exactly how the pieces fit.

Until suddenly something clicked and her body connected, and she was staring into the planet's core. Their people, their history, their memories. It all became hers. And even more terrifying and satisfying—their power.

She swallowed. *I can do it.*

Attack Delon and Earth, or shut it all off with one virus.

She seized up and gasped.

Delon's reaction to her intrusion was surprisingly swift. Icy.

Its systems and people lashed back with electrical pulses of their own, working to cut her off and push her out, protecting themselves from what she was about to do. What she was capable of doing.

There was something infinitely satisfying in that. To have stirred the already infuriated hornet's nest.

A hand touched her arm and she felt Miguel push whoever it was off, as the peacekeepers and politicians and security teams rushed past and around them. Yelling and trying to keep control of a world that was completely and unequivocally out of control. And of a people who were more obsessed with controlling others than themselves.

Danya's voice stirred her mind. *"Sofi, do you know how you're able to connect with my planet? Or what they altered inside you as a child that causes that ability?"*

Was she joking right now? Sofi tried to push her from her thoughts and lean into the planet core.

"Sofi—"

"Danya, I was only a freaking child. I have no idea."

The Delonese woman mentally whispered, *"Because I can feel what you're doing. In my blood, I feel what you're tempted to do, and I'm asking you not to. It's not who you are. There are children. Do not bring this harm on them."*

The children.

Sofi peered up at the Colinade.

If she took down the tech woven through the stadium, thousands would die in those stands. If she took down the planet, everyone could die.

None of whom deserved it. Some of whom deserved it.

She blinked and took a breath.

Then leaned back. Swallowed. And suddenly noted the *beat, beat, beat* of Miguel's steady heart pressed against her spine. Easing. Staying. Not saying a word. Like he'd been there for years in the bass of a song.

Sofi mentally disarmed Delon's weapons with one blink, then retracted from the virtual firewall codes and pathways and released her hold on the planet and the tech inside the stadium— and tried to picture the faces of those watching her right now. Still young and innocent, full of trust and life and belief. Like little seeds of hope in a love-starved land.

You're not finished yet.

"This is why I said—"

Sofi jumped at the voice. From somewhere behind them CEO Hart was yelling again, closer this time. She cringed as her heart shook. For what he'd done to her mother and family. She felt Miguel turn toward Hart, who was now stepping off the hoverelevator and stomping toward them across the landscape. *"Hagamos esto."* Miguel rose, cracked his neck, and walked over to meet him. And punched him across the face.

Hart went down.

But his voice was still going. Up on the telescreens, as the audience suddenly quieted and slowed. The vids had turned back on, drawing interest over fear. And this one was clearly dishing out some solid gossip.

Sofi looked up at the screen to see Hart in private conversation with Inola on a vid dated yesterday. Confessing before the world outside the privacy of their CEO cabana terrace what more he was planning in betraying Earth's children. Sofi smiled.

He'd hid it with white noise—but Shilo's mind had found a way through it.

The telescreen flashed to another scene, this one a vid conversation yesterday between Ethos and the guilty parties of the Delonese Project, including some indicting words from Ms. Gaines.

She swallowed. At least it was coming out. They were being seen for what they truly were.

The world knew.

The world knew.

"Thanks for the vid backup, Vic and Ranger," she murmured.

"You got it, girl."

She turned back to her brother and mother.

And felt the slightest tingling in her arm. Right where the arrow had swiped her.

Glancing down, she noted the bleeding had stopped and the wound wasn't nearly as bad as it'd first felt. The wound was healing.

"Sofi—" Shilo's tearstained hand was pointing at his leg doing the same.

She frowned.

"Do you know what they altered inside you?" Danya's words whispered again.

She actually had no idea.

She placed her hand on the sand. And inhaled. Then shut her eyes to work her way back into the Delonese planet core—resisting the immediate rush of attack from their scanners. She reentered the Delonese history and memories and remedies, and sorted through them until she reached the series of files labeled "Snow."

Nanobots.

Their blood held nanobots.

According to their data, in Delonese blood the nanobots had been created to serve as physiological support and to unify their species. No wonder they all looked and sounded and thought so much alike.

But in Shilo and Sofi . . .

The bots had activated into something wholly different.

They had melded to their brain and blood in a way that—

Sofi leaned against Shilo, tightened her closed eyes, and imagined the inside of her veins and brain and heart working overtime on that wound seeping blood. She found where the bots had been cut and unraveled through the violence and loss of too much fluid. And too many shorted connections.

And watched them repair.

Slouching, she began to follow the patterns. Triggering the nanobots to make more of themselves. Replicating fifty at a time until they were back on course and knew their place and what to fix.

Then she retracted from the planet. And looked up at Shilo with an expression of wonder. He cracked a smile on that tear-streaked face.

A ripple of thunder above them shattered the heavens, and the sky about split in half. Sofi and Shilo lurched as everyone around her jumped back and fell. A light the brightness of a mind-numbing explosion followed and spread across the entire area, bathing them all in white and blinding Sofi's eyes for far too many seconds.

At the same time she could feel it. The tug. The pull. As if part of her brain and bones were being ripped from her skin and dragged beyond Earth's atmosphere at the speed of light. There was screaming. So much screaming—as people around her were cowering in fear while she and Shi just stood there, gasping for air as every nerve in her body flexed and lit on fire.

Until at some point she realized she was screaming too. And the endless, exhausting, begging-the-pain-to-stop cry that was louder than the rest was coming from her lungs.

Boom! The Earth shuddered, like a small quake rippling the atmosphere, and then the glare ended and the shaking stopped and the sky went back to blue. And Shilo was staring at her.

People were running, chaos already ensuing. She moved her gaze farther above them—to the spot just beyond the moon where the Delonese planet had sat for the past eleven years. Knowing what she'd find before she saw it.

Delon was gone. Disappeared through a wormhole.

Without a trace.

What have I done?

"Danya?" She reached out.

"I'm here. They left me behind."

"I'm sorry."

"I'm not."

A hand moved to Sofi's and squeezed.

She looked down to find Shilo blinking at her.

"Sof, these are some wicked powers we've got," he whispered.

As the vids of Ethos kept playing.

39

MIGUEL

ONE WEEK LATER...

"THANK YOU ALL FOR YOUR PERSPECTIVE SHARED HERE," THE
United World Corporations attorney general said. "It is the decision of this Council to pursue criminal charges against Senator
Finn, Corp 13's CEO Hart, Corp 30's vice president Ms. Gaines,
and the security individuals involved—for acts of treason against
the people of Earth."

The round, wood-paneled room was packed with every
single UWC leader, ambassador, senator, and advisor, and so
quiet you could almost hear the very slight *tap, tap, tapping* of
Claudius's finger against his drink.

Miguel glanced over and smirked. Claudius was eager for his
date with Vic—even if Miguel had no idea how the logistics of it
actually worked.

"However," the attorney general continued, "in regard to
Sofi and Shilo Snow, Ambassadors Claudius, Danya, Miguel,
and those of Corp 24, we find no reason to bring charges against

them at this time. Instead, the recommendation of this forum is to express our gratitude at their assistance in uncovering the illegal activities that have taken place."

Danya's sigh of relief slipped out beside Miguel, along with most of the rest of the audience's a second later.

Sofi and Shilo had spent the past three days being interviewed and investigated in this room, and most everyone seemed in agreement that the facts presented were the truth.

"But what *of* the Snows?" A senator from Eurasia lifted his hand without looking at either Shilo or Sofi. "What will be their involvement here on out, considering they can effectively shut down a good portion of our technology?"

"He does realize they just helped to save humanity, right?" Claudius said under his breath.

The UW attorney general stood. "Senator, thank you for your query, as it's the very thing we've wrestled with this past week. And we will wrestle with it for many years to come." He scanned the assembly's faces. "However, I think we can all agree their benefit to us cannot be remotely underestimated. To have individuals who can detect and protect Earth from those who might not have our best interests in mind—that's a defense system we couldn't build if we tried."

"I heartily agree," said the senator. "But I think it worth acknowledging that they contain the potential for both help and danger. And a week of investigations isn't nearly enough to explore those limits."

"Don't we all contain the potential for help and harm?" The attorney general gave a kindly grimace and spread his hands, provoking a chuckle from the assembly. "The fact is, Senator, we're in a new era that started before the Delonese arrived—where people and technological breakthroughs are capable of near anything."

From his seat four rows away, Miguel caught old Senator Kosame winking at him.

"All we can do is assure this Council we'll be keeping an eye on Shilo and Sofi. Just like we are keeping an eye on the rest of humanity. With the encouragement that we all seek to become and behave as our best selves. Thank you. And with that, this Council is adjourned today."

4□

SOFI

"SOFIIIIIIII!"

Shrieks and hollers echoed through the black-lit, music-thumping hall as she and Shilo stepped into the main room of Mom's Basement. The usual rainbow strobe lights and scrapp music blasted over her, pounding life back through Sofi's bones.

She inhaled. The noise, the chilly air, the groups of gamers and fans around tables, amid telescreens and game teams—and the oxygen bar along the far wall.

These were her people. This was a piece of her home.

"And *Shilo whaaaat*? We've got them both here!" someone yelled. "How freaky are you two?" another howled.

The questions and comments came just as fast as the cat-calls. "What was the planet like?"

"Where'd the Delonese disappear to?"

"Way to rock the free world, guys."

Sofi smiled and ducked as they came to smack her shoulder, and Shilo spread his arms out to welcome hugs from the girls fawning over him. She snorted and kept walking.

"Hey, don't be hating," he mentally defended. *"I've been stuck*

on an alien planet, wondering if I'd ever see humans again. I'm open to hugging. I'm a hugger. Let the people hug."

"Uh-huh." She smirked just as she caught sight of Ranger waving them down from one of the wall tables. She beckoned Shilo to extricate himself from the sea of love before flashing two fingers for a "number two" order from the bar waiter wearing his animated-skull apron.

"Hey, dude," Ranger said the moment she reached him. He wrapped Sofi in a bear hug, then rapped Shi's knuckles as the waiter brought over their buzz drinks and fries. The guy set down their food and smiled like he wanted to say something, but instead gave a shy shrug before sauntering back to the bar.

A quick blue flickering of the room's strobe lights, and suddenly the FanFight music took over, causing the place to erupt in howls and cheers. Ranger jerked his chin at the giant telescreen where the image had changed to the Basement's own gamer-created video announcement. "Nice timing. They're about to start the tribute."

Sofi stuck a fry in her mouth, then leaned her head on Shilo's shoulder, bracing herself for the vid the gamers here made every FanFight season to privately honor the players who'd lost rather than won. Tonight's would be all about her mother.

Sofi felt Shi sag beneath her chin, as if relaxing from his public persona back into her little brother.

Their mom's face flashed on-screen as the music soared then dropped, and a voice came on. *"This week we lost one of our own. A contributing creator of the FanFights and the mother of two of our best players."*

A muted cheer went up as faces looked kindly at Sofi and Shilo.

"*But Inola Snow was much more than that,*" the vid continued. "*A powerful person in her own right, she was a woman who'd survived the loss of her first child—and used her grief to discover the cure for a multitude of cancers. She built Corp 30 and this city into what it is today. And, in recent days, managed to begin waking the world to the levels of poverty and trafficking that are taking place. And for that, we salute you, Inola Snow. May you live on in our hearts.*"

Sofi peeked at Ranger. They hadn't mentioned her mom's involvement in allowing the child abductions or unethical testing.

"*That was nice of him.*" Shilo's thoughts sounded as choked up as her throat suddenly felt.

The tribute continued through more music and a display of photos of Inola. One after the other, all pictures Sofi'd seen before, but somehow they felt richer this time. Clearer. And dearer. Forgiveness had a way of doing that. Of releasing the hold one's actions had over the heart.

Even if trust wasn't a filter she'd ever view her mother's choices through.

The vid slowed upon one photo in particular. It was of her and Shilo and Inola playing at the farm in the dirt. It must've been on one of her mother's visits because Shilo couldn't have been more than three.

Sofi's mind drifted back to the memory it brought back. A moment she'd never even known existed because it'd been bottled up with the rest.

THEY WERE MAKING STICK AND DIRT HOSPITALS TO care for the handful of worms Sofi had collected.

"Sofi, be gentle." Her mother laughed.

"But we need to fix them, just like you leave to fix people, Mama."

"I'm not sure they want to be fixed, Sofi." Her mother smiled down on her. "I think they'd rather be loved. And sometimes loving someone means letting them go, to be as they are. For who they are."

"Like we love you, Mama?" Shilo said.

Her mother's eyes had blinked quick, then watered. And Sofi could see it so clearly—that expression of doubt. Of longing. Of being torn between two worlds.

Sofi blinked and refocused back on the lounge and the loud music surrounding them. What had changed between that moment and two years later when her mom had sent them to the Delonese? Or between that day and this past month, for that matter? Was it something big? Or was it simply the small choices her mother had made along the way?

One thing was certain—Sofi would never accept what her mother had done. But perhaps that wasn't Sofi's responsibility. Perhaps her job was to simply accept herself and the future *she* wanted. And to create that.

Forcing the warmth from her eyes, she cleared her throat. "Hey, Range. Thanks for taking care of my mom and all that. While I was on Delon."

"She was a good person, Sof. A lot wrong with her—but some was done for good reasons, you know?"

Yeah. She knew.

She took another fry and held it while she searched out more words. "Thanks for the tribute to her," she said after a moment. "It was kind of you."

"It's what I'd want."

Sofi nodded and pushed the basket of fries at Shilo before patting Ranger's hand and peering back at the tele that had returned to the news. Nadine was currently talking.

"While the medics rushed to save CEO Inola, unfortunately, they were too late." The i-reality star's voice softened to a note that seemed genuinely grieved. "I don't think there's a person on this planet who wouldn't agree that she was a courageous woman. And she'll be sorely missed."

"So, who do you think will take over for Mom?"

Sofi glanced at Shi and shrugged. "No idea."

"Maybe they'll elect you and we can be in charge of the Games."

She snorted. "No thanks."

"While the UW scientists will continue to analyze the data for years to come," Nadine continued, "it's believed Delon opened or discovered a wormhole in the system and used it to intentionally exit the Milky Way the same way they came. All traces and particulates seem to support this as well. And in light of recent revelations regarding their questionable intentions here, I think it's fair to say the shock of them leaving comes with a matched sense of relief."

Nadine's voice dropped in a note of exhaustion that hung about her entire body—even while her gaze displayed a strength and gentleness born of someone who'd been in the thick of the fight the past few days. She stared into the camera. "We'll continue to keep you updated as we know more. But for this evening, may you all breathe a little lighter, hug your loved ones tighter, and realize that, for tonight, the world is alright. *We* are alright. Much love to you all."

41

MIGUEL

THE COLINADE WAS PACKED. SUN SHINING, CABANAS GLITTER-ing, and the scents of sweat and cinnamon and organic coffee drifting up on the air-conditioned breezes. Miguel stood on the announcement platform that the organizers had connected to the CEO cabana and surveyed the coliseum, which was crammed tighter with people for this event than any in the past. And probably more than was actually legal.

He half listened as the UW attorney general finished inform-ing the crowd of what they already knew—the state of the world, its thirty corporations and regions, and the planet Delon fleeing with its citizens.

All of which had been talked to death during numerous sta-tus alerts and press conferences the last eight days. But still, the need for providing an official detailing and ensuring their gov-erning reputation stayed transparent was vital.

So here they stood, Miguel, the attorney general, all twenty-eight CEOs, and Ambassador Danya, who, as far as the majority of the world knew or was concerned, was as human as anyone here. And those who knew differently agreed to keep it that way in gratitude for what she'd sacrificed to help Earth.

"While we are grateful for the massive amounts of assistance the Delonese gave during their time in our Milky Way system," the attorney general continued, "we are also relieved to see them move on. And with them gone, we support Corp 24's voluntary decision to pull the Altered device off the market. In light of our investigations, we have unanimously voted that a person's genetic coding is a part of their private personhood—and to test, judge, or infringe on that without an individual's consent is an overstep in human respect. We believe you'll join us not only in understanding this decision but in supporting it as well. Thank you."

Voices rumbled like thunder from the crowd in cheers mixed with nerves and questions beneath the overhead telescreens. And from the base where—instead of the green-screens and virtual scenes—the rest of the world senators, VPs, and ambassadors sat in circular rows as part of the audience.

The attorney general lifted his hand for a quiet that didn't come and stated, "As you have heard from myself and each of the CEOs standing with me during the past hour and a half, we now turn the final podium over to Ambassador Miguel, who—"

The crowd just grew louder, their cheers and yells now more demanding. As if they still needed something.

Sofi and Shilo stepped out onto the stage and strolled up to stand on either side of Miguel. Dressed in matching black slim-suits, black hair swept back off their faces. An owl necklace around Sofi's throat, and a metal cougar around Shilo's. Together they shut their eyes and, in the same moment, discreetly shut off the telescreens of the attorney general's face.

The Colinade fell silent.

Miguel snorted. "You're going to get yourselves in trouble."

"Just helping you out, dude," Shilo said.

Sofi tipped her head and turned them back on—causing the screens to flicker with static before they zeroed in their telefocus on Miguel, as behind them one of the CEOs cleared her throat and said, "Good gad, please tell me that wasn't you two."

"Corp heads, peacekeepers, media, and highly respected friends." Miguel's rich voice echoed through the Colinade. "As well as friends of friends, friends of mine, and friends with *benefits.*"

The silence broke and the audience laughed as Miguel swept his gaze over all thirteen levels and the thousands of people standing among the glitter and pomp and sun-drenched cabanas. He then stared straight into the camera for the other few million watching across the globe via their telescreens.

Beside him, Sofi slipped her hand into his in a symbol of trust.

The crowd must've caught the gesture on the giant teles because they began shouting, "Sofi! Sofi!" then erupted into a thunderous round of applause.

Miguel squeezed her hand and waited for the cheers to die before lifting his chin and extending his voice even further. "The fact that you and I are standing here today—on this planet, on this soil that is far older, with far more history than any of us— should give me and you pause. That we are here, in this time, is a gift. And one we cannot take lightly."

"*You're* a gift, Miguel!" some rabid guy yelled from the sixth level, sparking laughter—even from Sofi.

"He's got that right," Sofi said, with a wink at the camera.

If the audience had been tense and hopeful before, they were beside themselves in their level of approval now. Miguel gave Sofi a shy side glance that quickly became an enormous smile. And the crowd ate it up.

He dropped his gaze and scanned the arena of officials and held up his hand for calm. "That we are alive at all is a testament to the ingenuity of our forefathers, the advances in arts and sciences—like technology, cellular exploration, and education—and the mercy of something that is far bigger than our universe."

He took a breath and recentered his gaze on the camera. "It's also a tribute to the belief that life is precious. Your life is precious. So is mine. So are our neighbors', and coworkers', and those who disagree with us. And the minute I elevate my life above another's—the moment I choose mine as more valuable for the survival of humanity—is the moment I begin to give away my humanity. And that is the moment we all begin to lose."

Sofi gripped his hand tighter. They were quiet now. All listening. Staring at him. All breathing the same air as him. Beating with the same heartbeat as his.

"The questions for you and me—the questions for all of us—are: What choices do you or I make that emasculate the very heart of what it means to be alive? What do *we* contribute to the tearing down or building up of people on a daily basis? How do we decide who is worthy or not to have the same benefits as the rest of us—the same food, same joy, same prosperity? And who do we sacrifice in order to achieve what you or I think is best? Is it nobler to sacrifice another in the name of the needy—or to serve and sacrifice of ourselves?"

He stared at their faces. As if he could speak to their hearts one by one—to ignite conviction and compassion in a world that had clearly forgotten both far too often and for far too long. Just like he had.

"My friends, we have become so busy taking care of people that we've too often forgotten to care *about* them. To know them at a heart and face level. They've become means to a cultural end rather than the measure of health on the journey. And I no longer want anything to do with it."

The audience erupted again. He glanced at Sofi, who nodded as if to say he was doing fine, while beside her, Shilo stood on one foot as if to say, "Can we get lunch soon?"

Miguel grinned and strode to the edge of the stage. "Because arrogance at its worst masquerades as goodness. It deceives itself and others that it is for the people rather than accomplishing things off the backs of the people. But, my friends, business part-ners, political associates . . . somewhere along the way we lost sight of what exactly it means to be good. And we simply aimed for being right."

He swallowed. And looked straight at the camera again. "If the Delonese gave us anything, it is this: the reality that they are no different from us. Did you hear me, friends?" He raised his voice to a shout. "For as appalled as we are that they, and a few of our top corporate leaders, would use and abuse our children in such brutal ways—at least they were doing it for survival, you know? So what's *our* excuse? We're doing it every day—in our black markets, in our trafficking parlors, in our own neighbor-hoods. And even if we're not partaking, we're certainly allowing it. Because what are you and I doing to stop it? So thank heavens for the Delonese. For their gift of technology and environmental cleanup. But more so for the mirror they held up."

"May God help us all," he heard Sofi mutter over the silence that was now uncomfortable.

Miguel licked his lips and finished. "The question I've been asking myself recently is what does it mean to exist for a very brief time in this place we call the Milky Way? What does it mean to be in a community—to contribute to that community—and to fight for it rather than against each other?" He rubbed a hand across the back of his neck. "So, friends, the question I leave you with is simply this:

"How do we lose our humanity? And how do we gain our humanity back?"

42

SOFI

"SOF, CHECK THIS OUT!" SHILO'S BLACK HAIR RUFFLED IN THE breeze on the old weathered porch of their farmhouse, nestled on the border of Old North Carolina and the rest of the world. "Found it under the floorboards of the basement!" He held up a metallic black box as his shadow filled the same spot where Sofi'd cradled her father's head as he quietly passed from this world to the next. "It's a radio. I'm going to pull it apart and see what I can do with it."

She squinted. Man, Shilo looked like Papa. Those broad shoulders and long legs—and that little bit of sparse hair above his upper lip. She twisted her mouth. He needed to shave that thing.

"Not a chance," his voice said inside her head. *"It looks manly."*

She shielded the blaring sun from her eyes and wiped a stray ponytail strand away. *"Says the twelve-year-old boy waving a boom box at me. You know we could just buy a new one."*

He grinned. And said aloud, "Just think how old skool we'll be. Actual radio waves. We could make our own music station."

He flashed a rock-on sign at her, then sat down on the steps to disembowel the thing.

"He does realize the types of radio towers it uses aren't the same these days, right?" Miguel said, not looking up from where he squatted nearby, mid-sending something on his handscreen to Vicero.

"Leave it to him to bring them back." Sofi smiled and turned to analyze the half-fallen-down barn. "Just like they were going to bring back this place." Sofi wiped the sweat from her neck, then picked up her glass of melting iced tea.

"So I'm thinking you should keep some of those old barn beams for lining the rafters." Miguel leaned up and handed her his screen with a 3-D architectural draft Vic had just sketched of the barn, exactly as it'd been in its former glory. Including that one missing slat in the roof through which Sofi and Shilo used to watch the fireflies and their half sister's star glimmer down at them.

Sof swallowed and wanted to say the design was more than perfect, but ended up saying nothing at all. Just let the emotion sit in her throat.

His expression widened to a grin. "I'll take that as a yes." He stood and stepped over beside her. And studied her face.

She let him. Until after a minute she moved to lean her head into him and felt for the warmth of his heartbeat that was the only thing she wanted to hear right now.

He pulled her close and kissed the top of her head. The simplicity of which, she thought, might as well have ignited the summer skies. This man she'd never wanted to see again, never believed she'd need again, was here. And she'd been wrong.

She'd never in her life been so glad to be wrong.

Because somehow they'd grown. Through the brokenness, through the loss and finding of themselves, through the memories that had unmade then remade them. And perhaps this was what she'd wanted—waited for—all along. She just hadn't known he'd already chosen it too, a year and a half ago.

Her handscreen buzzed, causing them both to jump. "You've got to be kidding," he murmured. "Tell them we're busy."

Sofi held up her screen. "It's Danya."

"Like I said—"

Congrats. They've just voted you and Miguel in as the new Corp 30 CEO unit, Sof.

Sofi stared. *What?*

Miguel raised a brow.

"Are they joking?"

He looked over her shoulder at the message. "The UW rarely jokes, love. But perhaps they've made an exception due to your mother's untimely death."

"You're so not even funny."

"Yes, I am. At least your old lady neighbor who's been watching through the fence for the past hour seems to think so. That or she's ogling my frame."

"Pretty sure it's the fact your shirt's been inside out all day."

"It—what?"

Sofi laughed and texted back:

Thanks, but no thanks. Miguel can take it, though, if he wants.

Right. Not sure you have a choice.

Excuse me?

You really want to leave it to someone else?

Sofi scowled and looked away, out over the horizon of the green fields and broken-down homestead and memories of the first half of her life spent here. She didn't want it. The pressure, the people politics.

She glanced at Miguel, who'd taken to sipping his tea and fluttering a wave at the old woman who was indeed spying on them through the fence.

Sofi snorted. "I take it you knew the UW would ask."

"You'd be good at it," was all he said.

Of course he knew.

"Yeah, well, the world doesn't need more CEOs," she muttered and kicked the crunchy dirt with the tip of her black boot that came up over her knee, almost as high as her shorts.

He winked at the lady, who seemed to remember she had to be somewhere, then returned to his handheld and messaging Vic.

"Nor does it need more politicians. No offense." She glared at him.

"Quite true. And none taken." He tapped his screen.

"Besides, I'd hate it."

He nodded again and kept tapping.

"Except—I'd be with *you*, obviously."

"Not sure that's a plus for you."

"But even if I took it, I'd still want to live here and I'd run things differently."

The smallest smile flickered as he sent off the note he'd been formatting, only to be interrupted by a hologram popping up from his screen.

Claudius's head assessed Miguel and his iced tea with a strafing gaze. "Ah, good. Nice to see you drinking your sissy tea, dude. I was worried you might've gone hard after spending so much time with the gamer-chick. But here you are, sexy as always."

Miguel sniffed. "Vic's got you hanging out with her today, eh?"

"You know it. Except she's all about work work work all the time. It's all she does, and apparently I'm only here to be eye candy." He sighed dramatically.

"Darn right," Vic's voice rang out from the handscreen's microphone.

Claudius smoothed his plaid collar and smiled pleased-like, then turned to Sof. "Anyhow. I hear you're both the new Corp 30 CEOs. Congrats. Remind me to send you my brief on food carts and dress codes for the UW meetings. Very classy. Very important."

"Don't let him," Vic interrupted. "They look like a cat threw up on his grandma's afghan and turned it into an outfit."

Sofi let out a laugh.

"Okay, but for reals," Claudius said. "You two are going to take the position, right? Because I need someone to entertain in those meetings."

She bit her cheek, then shook her head. "Not sure," she said, before peering over at Shilo. He already had the radio apart in clunky pieces.

"*Thoughts?*" she asked silently.

He didn't look up. "*What are you afraid of? Becoming Mom?*"

"*Becoming like everyone.*"

"*Policies and politics don't change people, Sof. Choices do.*"

"*You're not answering my question.*"

"*And I'm not going to. But I don't think you can actually hide from the world if you want to help change it. Seems like you gotta be in it to do that.*"

"*Yeah, well, the world's a mess.*"

She felt him chuckle. "*So are we.*"

Good point.

"Jerk."

This time his chuckle was audible from his spot across the yard. She looked out over the fields dotted with sumac bushes and shadows from the sweltering sun finally making its way toward the tree line for the day. Then across the broken homes and tents and—far in the distance—the cities that lay like gorged gems in the midst of everything else that was still so desperately in need.

A mental image of the black markets popped up. Full of children and homeless.

She firmed her jaw and opened her screen to pull up Ranger. Hey. You interested in a job?

Thirty seconds went by before he replied, Maybe. What would I have to do?

Oversee tech for Miguel's and my company. Help me end the black markets.

Would I have to wear a suit?

Nope, she answered.

Yeah, I'm in.

Oh, and you'd be responsible for keeping Miguel in line, she added, since Miguel was eavesdropping over her shoulder after hanging up on Claudius.

She clicked the device off as Miguel chuckled and glanced up at the day-lit moon, then beyond, to where Delon used to be. She'd spent so much of her life despising the thing, she'd not noticed the permanent pull it had on her. The noise it left in her brain that only her headphones could block out. Now that it was gone, there was the permanent void of something missing.

She pressed out her mind, like she had multiple times over

the past week, to see if she could pick up a vibration or speck of something more.

The impressions that bounced back were only of the imprint they'd left upon Earth—their environmental additions and expansive technology. And Danya halfway around the world with her family. She pushed farther, past Earth's atmosphere and into space, but was met with a cold sense of emptiness. Not even a lingering wormhole trace.

Miguel swiped up a song on his handcomp, then slipped his hand into hers. "Hey. Where are you?"

Sofi inhaled. And picked up his vibration as his pulse struck softly. His heartbeat in cadence with hers.

"You okay?"

She shut her eyes and nodded. "I'm fine."

Then said good-bye to them. To the visitors who'd stolen so much of her life and the lives of far too many others. She said good-bye to her mother, and father, and Ella. She said good-bye to the history she could not change—the former things that were no longer her. And released her mind to come back home—to here. This place where Shilo was destroying a radio and Miguel was helping create a new life in this wilderness of humanity, but only if she wanted it. He wouldn't push her, she knew. He was there to be hers for whatever she wanted. Or not, if she wanted that too.

Of course she wanted him here. She pressed out to him with her feelings and got back what she'd expected. Contentment. Because she was his family now too. And this was their home, with the scent of warm earth and farm fields and sun-touched skin and the low sound of music thumping.

"Leaving shadows of our former selves and former loves . . ."

the music crooned. She opened her eyes and peered up at Miguel's face, and caught that quirk of a smile. The one that said even though all was not perfect in the world, the world was perfect in this moment.

And that was enough.

It was more than enough.

To have a life full of perfect moments in between the hard and painful and fearful. To live tasting the in-betweens like these, and to create them. And to believe again that there was something bigger to all this—bigger than aliens and humans and hate and hope. Something that held them, like melodic strands, in the unwavering hands of Love.

Sofi raised a palm to Miguel's chest and pressed into the heartbeat that had over the past few weeks become a rhythm to her own pulsing refrain. And stood beside him as the song played: *"But what if just for tonight we forget the brutal and be true to ourselves? Souls sharing skin and something bigger in this moment?"*

The sun slipped lower and the music thumped on, carrying with it the promise that tomorrow would hold a whole new set of breathtaking moments all their own.

And *that* was her future.

TEN MONTHS LATER . . .

SOMEWHERE IN THE SOUTH MIDDLE EAST REGION, ON A WARMER-than-normal afternoon, a baby's cry erupted through the maternity wing of an already-noisy hospital.

The father leaned down as the midwife placed the baby on the mother's bare chest, skin radiating warmth and maternal connection that ran deeper than merely mental logic. This was her child. Her gift. Her miracle.

"She's beautiful." Salim brushed his brown hand over the baby's skin, then on up to his wife's face. "She will be a mediator, and an advisor, and a strong woman of hope, just like you, my love."

Danya peered up at this man who'd been her husband only six years—chosen when she'd begun her life here on Earth for the purpose of learning more about their culture, their security, and their beliefs. What she learned about more than any of that, however, was how to love.

And it was the gift she'd given him to learn in return.

She looked down at her baby—this impossibility of Delonese and human DNA. She kissed the black hair and brown skin and tiny nose. Love had done what all the technology of Delon could not—created life and a future for her species.

Little voices chattered out in the hallway, and suddenly the door flung open. "May we see, Mama?" The children she and Salim had adopted ran into the room. "Can she talk yet? Can we hold her?"

Danya smiled at these faces she loved more than the entirety of life. These faces beaming like the hearts their bodies housed— which had taught her even more the meaning of love.

She placed the baby onto the clean linen in her lap and scooted over for them to climb on the bed beside her. "She's watching you. Look, she already likes you."

"Why's she all pink? What's her name?"

Danya looked at Salim. "I don't know. What shall we name her?"

"Name her after me!" squealed her daughter.

"Name her after the stars," whispered Danya's son.

Danya's handscreen suddenly clicked on and a message scrolled across the face of it.

Congratulations. Shilo, Miguel, and I are so happy for you.

Thank you, friend. **Danya responded.** We hope that like her siblings, she too will one day change the world.

Sofi's text came back: She already has.

MY PLAYLIST OF THANK-YOUS

Dearest Reader . . .

I wrote this story over a course of months when my heart felt laid open and raw, and I'd just about lost my faith in humanity (which, if you know me at all, is near impossible). Like I was ready to simply walk away and live in a cave.

It was the kindness of a few friends that held my soul in place, held me steady, held my head up amid a culture that seems to have forgotten what we're all here for. It was kindness that said, "Sweetheart, this world is so bloated with itself, you'd think it ain't got room for anyone else—and yet it's wasting away for lack of love. Cuz we can't live on rage and hate. There's no sustenance in it. So come sit here with us where there's room. We're not as loud or shocking, but we're real. Come feast on our belief that even where evil abounds, grace will always abound more."

So I sat at the table, and ate, and bled. And they sat with me and set the music to "play."

There are still days I remind myself to stay seated. But those are the ones I force myself to look around and see just how big the table of kindness is. And it's growing. Because grace abounds even more.

So, here's my invitation to you.

If you need it, we're here. You can sit with us. <3

Here's a list of friends already at the table:

Peter, my husband. My children Rilian, Avalon, and Korbin. Dad and Mom. My siblings and their families. Kati.

Courtney Stevens, Jay and JoanMarie Asher, Maggie Stiefvater, CJ Redwine, Katie Ganshert, Allen Arnold, Ted and Leeann Dekker, Kevin Kaiser, Jim Rubart, Caleb and Brittney Breakey, and my sweet cookie sisters, Nadine Brandes and Sara Ella.

Lori and Will Barrow, Jeanette Morris, Robert Perez, and the entire Father's House and Rise leaders, teens, and family. My agent, Danielle Smith. My publisher, Bex, Amanda, Jodi, Paul, Allison, Kristen, Julee, and the TN team.

Every reader, blogger, bookstagrammer, interviewer, and human who has read my books, showed up to events, or reached out simply to say, "I see you. I'm here too." Y'all are far more treasured in this world than you can know. Thank you.

Jesus. Because you are all this heart exists for.

~m

DISCUSSION QUESTIONS

WARNING: SPOILERS AHEAD!

1. In chapter 16, Jerrad tells Inola that she's not lost Sofi—rather, Sofi's actions have simply been attempts to gain her mom's attention. Do you think that's true? That she wants a relationship with her mom beyond just being corrected or ignored? If you could say anything to your parent(s), what would it be? If your parent(s) could say anything to you, what would you want to hear?

2. There's a quote often attributed to Edmond Burke that says, "The only thing necessary for the triumph of evil is that good men should do nothing." In the black markets Inola discovers firsthand a very dark reality to life—the fact that people are literally trafficking (selling) others, particularly children. When the question is posed to her, "Whose fault is it?" she's left to consider the answer. Is it hers? Is it those directly doing the harm? Is it those who knowingly go back into harmful lifestyles? As members of the human family, what is your and my responsibility when it comes to this issue?

3. In chapter 15, we read how Sofi's belief in the goodness of humanity altered Miguel's perspective on life. And yet, people are not always good—in fact, as mentioned above, and as we see in the news regularly, people do hurtful things. How can both of those be true? Can a person have goodness within? Can that same person do harmful things? Why or why not? And what do *you* believe about people? What do you think ultimately causes humans to choose good over harm?

4. Sofi and Miguel have a complicated relationship in which both of them are learning to become truer to who they are. Part of this is identifying negative aspects of their past and then releasing those. Part of it is viewing the future through the lenses of the people they are choosing to become. And part of it is learning to love oneself. What do you think it means in a practical sense to do this? Can a person actually be "true to oneself"?

5. Another theme presented in this story is that of family. What breaks a family—and what makes a family. In your perspective, does family always have to be biological? What characteristics make up a "healthy" family unit?

6. One of the topics this book wrestles with is that of genetic engineering—an issue people across the spectrum, but especially in the sciences, are continually debating. What rights do we have to genetically engineer things (including humans, animals, plants, etc.)? How far do those rights extend? Is there a chance we might go too far? What are the potential impacts—both positive and negative? Should it be regulated, and if so, who should be responsible to do so?

7. In Miguel's speech in the FanFight arena near the book's end, he states that all life is precious, even the lives of those we

disagree with—adding that the moment we elevate our lives above another's is the moment we all begin to lose. In light of our current online, cultural, and political surroundings, do you think those statements are true? What would change if people actually lived like that?

8. In the second part of Miguel's ending speech, he poses two questions: "How do we lose our humanity? And how do we gain our humanity back?" How would *you* answer those?

IF THE IDEA OF THE BLACK MARKETS OR THE DELONESE EXPER-iments in this book made you or others uncomfortable, it was for a reason. A large part of this series is centered around human trafficking, which is a very real crisis across our globe today. At the time of this writing, nearly 30 million humans are enslaved and oppressed—in the most horrific circumstances one can imagine. And they need voices to speak up for them.

To learn more about human trafficking and how you can (1) protect yourself, (2) protect others, and (3) help bring freedom to those who desperately need it, visit www.A21.org. And if you are currently one of those millions, then please know this: This series is for you. It is your voice being raised for the world to hear because you are not alone. We're here fighting for you. And. We. Will. Not. Stop.

Teachers and Librarians—for more resources,
please visit www.MaryWeber.com

CONNECT WITH ME

Mary loves to connect with readers! Here's where you can find her online:

maryweber.com

Instagram:
MaryWeberAuthor

Facebook:
Mary Weber, Author

Twitter:
@MChristineWeber

School, Skype, or conference visits:
mary@mchristineweber.com

ABOUT THE AUTHOR

MARY WEBER IS THE AUTHOR OF THE Scholastic Pick, Christy, Carol, and INSPY Award–winning young adult novel, *Storm Siren*, and the Storm Siren Trilogy. As an avid school and conference speaker, Weber has a passion for helping others find their voice amid a too-loud world. In her spare time she sings '80s songs to her three muggle children and ogles her husband who looks strikingly like Wolverine. They live in California, which is perfect for stalking tacos and the ocean.

31901062746310